Soda Fountain Blues

Soda Fountain Blues

by L.D. Whitaker

Scrivener Oak Press

This is a work of fiction. Names, characters, and incidents are products of the author's imagination or are used fictitiously and are not to be construed as real. Any resemblance to actual events, locales, organizations, or persons, living or dead, is entirely coincidental.

Published by
Scrivener Oak Press

Paperback ISBN-13: 978-1-7332029-3-0
Kindle ISBN-13: 978-1-7332029-4-7

Book design: Eddie Vincent/ENC Graphic Services
Cover design /ENC Graphic Services
Cover images © Shutterstock

For Mary Ellen

ACKNOWLEDGEMENTS

I owe thanks to many people for their encouragement and support in writing this novel and will mention a few.

Eddie Vincent and the staff at Encircle Publications for outstanding support and direction in the publication of this novel.

Gina Keckritz, editor par excellence, whose deft hand always improves my writing efforts.

Rochelle Wisoff Fields, accomplished author and artist, for reading an early draft, sharing her insights, and making valuable suggestions.

Deborah Schott, my friend and critique partner, for her excellent comments and corrections.

Linda, Michelle, Chad, and Jana at the Writers' Colony at Dairy Hollow, where this novel got its start, for providing the ultimate writing retreat.

My wife Mary Ellen for her love, patience, and proofreading skills during the long haul and countless drafts of this novel.

PROLOGUE

The 1960s marked the twilight of the conformist, buttoned-down fifties, the decade of tailfins, hula-hoops, *The Creature from the Black Lagoon*, ducktail haircuts, girdles, and sock hops. Many cite the 1963 assassination of John F. Kennedy as the turning point. Others say the 1950s began collapsing on itself with the advent of Elvis.

But in many ways, the fifties lingered for another five years beyond its closing date, keeping its hold on the first half of the sixties. Acid hadn't yet hit rock and roll—Tammy Wynette, the Beatles, the Beach Boys, and folk music ruled the scene. The drug culture and civil rights protest movements were nascent. Still, beatniks and coffeehouse poets preached that the times were changing.

Vietnam was a distant drum, at least for those bound for college. Turn eighteen, register with the Selective Service Board, and get your 2-S classification—just keep your grades up because Uncle Sam was watching.

For 18-year-old Wesley Sanders, the world began changing in early May of 1965, two days after graduating from high school in a sleepy Missouri Ozark town. With a guitar and two suitcases, Wesley and his classmate Cliff Westin boarded a Trailways bus hoping to find summer jobs in Yellowstone Park. And like the Beach Boys, they were ready to have fun.

CHAPTER ONE

Wesley's mind wandered as Brother Jackson droned on with his sermon. In two hours, he would be on a Trailways bus with Cliff headed toward Yellowstone Park. It had seemed like a good idea to attend church before the trip, but now, he was second-guessing that decision.

Doubts had started creeping in earlier that morning during the young men's Sunday school class. It seemed to Wesley the class, ultimately about sins of the flesh, had been specifically designed to put a damper on his trip. Brother Jackson taught the class. Because he also performed premarital counseling, Brother Jackson was well prepared.

He began by proclaiming God was everywhere, and then added, "Even when you go out of town, God is there—even in Yellowstone Park." With this statement, he directed beady-eyed stares at Cliff and Wesley. Wesley squirmed in his chair, and Cliff grimaced.

Next, Brother Jackson progressed from the ubiquitous nature of God, to sins of the flesh, focusing on the prohibitions of premarital sex. To underscore the matter, he quoted Matthew 5:28, "But I say to you that everyone who looks at a woman with lustful intent has already committed adultery with her in his heart."

Wesley glanced at Cliff, who mouthed, "I'm doomed."

Now, in his sermon, Brother Jackson was at it again, quoting from Corinthians that the body is a temple of the Holy Spirit, which generated a few "Amens" from older folks in the congregation.

Thankfully, it was nearly noon, and he would have to wrap up soon—his sermon was being carried live on the local radio station. Still, Brother Jackson had planted seeds as he, no doubt, had intended.

*   *   *

Wesley and Cliff's journey crossed the flatlands of Kansas to Denver, and then northward, diagonally, across Wyoming, and finally stopping in Ashton, Idaho—the seed potato capital of the world. Until June, and the likelihood of snow in the mountain passes waned, this was the turnaround spot for Trailways.

They checked into the Horton hotel, built in 1913. According to Wesley, Doc Holiday and Wyatt Earp might have stayed there. Cliff quipped, "That desk clerk smelled like he was nipping from some of Doc's old hooch."

That evening the boys struck up a conversation in the hotel coffee shop with a stocky guy from Nebraska named Bob. Bob wore a Creighton University sweatshirt and had returned to work for a second year in the park. The boys had plenty of questions, and Bob was happy to share, with the air of an old sage.

"Yeah, I got in yesterday," Bob said, "and just missed the employee bus, but another one will be here tomorrow morning. Since I'm experienced, they'll hold my job." He uttered a smug laugh. "So, where are you guys planning to work?"

"We don't know—we don't have jobs yet." Wesley said.

"No," Cliff added. "We hope we're there early enough to nab one. Where are you working?"

"I work in the grocery department at the Hamilton Store on Yellowstone Lake. In case you haven't heard, Hamilton Stores is a park concessioner that sells food and souvenirs to tourists."

"That's one of the employers we heard about. One of our coaches worked for them in the 1950s. He wrote reference letters for us," Wesley said.

"You guys be out front tomorrow at 10 o'clock when the bus arrives, and I'll tell the driver you both are going to work for Hamilton Stores."

Slowly, the angst that had been building in Wesley eased a bit. It had been a long trip that had ended in a creepy hotel, and they had no plan other than hitchhiking the last fifty miles. Now, the prospect of a bus ride gave him hope.

A Yellowstone Park bus arrived the next morning to pick up employees, and an hour or so later, the bus stopped at a storefront office in West Yellowstone. Bob said, "Here's where you boys get off. This is the Hamilton Store office. As I mentioned, my job is at Yellowstone Lake so I'm staying onboard. Mr. Smith is the personnel director—ask to speak to him."

Inside the office, a secretary gave them application forms. After they filled out their forms, she collected them and said, "I'll take these to Mr. Smith. Wait here." Twenty minutes later, she returned and said, "Mr. Smith will see you now. Follow me." She escorted them to his office, made introductions, and excused herself.

From behind his desk, Mr. Smith pointed toward two chairs in front, and the boys sat down. He glimpsed at their applications—first one, then the other—and then at them. "Normally, we don't hire personnel on the spot, but since you two are here before most of the seasonal help has arrived, I might make an exception. I've reviewed your applications and recommendation letters, and they are impressive. Athletes, good grades, leadership positions. We can always use a couple dishwashers. How does that sound?"

Wesley sat up taller. "That doesn't sound too good." Mr. Smith raised his eyebrows, seemingly surprised by the spunk. Wesley kept talking. "I have enough money to get back to Kansas, where I can work in the wheat harvest. I'd rather drive a John Deere tractor than wash dishes."

"I take it you have worked there before."

"Yes, sir. The past two summers."

"Interesting." Mr. Smith nodded at Cliff. "What about you?"

Cliff shifted his weight and leaned forward. "Well, we've come a long way just to wash dishes, and Wes says he can get me a wheat harvest job, so I agree with him."

The personnel director didn't reply right away, but he kept his gaze focused on the boys, as if judging their merit. "You two young men have some pluck—I like that. How would being soda jerks at the upper Hamilton Store at Old Faithful sound to you boys?"

Wesley could feel his lips relaxing into a smile. The on-edge feeling from sparring with an adult slipped away. "That sounds great."

"Sounds good to me, too," Cliff said.

"Then it's settled. A company truck will take you fellows to the boys' dormitory. Pick out a room and drop off your suitcases, but then go to the store and introduce yourselves to Betty, the fountain manager. You'll come to like her eventually. Just be sure you shoot straight with her."

The dormitory, a two-story barracks-style building, sat behind the store and formed the back side of a courtyard. Inside, they selected a first-floor room with two sets of bunk beds. They threw their gear on the lower bunks, staking their claims, and headed to the store to meet Betty.

The Hamilton Store, a huge log structure sitting among tall pine trees, resembled a rustic inn or ski lodge. The shake roof sloped downward from a central ridge, with a gable at either end.

The interior boasted a high cathedral ceiling that revealed the exposed underside of the roof, supported by massive lodgepole pine girders trussed with iron plates. Wesley could imagine it as the great banquet hall for a medieval giant.

"This is as big as our basketball gym back home," Wesley said.

Cliff nodded, as he gawked at the ceiling.

The food and dry goods departments covered the front part of the store, where older men and women dusted and stocked shelves. Meandering through aisles cluttered with cardboard boxes, the boys found the soda fountain tucked in a smaller wing at the back of the store.

For the most part, the soda fountain bore little resemblance to an old-fashioned ice cream parlor. It was enormous. The service counter had five U-shaped bays, with barstools for eight customers at each bay. However, the mirrored back bar, with tall fizz-water faucets and milkshake mixers, could have been from the 1940s.

A chunky woman wearing tortoise-shell glasses and her hair tied back in a madras scarf sat at the rear bay unpacking glassware from a cardboard box. She appeared to be in her mid-thirties. Two college-aged women, a blond and a brunette, and a woman in her late twenties with a mouse-brown bob-style haircut, stood near her. The brunette stacked glasses on a tray and threw packing paper in a trash can, while Mouse-Brown marked on a clipboard, apparently taking inventory. The blond turned and walked a few feet to a back room.

With the coarse voice of a smoker, the older woman said, "Are you boys just here to admire the scenery?" No doubt, the voice belonged to Betty.

Wesley said, "I'm—

"I know who you are." Betty stood up and faced the two boys. She was stout and only average height, but she barked like a drill sergeant. "Get your butts over here and help out."

The boys marched over.

Betty introduced the woman with the mouse-brown hair as Margaret, a third-grade teacher from Iowa, and the brunette as Vivian. She pronounced Vivian with a French accent, which prompted the brunette to smile and say, omitting the accent, "Most people just call me Vivian. My father loved Vivien Leigh in *Gone with the Wind*, but mother's ancestors were French, so I answer to either."

Cliff's gaze locked on Vivian, but Wes kept his eyes on Betty. Wesley knew the drill—his stepfather had been a Navy man. He suspected Betty had a military history.

"Just so you boys know, I spent four years in the United States

Marine Corps—as a drill instructor." Betty had the attention of both boys now.

Wesley pictured her in a Smokey Bear hat, and he stood a little straighter. Eager to demonstrate his military knowledge," he said. "You were a BAM."

"What?" Betty's face contorted and turned scarlet, as if she had swallowed something offensive and was about to gag. "Young man, do you know what that means?"

"Not exactly, ma'am . . . I thought it was an abbreviation for women in the marines, like WAC for women in the Army."

"No, son, it's a vulgar, derogatory term. Where did you hear that?"

"A guy from my hometown came back from bootcamp, and I heard him say it." When the high school's biggest greaser-hoodlum had returned home from the Marine Corps, squared away and clean-cut, some of the boys picked up his lingo.

Silence loomed in anticipation of what Betty would do. The other women's eyes locked on her like children anticipating the wrath of a vengeful head mistress. Cliff shot a glance at Wesley and then looked sheepishly back to Betty.

Wesley stood at attention, with his eyes not wavering from Betty. What had he said that upset her so much?

After a moment of stony silence, Betty's color faded from red to pale. "Young man," she said, in a gentler voice, "I'll cut you some slack this time, since it's pretty obvious you don't know what you're talking about. But it is my strong suggestion that you wipe that term from your vocabulary."

"Yes, ma'am."

"At ease, and my name is Betty."

Oh, great. First five minutes on the job and I've already stuck my foot in my mouth.

As the boys stood more relaxed, the blond, a tall female about their age, with her hair styled in a flip, emerged from a back room struggling to carry an electric meat slicer. Betty pointed toward the girl and said to the boys, "You two, go help Sue. Set that slicer on the back bar. It needs to be cleaned."

As they maneuvered around to the back bar, Cliff nudged Wesley with his elbow and in an undertone said, "Dibs on the blond."

"No problem—the brunette's cuter," Wesley said, under his breath. From Wesley's perspective, the brunette in question, Vivian, was drop-dead gorgeous. Every inch of her curvy five-foot-something frame said *cheerleader.*

Later, Betty, seemingly over her aggravation with Wesley, assembled the crew around her. "Listen up, everyone. In less than a week the soda fountain opens, and every time Old Faithful blows, ten minutes later we'll have thirty customers at the counters. No sooner than we get them served with milkshakes and banana splits, the geyser goes off again, and we start all over. Here are my rules. Rule number 1: No slackers, whiners, or liars. Rule number 2: Never be late for your shift. And Rule number 3: No eating or flirting with the opposite sex while on duty. Any questions? I didn't think so."

As the meeting broke up, Vivian sidled next to Wesley. "You made quite an impression on your first day." Her eyes sparkled as she flashed a smile with perfect teeth.

"Yeah, it's too bad the boss doesn't like me."

"Oh, she likes you okay."

"What makes you say that?" Without thinking, his eyes moved to her exposed cleavage.

With one finger she pushed his chin upward until their eyes met. It was an unsubtle message, but the smile never left her face. "Because if she didn't, she would have fired you on the spot. Yesterday, she fired a girl for an impertinent comment."

"What'd the girl say?

"I don't know exactly, but it doesn't matter. The personnel office transferred her to West Thumb. Which is fine with me, because she goes to the University of Georgia."

"Don't you like people from Georgia?"

"I go to the University of Alabama. Students at UGA are an acquired taste."

Over the next few weeks college students from all over the country arrived to fill summer jobs in the park, and soon the fountain was mostly staffed.

During the second week, after Wesley finished his shift, he cruised back to his room. The door was open. What the heck was this? From the looks of things, some trespasser had unrolled the cotton mattress on the top bunk of Wesley's bed, covered it with a Coleman sleeping bag and a moth-eaten, olive-drab wool army blanket. And the claim jumper had tossed some of Wesley's gear from the top bunk to his lower one and left a pair of beaten-up cowboy boots on the floor next to the head of his bunk.

The boots provoked the greatest irritation. At one time they may have been the height of Western style, with their under-shod heels and orange sunburst inlays, but not now. The heels were worn down, the toes bent upwards, and the shafts flopped sideways. The image of a sodbuster, and not Roy Rogers, formed in Wesley's mind.

Wesley hightailed it back to the soda fountain, where Cliff was on duty. They had staked claim to the room and weren't looking for any interlopers. He got Cliff's attention at the fountain and motioned him over. "Looks like we have a roommate."

"Have you met him?" Cliff asked.

"No, but he stashed a bedroll on my top bunk and left a pair of crappy-looking cowboy boots on the floor."

The jukebox blared Mick Jagger singing the Rolling Stones' "Satisfaction." Cliff's eyes went to the sound, and Wesley's eyes followed his lead. A guy wearing a cowboy hat with the brim bent up on both sides and folded down in front stood by the Wurlitzer making selections.

"Partner," Cliff said, "any chance that's our cowboy?"

One look confirmed it for Wesley. Wrangler jeans with a wide leather belt. "You might be right . . . but Converse tennis shoes? He must be saving his boots for the next hoedown. Maybe he's just a tourist."

"He doesn't look like a dude to me," Cliff surmised. "Maybe he's one of the wranglers that leads trail rides for the dudes."

"Here comes Betty. Let's ask her. Hey, Betty, do you know that guy at the jukebox?" Wesley asked.

"Yeah, he's a new fountain guy from Texas. His name is Hezekiah H. Beckett."

"Are you kidding me?" Cliff asked.

"No, that's what he put on his application form. He says his friends call him *Hez*."

"Since it appears he's our new roommate," Wesley said, "I suppose we should introduce ourselves."

That evening after the fountain closed, Wesley, Cliff, and Hez lounged on their bunks before turning in. Cliff and Wesley quizzed Hez about his background. He seemed friendly enough but was visually a few years older, and they were more than a little curious.

"So, just where in Texas are you from, Hez?" Wesley asked.

"West Texas mostly. I spent a couple years at Texas Tech—"

"Ah, that accounts for the 'Property of Red Raider Football' jersey in the closet," Cliff said, scrutinizing Hez's slender six-foot frame. "Did you play football there?"

"I walked on and played some on the freshman team as a defensive back. I dropped out my sophomore year to earn some money working the oil fields. I didn't want to spend another summer in the heat and dust of the Texas Panhandle. My uncle worked here in the forties and made it sound like fun."

"So far, it has been okay," Cliff said.

Hez scooted back on his bunk, bracing his back against the wall. "Fellas, what's the chick scene at the old soda fountain?"

"You've met Betty—"

"Whoa there, son," Hez said. "Surely, you don't consider Betty chick material?"

"No way, of course, I don't, but she's in charge and doesn't want any fraternizing during work. That's all. At least she seems to have gotten over me calling her a BAM—you know she was in the Marine Corps."

"You called her that? It's a wonder she didn't deck you."

"Why? What does it mean? I still don't know."

"Broad ass marine. The uncle I mentioned was a marine."

"No wonder she was ticked off. I hope she doesn't hold it against me."

"I wouldn't worry," Cliff said. "I can tell she likes you."

"Back to the chick situation," Hez said.

"Vivian and Sue are the two cutest," Wesley said. "Vivian is petite with dark hair. She's a cheerleader and sorority girl at the University of Alabama. Kind of hoity-toity, but I love her Southern accent, and she's definitely sexy."

"She's sexy and flirty, for sure," Cliff said, "but she lets you know she's in a different league."

"She says I am her naïve protégé," Wesley said.

"Naïve protégé?" Hez chuckled. "Vivian doesn't sound like my type. What about Sue?"

"Sue is the tall blond who likes Wes," Cliff said.

"Maybe so," Wesley said, "but remember, the first day here, you called for dibs on her."

"Well, I changed my mind. She's too tall for me, and besides, she's always looking at you."

"I like her, but not to date."

"The way I see it, the park is full of birds, and I'm ready to go hunting," Hez said.

To Cliff's annoyance, Hez had fired up a hand-rolled cigarette. "Hez, what kind of tobacco is that? It smells like you rolled up a dog turd."

Wesley tilted his head upward, and his nostrils flared as he sniffed the air. "Geez, Hez, that stuff would gag a maggot on a gut wagon."

"Okay, fellas, I'll put it out and open the window. I just wanted a few drags before I went to sleep." As he opened the window, he said, "By the way, I've been meaning to ask you boys about something. I saw this dude with a T-shirt that had *I-P-I-O-F* on it." Hez sounded out each letter. "What's that?"

"You mean *ippyoff*." Cliff grinned at Wes. "You want to tell him?"

"No, you go ahead."

"First of all, Hez, I doubt it was a *dude* wearing the shirt. In Texas, a *dude* may be any non-cowboy type, but in the park, it means someone who doesn't work here. Park employees are called *savages*."

"I get it, but what's *ippyoff*?"

"It's sort of a club."

"And it has an initiation," Wesley said. "Sort of an 'initiation by urination.' You see, Hez, the letters *I-P-I-O-F* stand for 'I Pissed in Old Faithful.' To join, you have to take a leak in the geyser."

Hez broke out in laughter. "Do you boys belong?" Cliff and Wesley said that they didn't. "Hells bells, fellas, I think we ought to join."

"Not so fast, cowboy. Cliff and I have discussed this, but it's not as simple as it sounds. You've got to time it just right, and for sure, it has to be done at night. You have to know where to step, too. A lot of the surface area around Old Faithful is a thin crust you can fall through into scalding water."

"And another thing," Cliff added, "if a ranger catches you, you'll be thrown out of the park, or worse. I'm sure it's some kind of federal offense."

Hez's eyes gleamed to the challenge, and a Texas-sized smile spread his mouth wide. "Do any girls belong?"

Cliff and Wesley started laughing. Nothing more needed to be said. A confederacy was formed. The boys would join the IPIOF Club.

Over the next few days, the boys conducted reconnaissance missions and made plans: cover of darkness, no flashlights, dark clothing, enter from the backside.

In their last strategy session, Wesley cautioned, "Timing is everything. Old Faithful is *faithful*, and it's been erupting for many years, but the intervals between eruptions can vary from 45 to 90 minutes. And when it blows, it can spew 8,000 gallons of boiling water in the air. The steam alone can peel skin."

"Don't worry. We'll just hide until it erupts and then rush over," Cliff said.

Shortly after 2 a.m. on "P-Day," as Hez had started calling initiation day, the three boys hid behind a utility shed on the north side of the Old Faithful basin outside the restricted area. They had no way of knowing when the previous eruption had occurred. The ranger's station, with the large clock that showed the estimated eruption time, was closed. Even if it was open, the last thing the boys wanted to see at this time of night was a U.S. Park Service Ranger.

"How long ago do you figure it went off?" Cliff asked.

"Hard to say, but the ground surface looks pretty wet, like it hasn't had time to drain yet," Wesley said.

"Yeah, but as you said, it can go as long as 90 minutes or as short as 45 minutes. What if it decides to get speedy and have a premature ejaculation and erupt in 30 minutes tonight? Our weezers will be cooked—literally."

"You two boys are a couple of pansy asses," Hez said. "It'll be daylight before you two decide what to do. I'm a gambler. I say let's go."

"You gamble with your own wiener and get it boiled, cowboy," Wesley said.

Without another word, Hez stepped over the split-rail fence, crouched down, and sidled toward Old Faithful.

A few yards in, Hez became a barely visible specter against the geyser's steam, backlit by the lights of the Old Faithful Inn in the distance.

"Ah, hell, Cliff, we can't let him go alone."

"It hasn't gone off in the last 15 minutes, so I guess we're safe," Cliff said.

They caught up with Hez about 20 yards from the geyser's blowhole. In the cloud-covered moonlight, the slick calcified surface shone like milk-colored glass. The opening resembled a half-domed stalagmite that had been frosted with layers of wax.

At ten yards, Hez said, "Get a load of that opening. That sucker's huge. I'll bet it's eight feet across."

"We better be careful. If we slip and fall, we're goners," Cliff said.

As the boys inched toward the opening, the sulfurous steam coming from the hole smelled like rotten eggs. Wesley said, "This must be what hell smells like. The Bible calls it brimstone."

"You could fart without detection," Hez said.

"Or smoke your stinky tobacco," Cliff added.

"All right, let's get on with it," Hez said.

"What's that noise?" Cliff said. "Do you feel that vibration?"

The vibration became a rumble. It sounded like a freight train roaring deep below.

"Let's get out of Dodge," Hez yelled.

Sprinting and hopscotching across the drainage pools, they were nearly to the edge of the basin when Old Faithful erupted. As it blew, they instinctively dove to the ground as if escaping from a bomb blast.

Out of breath and shaky, Wesley rose up on his forearms and said, "Damn, that was a close call."

"Yes, it was, boys." The voice came from a U.S. Park Service Ranger—an enforcement ranger with a sidearm—not one of the "flower pickers" who gave wildlife lectures to the tourists. A tall, uniformed ranger wearing a Smokey Bear hat.

The ranger sauntered over to the boys as they were standing up. "What are your names?"

The boys told him who they were.

"Well, now, Cliff, Wesley, and Hezekiah, you three just put your lives in danger, and in the process broke a handful of federal statutes and regulations. I have seen young men such as you prosecuted by the United States Attorney for something as minor as chucking pebbles at some girls' tent. What do you think will happen when I report this incident?"

Hez stretched to his full height and said, "Well, officer, back in Texas—"

"Knock it off, Hez," Cliff said.

"What were you boys doing out there?"

"We just wanted to see how big the opening was to Old Faithful," Wesley said.

"Come on, now. Do you expect me to believe that? I've been working this park for ten years. All you needed to do was ask about the dimensions at the ranger station over there. Where do you boys work?"

"At the soda fountain," Wes said.

"So, you're Betty's boys. Is that right?"

"Yes, sir," they all said.

"I ought to arrest you all right now." The ranger grunted. "But I have to be over at West Thumb in 20 minutes, so I'm going to cut you a break and let you off with a warning. However, if I come back in an hour, and you yahoos are hanging around, I *will* arrest all of you. Now, get back to your dormitory."

The ranger snickered as he monitored the boys slogging toward the dorm, grumbling to each other. What he didn't see, as he drove off, were the three yahoos peaking from behind Hamilton Store.

Nor did he see, 90 minutes later, the newest members of the IPIOF Club leaving the Old Faithful basin . . . but he, no doubt, imagined it.

The next day, when Wesley and Cliff arrived for the afternoon shift, Betty said, "I hear you two boys met my ol' buddy, Ranger Brett."

The two boys glimpsed at each other, and at the same time said, "Hez!"

"It wasn't Hez. Brett often stops by for coffee when there's some gossip worth sharing. You boys need to realize nothing stays a secret in this park . . . at least not from me." She paused and emitted a wistful sigh. "But I guess, now, you two are genuine *savages*. Get to work."

Chapter Two

Flyers posted around the Old Faithful area advertised a "5th Monday Hootenanny on Memorial Day." It encouraged people to bring their guitars and singing voices to the Old Faithful Inn.

Wesley had been in the park for over two weeks and hadn't opened his guitar case. Hez and Cliff said they weren't going, so Wesley hoofed it over alone.

The Old Faithful Inn enamored Wesley the first time he saw it. Even from the bus a half-mile away, the log hotel, built in 1903, stood regal with its steeped-pitched roof and dormers. And on the inside, the architect had engineered rustic magnificence. The lobby soared 65 feet to the ceiling through three levels of exposed balconies, with bannisters and balusters constructed of oddly shaped limbs from lodgepole pines.

A mammoth stone fireplace in the southeast corner, the focal point and emblem of the lobby, seemed to grow out of bedrock. Rhyolite volcanic rocks resembling granite, most of which were three or four times bigger than concrete construction blocks, formed a 16-foot square base, with hearths on all four sides.

An imposing wrought-iron clock with bold Roman numerals was mounted on the exposed chimney, which extended past the balconies through the roof. This turn-of-the-century timepiece, with its 12-foot pendulum and even longer counter-balance weights, by contrast, added a modern statement against the million-year-old stones.

As the premier place to stay in the park, the Old Faithful Inn was also the most popular place to be employed. A rumor circulated that bellhops could haul in fifty dollars a night toting luggage for rich tourists because the OFI didn't have elevators. A soda jerk, whose share of the tips might only be a few dollars on a busy day, could only dream of such a fortune.

Off-duty savages employed the lobby as a trysting place or hunting ground to advance their romantic lives. Wesley hoped his guitar would help in that pursuit.

It was nearly 8 p.m. when he arrived. A dozen or so college-aged kids, not the size of group he had anticipated, sat around the fireplace, where a fire in one hearth took the chill off the mountain spring evening.

A guy sporting a blond flattop haircut and playing a guitar appeared to be leading the singing. Wesley thought he resembled Dobie Gillis from the TV show. Early twenties, maybe. He checked out Flattop's guitar. A Gibson. Harrumph. Wesley knew his Silvertone would appear cheap in comparison. Maybe he wouldn't unpack it.

Wesley sat in an empty mission chair inside the log railing surrounding the fireplace, several yards from the singers, and stowed his guitar case behind the chair.

Flattop began singing "If I Had a Hammer" and was joined by most of his audience. Wesley envied Flattop's skill at making barre chords down the neck of the Gibson flattop. A flattop with a flattop, he thought, but then his grandmother's words chided him: *Jealousy is not becoming, Wesley.*

Several cute girls all seemed reverently focused on Flattop. Without thinking, Wesley sang along, initially whispering, but in full voice by the second verse. When they finished the song, Flattop gestured with his hand to Wesley. "Hey, come on over and bring your guitar—I need some help."

Nervousness struck him. He wanted to join in, but he wished he had not brought his guitar. His Silvertone that came from a mail-order catalog. His Silvertone, on which he had only mastered the keys of G and C.

"Don't be shy," Flattop urged. The welcome felt more like a challenge to Wesley.

One of the admiring girls, maybe Wesley's age, gave him a congenial smile and said, "Yeah, come on over." He took a mental snapshot of the girl. Long blond hair, parted in the middle like Mary Travers of Peter, Paul, and Mary, and pulled from her face with a thin leather headband. Without any makeup, her face was pretty and intriguing. Her eyes gave the impression she had met you before and you weren't a stranger.

Wesley got up and stepped toward the group. "Bring your guitar," Flattop, said. Wesley picked up the case and moved forward. He started to sit at the perimeter of the group, but Flattop said, "Come over here and sit next to me."

At Flattop's insistence, Wesley unpacked the Silvertone. His mind skipped back to a botched performance at a church songfest when he was a freshman in high school. His mouth went suddenly dry, and his throat tightened.

"By the way, my name is Michael," Flattop said. "Just call me Mike. What's yours?" Wesley told him. "Okay, Wesley, what do you want to play?"

"How about 'Michael Row Your Boat Ashore'?"

"Good name, good song," Mike said. After they finished the song, he said, "Nicely played, Wesley. You've got a good voice, too."

The compliment buoyed Wesley's feelings and his attitude toward Flattop. "Thanks, Mike, but it wasn't much. I can't play as well as you."

"Well, I suspect I've been at it a bit longer—that's all."

After an hour or so of singing, with Wesley able to play most of the songs, Mike announced, "I'm ready to call it a night—I have an early morning ahead of me, but we can sing one more. Let's get Lizzie up here to sing." He pointed at the girl with the long blond hair. "Hey, Lizzie, how about doing 'Five Hundred Miles'?"

The girl pressed her lips together in the pained look of an unprepared student called to recite. "Come on, Lizzie," Mike said.

"Well, all right." Her tone suggested she didn't have a choice.

When she stood up in her cowboy boots, Wesley thought she must be at least 5-foot 7-inches tall. She moved to the front and sat next to Mike. Wesley's suspicions were confirmed—she was Flattop's girlfriend.

"Wesley, I usually play this in the key of G," Mike said. Wesley curled his fingers into a G chord.

Her voice was soft as a gentle breeze that could brush snow off the tops of pines. A whisper that somehow could be heard with ease above the other singers. With the lyrics, a notion of time and place and how far he had come settled on Wesley. And his attraction to Lizzie would have been obvious, had anyone been looking at him instead of her.

"Great job, Lizzie. Let's give her a hand," Mike said. After the applause, Mike packed his guitar in the case and stood up. "Lizzie, are you coming with me?"

"No, I think I'll stay a little longer."

"I'll see you tomorrow morning—early," Mike said as he strode away.

The hootenanny crowd began dispersing, leaving Wesley sitting next to Lizzie by the fireplace. "I figured you would leave with Mike."

"Why would I?"

"Isn't he your boyfriend? He seemed a bit annoyed that you were staying."

Her face became quizzical. "Not that it is any of your business, but Michael is not my boyfriend—he's my *brother*. And he's also my boss."

Wesley's throat tightened and some unknown force rendered him speechless. He had stepped in a snare that had hoisted him upside down and flopped his tongue to the back of his mouth, leaving him struggling for something clever to say.

"Oh, quit looking down at your shoes," Lizzie, said. "Has the cat got your tongue, Miles Standish?"

His mind raced. Back in school, he had been forced to read Longfellow's poem, *The Courtship of Miles Standish*, and knew she was referring to the part where John Alden was sent to speak to Priscilla Mullins on behalf of the inarticulate Miles Standish. Wesley resumed the conversation. "My grandpa always told me when I was in a hole to quit digging."

"Your grandpa was right, but the fact of the matter is I work with my brother. We're both wranglers at the Old Faithful stables. We lead trail rides, and I have one tomorrow morning at 8 a.m."

"Wow, that's a cool job—you're a cowgirl. Better than dipping ice cream."

"Let me guess. You're a soda jerk at one of the Ham Stores."

"That's right. How did you get your job? I thought only men had those jobs."

"Why would you say that? Heck, my older sister is a wrangler at Grand Canyon National Park and leads overnight mule rides to the bottom of the canyon."

"Hey, I didn't intend to dig a deeper hole. I just didn't know they had girls as wranglers and was curious how you got the job. I didn't have a job before I got out here. I hopped on a bus and gambled I'd find one."

"Why don't we go to the coffee shop and get a Coke, and I'll tell you."

In the coffee shop, they sat at an empty table with a view of the fireplace. A waitress came and Lizzie ordered a 7-Up. Wesley, said, "Make it two." After the waitress left, he added, "I thought you were going to get a Coke."

"I don't drink Cokes."

"Why?"

"I'm Mormon and our *Doctrines and Covenants* speak against drinking tea or coffee, and many Mormons—my father included—

say it applies to anything with caffeine in it."

"That's interesting."

"What? That I'm a Mormon?"

"No, I didn't know Cokes had caffeine."

"Does it bother you that I'm a Mormon?"

"I don't think so. I've never met one before. All I know about Mormons is what I learned in school. That they crossed the desert with Brigham Young, and the men had more than one wife."

Lizzie rolled her eyes. "You need to be brought up to date. Technically, it's the Church of Jesus Christ of Latter-day Saints, but Mormon or LDS is okay. Polygamy was outlawed within the Church before it was made illegal by the state. We're quite modern. How about you? Where are you from, and what's *your* religion?"

"I'm from southern Missouri, and I'm Baptist."

"A hillbilly. Do your folks make moonshine and speak in tongues?"

"No," Wesley blurted. He had nearly added, "Hell, no," but he held up. Nonetheless his irritation was apparent.

"Touché, Monsieur Standish."

Almost to himself Wesley said, "I seem to keep digging." Attempting to climb out, he said, "You have a pretty singing voice. Maybe you could sing in the Mormon Tabernacle Choir. I saw them on TV."

"Oh, so you do know something about Mormons. To be on the Tab Choir you need to live in Salt Lake City because of the weekly practice sessions."

"That makes sense." Wanting to move on from religion, he said, "You were about to tell me how you got your job. And is Lizzie a nickname?"

Smiling, Lizzie said, "Now, what? You don't you like my name?"

Wesley flinched.

"Hey, I'm just kidding you." She poked his arm, and Wesley relaxed. "It's short for Elizabeth, but that's what teachers and my mother call me. Friends and my dad call me Lizzie. Mike calls me Lizard when nobody else is around."

"I'll call you Lizzie, then. Tell me how you got your job."

"Originally, I wanted to go work with my sister at the Grand Canyon, but I'm pretty sure she didn't want my company there. This is Mike's second year in the park, and he said he could get me on here, since I'm good with horses."

"You *are* a cowgirl."

"I guess so, I grew up on a Wyoming horse and cattle ranch. My mom thought spending the summer away from home before going away to school was good preparation—sort of a warm-up act. My dad didn't, but he gave into the idea since I would be working with Mike. And Yellowstone is a lot closer than the Grand Canyon."

"Where are you going to college?"

"Colorado State University. They have a vet school there and offer a major in zoology."

"I'm going to the University of Missouri, but I haven't decided on a major. Maybe business. I've been told that all freshmen pretty much take the same courses the first year."

"That's what I've heard, too." Lizzie pointed at the clock. "Looks like they're getting ready to close here, and I have an early ride tomorrow, so I better get moving."

"May I walk you back to your place?"

"Sure. That's pretty thoughtful for a hillbilly . . . just teasing."

Outside, the crisp night air had a slight chill. As they left the light of the inn, the sky blazed with stars, and the moon was a waxed crescent.

"You can't see a sky like this, with all the stars, back in Missouri."

"We see them all the time in Wyoming. I guess I'm so used to the stars I sometimes don't appreciate how spectacular they are. Although, tonight, they do seem awfully bright."

They continued to chat, and in what seemed like no time at all to Wesley, they arrived at Lizzie's dormitory.

"This is where I live, so I guess it's goodnight." She extended her hand to be shaken. Wesley took her hand and held it. Her lips formed a tight line, her eyes sparkled with curiosity, but she said nothing.

Wesley waited before speaking, weighing his next move. "Are you going to be at the Old Faithful Inn tomorrow night?"

She seemed to study him before responding. "Maybe. I haven't decided if you are worthy yet, Monsieur Standish. Goodnight." After giving his hand a gentle squeeze, she unlocked the door and went inside.

All the way back to his own dormitory, thoughts about Lizzie swirled in Wesley's head. *I should have kissed her. She must not be too prim and proper since she's a cowgirl. But she was so fast with her outstretched hand. Maybe Mormon girls aren't big on kissing.*

When he got back to his room, Hez had donned his cowboy hat and smelled of Old Spice aftershave lotion. He wore washed jeans and an ironed shirt. "Where are you off to, Hez?"

"I've got a date with a waitress from the lower Ham Store."

"It's past 10, everything is closed. You're too slicked up for a date on your old army blanket."

"An astute observation, my friend. I have a private room lined up."

Wesley's interest peaked. "Last I heard, you were broke until we get paid. Where are you getting the do-re-me for a room?"

Hez tapped the side of his head with his finger and assumed a professorial aura. "Who said I was *paying* for a room?"

"Come on, Hez, what kind of angle are you playing this time? We're already on thin ice from our Ippyoff adventure. And if Ranger Brett ever finds out you and Cliff dumped laundry detergent in that little geyser, you'll get booted out of the park, for sure."

"Yeah, that was great. The foam on the trees made it look like it had snowed."

"Maybe so, Hez, but that stunt probably violated some federal offense that could get you put in prison." As soon as he said prison, Wesley felt sudden shame recalling that his father had done a year in the Missouri state penitentiary.

"Take it easy, Cuz. Only three people know, and none of them are talking. Am I right?"

"Yeah, I guess so."

Hez extracted a ring of skeleton keys from his pocket. "These, my friend, are the keys to paradise. With one of these babies, I can get in an empty Yellowstone Lodge cabin."

Wesley ogled the keys and pictured the rustic one- and two-room tourist cabins scattered around the Old Faithful area that were less expensive than staying at the Old Faithful Inn. "You've got enough keys that you can likely get in, but how will you know if the cabin is occupied."

Hez tapped his head again. "You see, partner, the keys to the cabins hang on a pegboard with the cabin numbers behind the registration desk. If there is a key hanging over a number, it means that cabin hasn't been rented."

Unconvinced, Wesley said, "Yeah, but they could rent it after you went in the cabin, and then what would you do? It would be your ticket back to Texas. And quit tapping your damn head, Hez."

"Here's the trick, pal. They won't likely be renting any cabins after 10 p.m. Very few tourists enter the park after 9 p.m. So, you cruise by about half-past, and if the key is still hanging, the cabin hasn't been rented and it's all yours."

Wesley lapsed into thought. Why didn't it seem like such a great idea? By now, even though Hez was a friend and a roommate, Wesley had learned to be skeptical of his "great" ideas.

"Hez, your plan has one big problem."

"What?" Hez asked. He sounded surprised, as though he was certain there could be no flaw in his planning.

Wesley tapped the side of his own head, mocking Hez's gesture. Hez rolled his eyes as payback. Wesley continued. "When the word gets out, the lodge management will change the system. In other words, you can't tell anybody else."

"Good thinking. I haven't told anyone else."

"Then it's our secret pact. How do I get some of those skeleton keys?"

"Not a problem, Wes. I have plenty." Hez removed several of the keys from the ring and gave them to Wesley. "Me and you, partner." The secret pact was sealed.

"By the way, Wesley, where have you been?"

"At the Old Faithful Inn. I met a girl."

"Well, now, these keys will come in handy."

"I'm not sure she's that kind of girl—she's a Mormon."

CHAPTER THREE

The next day at the soda fountain Betty stopped her conversation with Vivian as Wesley walked in. "Speaking of the devil, here he is."

"Hey, what'd I do?" Wesley held up both hands, fending off imaginary blows.

"Rumor has it that you have a new girlfriend," Betty said.

Vivian chimed in. "Is she cute? And I thought I was your true love. Here you are, two-timing me."

Wesley did have a crush on the Alabama cheerleader, who dripped with Southern personality. Although Vivian claimed he was like a younger brother to her, it didn't stop her from flirting with him for sport. According to her, he needed grooming before he arrived on a college campus, and he had become a project for her.

Avoiding her girlfriend question, he said, "What are you two talking about?"

"Wesley, don't act so innocent—a handsome fellow like you is bound to attract the ladies," Betty said.

"Oh, I'm not very good-looking."

Vivian wagged her finger at Wesley. "Haven't you learned anything from me? Never reject a compliment—it's essentially telling someone they don't know what they're talking about. You should say, 'Why, thank you. How nice of you to say so.'"

"Got it. I'll remember." Wesley started for the storeroom to get an apron.

Betty grabbed his arm. "Not so fast, kiddo. Who's the girl?"

"Her name is Elizabeth." He immediately regretted divulging the information. He knew it would not stop their curiosity.

"Pretty name." Betty said.

"Did you kiss her?" Vivian grabbed his other arm and leaned into him.

"Hey, why are you two giving me the third degree? I just had a Coke with her. To be accurate, we had 7-Ups—she's Mormon."

"What's wrong with that?" Betty asked. "Some of my best friends are Mormons."

Vivian laughed, "At least I don't have to worry about this Elizabeth getting Wesley drunk and taking advantage of him. A Mormon and a Baptist."

"Enough chatter," Betty said. "You've got a customer, Vivian. Go get an apron, Wesley. Cliff's shift is about over."

Cliff moseyed over. "Yeah, that's right. My shift is over." He threw a dish towel at Wesley. "When can I see this new chick? Maybe she's got a friend."

"I don't know. I've only met her brother."

Vivian piped up. "So, you've already met the family. Sounds serious. Now, I'm really getting jealous."

Cliff smirked. "Vivian, you're a Crimson Tide cheerleader. You know you wouldn't give either of us the time of day back on campus."

"Why, Cliff, you old grump. I'm sure I don't know *what* you are talking about. You two are my buddies." The cheerleader's big smile followed and ended the discussion. As always, the boys melted. Five-foot-two, bug cute, and sexy. They never stood a chance.

That night after his shift was over, Wesley hustled over to the OFI. By this time, the crowd around Mike had already thinned and he was closing his guitar case. Lizzie was not there.

Mike gave Wesley a once-over. "Are you looking for my sister?"

"Well . . . uhm . . . just thought I'd come over and hang out."

"In case you were, I haven't seen her since supper. I think she has a date."

Perhaps it was just an offhand comment, but somehow, Mike seemed less friendly than the previous night. It hadn't occurred to Wesley that he might have competition, and the sudden awareness of this possibility sent his imagination on a wild goose chase. She was probably kissing some guy she had deemed *worthy*. She wasn't interested in him, after all. Surely, she wasn't with Hez. Then a rational thought came to his mind: Why was he angry at Mike? Mike had been nice to him last night.

Trying to appear nonchalant, Wesley said, "Well, looks like the action has slowed down here for the evening, so I guess I'll head back to the dorm."

"Suit yourself."

From the east entrance, Lizzie appeared. Alone. Wesley's spirits lifted as she proceeded toward the fireplace.

Wesley took in every step. Every feature, from the way the Lee Rider jeans accented her long legs and feminine shape to the cascade of blond hair on her shoulders. And the inscrutable smile that considered whether you were worthy . . . or not.

"It looks like I missed all the singing. Mike has packed up his guitar, and Mr. Standish doesn't have his."

"Not much of a crowd tonight, anyway," Mike said, as he picked up his guitar case. "It's getting late. Do you want to walk back with me?"

"No, I just got here. Think I'll stick around for a while."

"Don't be late tomorrow, Elizabeth." Mike said, and left without looking back.

"Hi, Lizzie. I'm surprised to see you. Mike said you had a date."

"That rat. He just made that up. He is beginning to try my patience. Did you notice he called me *Elizabeth?* Lately, he has started acting like my dad and not just my boss. That's fine at work, but not after work."

"Maybe he just doesn't like *me*."

"He misses his girlfriend back home and gets jealous if a boy looks at me. Misery loves company. Don't take it personally."

"He asked me if I was looking for you—"

"Were you?"

"I supposed you might be here."

She stepped next to him and seized him by the shirt collar with one hand. "I not sure if you are worthy or not, Miles Standish. A girl waits to come out until you get off work, and you can't say whether you were looking for her?"

The soft scent of her perfume disarmed him. Everything *about* her disarmed him. He didn't want to dig any more holes, but he wanted to respond. To say *something*. Not even something clever, just something not dumb. "You smell nice." *Oh, that was lame,* he thought.

Still holding him by the shirt, she said, "You don't get off that easily, Mr. Standish. Were you looking for me?"

"Yes. As a matter of fact, I thought about you all day," Wesley said." *Oh God, talk about uncool.*

She released her grip on his shirt and began smoothing out the wrinkles. "You might be worthy after all."

"The coffee shop is about to close, but the geyser should blow in twenty minutes or so. Do you want to join the dudes and watch it?"

"Sounds good to me." Lizzie hooked her arm in his to be escorted.

Outside, a partial moon lurked behind scattered clouds. Moonlight glistened off the geyser basin, and the ever-present sulfurous smell saturated the air. They sat on an unoccupied split-log bench facing Old Faithful. Twenty yards from them, a park ranger answered inane questions from the tourists.

He watched the geyser but felt her warmth as they sat shoulder to shoulder. Her fresh scent softened the sulfuric odor around them— she did smell nice—and if they had been in a movie theater, it would have been a perfect opportunity to reach over and hold her hand.

It wasn't necessary. Lizzie took his hand and appeared to be examining it. "Let's see what I can tell about you. Hmm? Not many calluses—must be that indoor soda fountain work."

"Your hands are soft, and you work with horses."

"Because I wear gloves. Otherwise, I would have paws like a farmer. A girl doesn't want that. I should have brought a sweater, it's chilly out here."

"Yeah, it is kind of cold. I should have brought a jacket myself."

"Boy, some guys can't take a hint."

"Oh, I can take a hint, I just didn't know if I had been deemed *worthy*."

"Touché, Mister Standish."

As Wesley circled her shoulder with his arm, Lizzie got closer and leaned her head against his shoulders. It seemed impossible to Wesley that this spunky girl, who always seemed to be in control of any situation, and who constantly kept him on the defensive, snuggled against him now.

Everything about her felt perfect. Wesley angled closer and nudged her cheek to his lips. She seemed frozen. He tilted his head so he could kiss her lips, but she sat taller and brought her lips to his ear and whispered, "Leave a tender moment alone."

She leaned her head against his shoulder again, as he put his other arm around her without speaking.

"Nice move."

"Thanks, Priscilla." He wanted to show that he could play along by referring to her as Miles Standish's love interest.

After they chatted for a while, she said, "You may walk me home, Miles."

Along the way to Lizzie's dormitory, she asked, "Do you know how to ride a horse, plowboy?"

"Yes, as a matter of fact, I do." He said it with a hint of authority. "When I lived on the farm, we had a saddle horse that doubled as a plowing horse."

"You really *are* a plowboy," Lizzie said.

Wesley ignored her comment. "My grandpa was a blacksmith. He taught me how to tie the cinch on the saddle. How to sit in the saddle. How to neck-rein. I rode several times a week. He shod her so I could ride her on the roads."

"My dad doesn't believe in shoeing horses. He says it binds their hooves. Says they've been running the rocky hills for centuries without shoes." She cocked her head in an appraising manner. "At least you know something about horses. Maybe we could go for a ride some time?"

"That would be great."

"This would be a good night for a ride. Moonlight rides are the best . . . I've got an idea. After dark some night, we could slip down to the stables and take a couple horses up to Hotpot Pool."

"Where's Hotpot Pool?" Wesley asked. "I haven't heard of it."

"It's not on the maps. You can only get there on horseback or by foot," Lizzie explained. "The question is whether you are up for a slightly illegal adventure."

"Maybe. I've already had one encounter with the park rangers, and if that Ranger Brett gets wind that I am involved in some shenanigan, he'll have my hide and maybe get me kicked out of the park."

"Oh no," she said with mock concern, "should I be worried that I am hanging out with a criminal? What did you do?"

"Let's just say it was an innocent case of being in the wrong place at the wrong time. Nothing to worry about."

"Oh, come on. I have to know these things to judge your worthiness."

Feeling cornered, he said, "A couple guys and I were on the wrong side of the warning signs at Old Faithful."

"Why would you do that?" After a moment, she burst out laughing. "Oh no, you guys were trying to join IPIOF. That's so funny." She began laughing again.

His jaw tightened as he gritted his teeth.

"Oh, I'm sorry. I'll quit laughing." Then she started again.

Her laughter was contagious, and Wesley joined her. After they quit laughing, he said, "I guess it is pretty funny."

"Back to the original subject," he said, "what about this Hotpot Pool?"

"It's a hot spring that the rangers go to during the winter. Some of the wranglers have gone there on night rides, so Mike knows about it, but I doubt he would approve of me going with you, or any boy, for that matter. We would have to cover our tracks, so to speak."

"It doesn't sound like something that would get us thrown out of the park, but it might get *you* fired."

"He wouldn't dare fire me for that. Dad would be furious with him."

"Sure, then, I'm up for it. When?"

"The next night you don't work late."

"That's Monday."

They strolled hand in hand back to her dormitory. Lizzie stood on the step and was at eye level with Wesley. She extended both arms to his shoulders. "Then we'll go for a ride Monday night. The sun doesn't set until 8 o'clock. Meet me at the laundry by the lower Ham Store. And bring your swimming suit."

"Swimming suit?"

"Just bring it. But remember this is about *horses* and not *horsing around*. And don't tell anybody about this—gossip travels with the speed of light in the park."

"I can keep a secret," Wesley said.

"Then I'll seal it with a kiss." She put both hands on his face, touched her lips to his, and in a flash said, "Goodnight, plowboy."

She unlocked the door and glimpsed back at Wesley. "Hey, I kissed you goodnight, why are you still standing there?"

"Just waiting for you to get inside. Will you be at the inn tomorrow?"

"See you tomorrow night."

Chapter Four

When Wesley arrived at a quarter of eight Monday night, Lizzie stood waiting outside the laundry, a concrete block building that housed the Hamilton Store washers and dryers. She wore her usual uniform of jeans and a flannel shirt but had added a denim barn jacket.

"Where's your swim suit, Plowboy?"

"Underneath my jeans."

"Did you bring a towel?"

"Err . . . I guess I forgot it."

"Don't worry, I left a couple at the tack shed."

"Where's *your* swim suit?"

"Don't worry. This isn't my first rodeo."

"You sound like my mother. She always says that."

Wesley pointed at Lizzie's feet. She had on low-cut sneakers, the kind cheerleaders wore.

"No cowboy boots?"

"They're too hard to put back on if your feet are wet. Let's go."

By the time they got to the stables, the evening had turned dark. Lizzie pulled a flashlight from her jacket pocket and opened the door to the tack shed.

"Can you ride bareback, Plowboy? It will save time, and these horses can navigate the trail in their sleep."

"Sure."

She retrieved two bridles from hooks on the wall.

"Hey, you're not going to put me on a horse named Geronimo that nobody has ridden before, are you?"

"Don't worry. These are as gentle as they come."

Lizzie clutched the mane of her horse and vaulted on like an Indian. Wesley did the same. It wasn't his first rodeo, either.

Away from the light of the campground, the spectacular night sky bloomed. The stars appeared much larger than in the Ozarks. They resembled asterisks instead of periods and their number was innumerable. Wesley thought this must be the same sky his stepfather Sam saw at sea, and maybe what drew him back each year, leaving his mother and him behind.

The sounds from the inn faded as they rode, and a mountain breeze carried the scent of pines. The moonlit trail was wide enough for them to ride abreast, with a couple feet between them.

"Do you know which direction we're going?" Lizzie asked.

"West."

Surprised, she asked, "How'd you determine that?"

"Easy. The stars. The Big Dipper is to our right."

"So?" Lizzie's tone became Socratic, a teacher probing the extent of his knowledge.

"You may live on a horse ranch, Lizzie, but my stepfather is a sailor—twenty years in the Navy and a merchant seaman afterwards—he's on his way to India now. He didn't teach me how to throw a football, but at night he lectured on the stars."

"I'm impressed. Another facet of this unusual hillbilly. Tell me more."

"The last two stars that form the bottom of the Big Dipper are the *pointer stars*. They point at a 45-degree angle to the North Star, which is part of the Little Dipper. It works whether you are on land or sea. Did you see the movie *The Big Country* with Gregory Peck?"

"Yes. I loved it."

"Remember when Gregory Peck, the sea captain, went on his

journey out on the prairie? And the ranchers thought he was lost?"

"Yeah, that's when he met Jean Simmons, who owned the Big Muddy."

"Do you know what he was doing?"

"Not exactly, but he had a compass."

"That's right. And he had a rough map. What he was doing was *dead reckoning*."

"Okay, sailor, explain."

"A compass is marked with 360 degrees, same as a circle. If north is zero, then 90 degrees would be due east. That angle of direction is called an azimuth. A 180-degree azimuth would be south. So to get back where you came from, you just add 180 degrees to whatever azimuth you had been following. That's why he was never lost."

"I get it. You just go back the same way you came. You might be worth a nickel after all." After some silence, Lizzie asked, "Where's your real father? If that's not too personal."

The question caught him off guard, and his mind went blank. The sound of the swirling breeze in the pines seemed louder. With hesitation in his voice, he finally said, "He's dead."

"Oh my. I'm sorry."

"That's all right. My parents divorced when I was in the fourth grade, and I lost track of him. I heard he might have gone to Texas. Then we heard he died."

"Still very sad. I can't imagine losing my father. I get a chill just thinking about it."

Wesley didn't respond, and Lizzie didn't pursue the subject further. They rode in silence until the trail narrowed at a copse of shrubs, and Lizzie indicated this was where they needed to dismount. They tied the horses to the bushes.

"All right, Smarty Pants, what kind of bushes are these?" She illuminated them with her flashlight.

He leaned toward the bushes for a closer examination. "They sort of look like the gooseberry bush my grandma had on the farm."

"Not bad. They're ribes bushes."

"Oh, yeah. Those are the ones that cause the white pine blister rust, right?"

"Yep. And that give jobs to forestry students to comb through the woods with their buckets of goop to eradicate them."

Wesley said, "I wish I could get one of those jobs—they are on a federal pay scale."

"Maybe so, but I would rather work with people."

They trudged single-file up a little-used path and came to a barren opening in a few minutes. The familiar scent of sulfur filled the air but with less intensity than the main geyser basin. Lizzie pointed her flashlight at a slight billow of steam twenty yards ahead, and the light reflected off the surrounding calcium hardpan like a white sand beach.

"There she blows, sailor." A round pool, twenty feet in diameter, awaited. An official-looking sign warned, *Danger: No swimming.*

"Go on and get your clothes off and get in. You said you had your swim suit on underneath your jeans."

"But the sign says . . ."

"I know what the sign says, but that's for dudes. It's not an actual government sign. The rangers put it up to keep out the tourists. As I said, they use it, particularly in the winter when they have more free time and want to keep it private."

Wesley began unbuttoning his shirt.

"In fact, they have a thermometer under a ledge just to be safe, but the water stays at about 104 degrees—not enough to scald you, but warm enough for you to sleep well."

She reached into the water for the thermometer. "Perfect—104."

Wesley said, "Good to know I won't get scalded. Where's your suit?"

"Just ease in, and I will be back after I change."

Wesley removed his shirt and jeans and stuck his foot in the water. "Hey, this is pretty hot."

"Get in, you'll get used to it."

Wesley put a leg in up to his knee. "How deep is this?"

"Not sure. The bottom is uneven, but it's at least four feet."

Wesley submerged to his waist and clung to the edge until he found a ledge he could sit on. "Come on in, the water's fine."

Lizzie clicked off the flashlight, but Wesley could still see her profile as she hung her jacket on a tree limb and slipped out of her shirt and jeans.

Through the steam Lizzie appeared as a silhouette as she tiptoed to his side of the pool. She flipped on the flashlight to light her path, revealing she was wearing a two-piece swimsuit, not as skimpy as a bikini. She slipped into the water, a full body length away.

"Ooh, this is nice."

"Come on over."

She scooted to within a couple feet and touched his shoulder. Wesley reached to embrace her, but she gave him a running back's stiff arm.

"My first rule of skinny dipping is keeping a respectable distance. Remember what I said about horsing around?"

"But you're wearing a swimming suit, so we're not really skinny dipping."

"Doesn't matter."

"Have you been skinny dipping before?"

"Maybe . . . but that's for me to know."

The buoyancy of the mineral-filled water floated her breasts to the surface and offered a modestly revealing view. He wanted to touch them and kiss her, but he dismissed the thought as outside the ground rules.

"Mr. Standish, don't you have anything to say?" She hesitated, and then added, "About the water?"

"It would be a whole lot nicer if you were a little closer," he said as he reached tentatively toward her.

"That, Mr. Standish, is a whole new level of worthiness," she said, with slight edge in her voice, but her closest hand found his and gripped it like a rein. Softly enough to be gentle but firm enough to demonstrate control.

"I know . . . and leave a tender moment alone."

"And your swimming suit on."

They sat in silence, but still held hands. Wesley searched the skies for a new topic, but instead of a solution, the stars were a kaleidoscope. The hot water soon calmed him, and he leaned back against the smooth calcite edge of the pool and flutter-kicked his legs.

After several minutes, Lizzie broke the silence. "What a beautiful night, and the water feels great . . . Wesley, I didn't mean to hurt your feelings."

He hated that phrase, *hurt feelings*. Children and girls got hurt feelings, and he would not acknowledge it. "Yes, it is a beautiful night, but it will be chilly when we get out."

With no response to her apology, Lizzie went along with his change of course and said, "Actually, it won't. Your body heat will still keep you warm until you dry off. Speaking of heat, I've had about all I can stand before I start getting dizzy."

She edged over to her towel and slipped out in the darkness. "You don't have to get out yet."

"No, I'll get out, too." He got out and began toweling off.

They got dressed in silence and got on their horses. The ride back produced only token bits of conversation.

After they had secured the door on the tack shed, Lizzie said, "You don't have to walk me to my dorm."

"Why wouldn't I do that?"

"You were so quiet on the ride back."

"I was just thinking, that's all."

"About what?"

"I can't figure you out. Last night, you said I couldn't take a hint, but tonight you wouldn't come close enough for me to kiss you."

"It wasn't the time or place for kissing."

"Well, when is?"

"You don't understand. I need to be sure about you—and me—before I let myself get all emotional about you. I probably shouldn't have taken you to the pool."

"What are you talking about?"

"It's about trust. Girls have feelings that are different than the way guys feel. There were some boys back home . . . never mind. It's late, and I have to go."

"I'm walking with you."

"That's a good start, hillbilly." She marched forward and Wesley followed.

"So, tell me about the boys back home . . . or is that another level of worthiness?"

"It's quite personal, and first I want to know more about you."

"To see if I am worthy?"

"Maybe." She hesitated. "I am curious about your real father. I can tell you respect your stepfather, but you almost seem indifferent about your real father."

Wesley's posture stiffened, and his pace slowed. He didn't respond.

"See what I mean?" she said. "Some things are personal, and they aren't easy to talk about unless we trust someone." She turned her head toward Wesley but kept walking. "I'll make a deal with you. First, you tell me more about your father, and then I'll tell you about the boys back home."

Wesley wasn't prepared for this development and stopped midstride. She took his hand, and without speaking, he followed her lead toward the dormitory.

As they walked, a sinking feeling fogged Wesley's thinking. If asked, he would have denied it amounted to fear, but it compared to the feeling he experienced before a big game or a schoolyard fight. He had never backed down before, because shame trumped fear. Suddenly, though, a bit of clarity crossed his mind: His shame caused his fear.

Halfway to her dorm he finally responded. "I think I understand what you mean by *worthiness*. It's about trust. Do I trust you enough to tell you about things I haven't shared? And if I told you, or you told me, would we keep it just between ourselves and still like each other?"

She pulled him into a full embrace and whispered in his ear. "That's one of the worthiest things I've heard you say. The question is whether it's worth the risk of uncertainty. I think so, and I promise you can trust me with your secrets, and I will still like you." Then she pushed him to arm's length. "As long as you haven't murdered someone."

He squeezed her hand, and they picked up their pace. "It's a deal."

She squeezed back.

A sense of urgency hit him. Somehow, he knew that if he didn't tell her now, he never would. In a near blurt, he said, "My parents got divorced when I was in the fourth grade. My dad was an over-the-road trucker, and he had a girlfriend on the side."

"How did you know that?"

"I met her."

"Really?" she said in a halting voice, and her eyes widened in surprise.

"Yeah, I was living on the farm with my grandparents, and one day, he pulled his rig into the front yard, with his girlfriend riding shotgun in the cab. She wasn't pretty like my mother."

Lizzie's mouth opened wide in disbelief. "Was you father always this bad?"

Wesley squirmed his lips, hesitating before he spoke. "Maybe not. He was gone a lot. My stepfather won't let me ever say anything negative about him. He says my dad was a veteran and deserves my respect. But he drank too much. I remember some good times, but then there were other times that . . ." Wesley's voice started to falter, and he quit talking.

At her front steps, she put her arm around him and said, "It's all right, you don't have to tell me anymore."

Wesley raised his arm to see his wristwatch. It was midnight.

Lizzie moved up onto the steps and turned toward him. Wesley had his head down and was feeling a little nervous to face her. She put both her arms around him, and her lips touched the top of his head. In a soft, caring voice said, "I'm sorry this happened to you. It wasn't your fault . . . and I still like you." She kissed his head.

In an exhausted voice Wesley said, "I've never told anyone that. People find out stuff about you, and they use it against you. Sometimes it's people you thought you could trust."

"You can trust me, Wesley, and I will keep my end of the bargain, but it will have to wait for another day. I have to get to bed. Six o'clock will come early tomorrow."

Before she opened the door, she put both her hands on his face, and brought her barely parted lips to his. The kiss lasted just a few seconds longer this time. "Goodnight, Plowboy."

Wesley began the walk back toward his dorm. He made it as far as Old Faithful, where he sat down on a bench at the perimeter. He was alone. The tourists had gone to their rooms and tents.

By now he was used to the sulfurous smell—he barely noticed. The temperature had dropped to the forties, and he crossed his arms against the chill. Although he was thrilled that Lizzy had kissed him, even if it was a quick one, his stomach churned at the same time. What had he been thinking when he told her about his dad? Girls liked to gossip. It would be all over the park that his dad was a drunk. He hadn't intended to tell her so much. At least he hadn't told her that his old man had also gone to prison.

CHAPTER FIVE

The next morning, Wesley woke with a sense of impending doom and a late-night confession "hangover." After some rationalization, his concern that Lizzie would broadcast the unflattering family secrets lessened. After all, she had promised he could trust her, and Mormons were religious, so she would probably keep her promise. He also thought he recalled some proverb in the Bible against gossip. But after a night's sleep, would she still think him worthy?

Wesley was glad he had the evening shift at the soda fountain today. Hez and Cliff had the morning stint, and they would have grilled him about his date. He certainly didn't plan to tell either of them what he had shared with Lizzie. He cringed when he imagined what Hez, the love 'em and leave 'em cowboy, might say.

After lunch he killed some time and roamed among the tourists watching Old Faithful. Even though he wanted to avoid Hez and Cliff, he was antsy to get to work. Staying busy was better than thinking.

When he arrived at the soda fountain, Betty huddled the incoming shift in the storage room for a pow-wow.

"Listen up, folks. We've got a problem. The food service company shipped a double order of bananas by mistake this morning, and they won't take them back. That leaves us with a huge pile of ripe fruit. So . . . we're gonna have ourselves a banana split contest. You'll work in pairs, and as a prize, the waitress and soda jerk from each shift who peddle the most banana splits will be my guests for dinner in West Yellowstone. Cliff and Margaret were the winners of the early shift. So let's see who will be joining them for dinner."

More than one set of eyes bulged with this offer coming from Betty, the self-admitted penny-pincher. However, she hadn't said *where* the dining experience would be. Hopefully, not some truck stop diner.

Vivian bumped her hip against Wesley to get his attention and then said, "We're going to win this." Her hip check gave him a pleasurable throb, and his morning angst crept to the recesses of his mind.

"One more thing," Betty said, "Cliff and Margaret had to sell 15 banana splits to be the champs of the early shift. So you'll have to get your hustle on if you expect to win."

Once their shift started, waitresses whizzed back and forth with their orders, and soda jerks dipped ice cream like miners digging gold. For a change, the girls even helped splitting the bananas. Vivian put her Southern charm into high gear, and after three hours, she and Wesley had sold 10 banana splits. If they were going to win, they'd have to scramble.

About the same time that Old Faithful blew at 5 p.m., the electricity suddenly went out, and a hum of confused voices buzzed inside the store. Worried department managers in the grocery and sundries sections of the Hamilton Store began ushering customers outside. However, Betty saw an opportunity and rushed to the main area and announced that the soda fountain would continue to serve customers. And tourists leaving Old Faithful piled in for sodas and ice cream.

Skylights furnished adequate light for patrons to see their way to their seats. The power outage proved to be a blessing in disguise. With no electricity, the milkshake mixers wouldn't work, and the popularity of banana splits soared.

By the time the lights went back on two hours later, Wesley and Vivian had sold 20 banana splits, five more than any other team on their shift.

"Hotdog, Vivian. It looks like you and I will be dining with Cliff and Margaret. The shift's about over—nobody will catch us," Wesley said.

With a matter-of-fact expression on her face, Vivian said, "Told you we'd win. And Betty says we're going to the Wagon Wheel. I haven't been there yet."

Giving her a suspicious look, Wesley said. "Just where else have you been in West Yellowstone?"

"Oh, a few places, but never you mind. Here's what I want to know. Will you have to get permission from your new girlfriend to go out with an older woman? I might try to take advantage of you."

"No. I've only seen her a few times." His inflection implied Lizzie was no big deal, but even as he said it, he felt like Peter denying Christ. And what made him feel worse was that he hoped Vivian *would* try to take advantage of him.

"Okay, then," she said in an insipid voice. Apparently satisfied with the situation, she changed subjects. "Hey, would you mind staying to clean up for me? I've got a date. That is, unless you have one, too."

Wesley forced an upbeat response. "I don't. Go ahead."

"Thanks, buddy, I'll make it up to you."

Wesley didn't have a date, exactly. Nothing had been said about meeting Lizzie this evening, but he suspected she would be at the Old Faithful Inn. The anxiety, which had vanished from his mind during the excitement of the afternoon, crept back in. Maybe he wouldn't go over. He wanted company but didn't want to face her, after what he had told her last night.

When Wesley entered the dorm room, Hez was applying aftershave, apparently getting ready for a date. "Who's the lucky girl tonight?" Wesley asked him.

"A cutie from the lower Ham Store. What about you? Going out?"

"Nah, I don't think so."

"Aren't you going to meet your honey at the OFI?"

"We never made any specific plans about tonight."

"Haven't you been meeting her regularly after work?"

"Yes, but we had sort of an unsettling talk last night."

"Cuz, if you got any ass in your pants, you ought to hustle on over there. Some other old hound dog's liable to be sniffing around."

Hez ran a comb through his hair and gave a satisfied look at himself in the mirror. "Good enough," he said to his reflection. He pulled his set of skeleton keys from his jeans pocket, displayed them with a jangle, and shoved off with a smile on his face.

Wesley lay on his bunk for a while, but he couldn't shake Hez's comment. The thought of some dude bird-dogging Lizzie did not sit well with him. He brushed his teeth, combed his hair, and beat it over to the OFI.

Inside the inn, Lizzie sat alone at a table in a small alcove on the mezzanine. She was writing in a spiral notebook. The light from two amber sconces highlighted her blond hair and created mysterious shadows on her face.

As Wesley approached, Lizzie said, "I was afraid you might not show up tonight for my half of our deal."

"No, I'm here," he said, not acknowledging his earlier reluctance. He had been so preoccupied with himself, he had forgotten about the bargain they had made, that she would tell him about the boys in her hometown. He sat down opposite her. "What are you writing?"

"My part of the bargain. It's a journal I've had for a while. I try to write in it every day. Sometimes it's just about what I did or where I went that day. But other times it's more about thoughts and feelings. And it helps me work through unhappy memories if I write them down. And one of the entries explains what I was talking about last night . . . about back home and some boys being different. If you are ready, I'll tell you."

A sudden sense of relief flooded him. She still liked him and had no apparent second thoughts about his worthiness. For some reason, that was enough, and he no longer cared whether she told the world about his father. "Yes, I'd like to hear it if you think I'm worthy."

"We'll see," Lizzie said. "All right, here goes … In high school, there was this guy I detested named Jimmy Leavitt. He was totally arrogant. The captain of the football team, and all the cheerleaders thought he was some dreamboat." Her mouth gaped and she faked a vomiting sound. "He was good-looking enough, but insufferable. Always smiling and winking and never staying with one girl for long. At one time or another, he had dated most of the cute girls in the school and some in neighboring towns."

"I know the type," Wesley said, nodding his head in sympathy.

"I never dated him," Lizzie said. "My father would have never allowed it, and my brother Mike said if a girl wanted her reputation to go down the drain, then Jimmy was the guy. But on the last day of my freshman year, I missed the school bus to take me home, so I started walking. It was about three miles, and I had just made it to the highway, a few blocks from the school, when Leavitt pulls over in his '55 Chevy Bel Air and offers me a ride."

Wesley listened without comment. He thought from her original reluctance to talk about the incident that it must be embarrassing, and he didn't want to say something awkward.

"So, I got in." Lizzie turned her head, avoiding eye contact. "At first everything seemed fine. I mean, we just talked about school and sports, but about a half-mile from the lane to my house, he pulled the car over to the shoulder. I asked why he was stopping, and he said we needed to get better acquainted. He said that he had noticed me for a while and thought I was cute."

Lizzie's expression dulled. "Now, I'm mortified to say that I was flattered . . . by someone I thought was a creep." She stopped talking and grimaced. Then she said, "This is harder than I imagined it would be," as she began nervously flipping through the pages of her notebook.

This was the first time Wesley had seen Lizzie hesitant, almost vulnerable, and it stirred his compassionate side. "You're doing fine. Remember, we made a deal—I'll still think you are *worthy*.

Wesley's use of Lizzie's word produced a wan smile on her lips. She looked at him and closed the notebook. And in a voice just above a whisper, she picked up where she had left off.

"Jimmy scooted next to me and put his hand on my shoulder. Then he touched a strand of hair behind my ear and smoothed it. 'Your hair is so soft,' he whispered, and he leaned closer until his nose and lips were next to my ear. It gave me a shivery feeling.

"Now, I grew up on a farm and knew about the birds and the bees, but it was a detached knowledge. This was *real*. It was exciting, but scary."

Lizzie continued. "His hand guided my face toward his. I knew he was about to kiss me, so I shut my eyes." Lizzie tightened her lips and shook her head slowly. "I look back, now, and wonder how I could have been so stupid."

Wesley touched her shoulder. "We've all done stuff we regret."

"Well, when Jimmy's lips touched mine, his mouth was wide open. It startled me. He stuck his tongue in my mouth, and I nearly gagged. My older sister had told me about French kissing, but it wasn't what I imagined."

Wesley's mind flashed to his freshman year when an older girl kissed him with an open mouth and her tongue. He didn't have an older brother to clue him in about such things, and none of his buddies had ever mentioned it. It came as complete surprise and was exciting, but definitely not scary. Now, he thought, most freshman girls wouldn't be the least bit surprised. Still, he could understand how Lizzie must have felt back then.

"Wesley, are you listening?"

"Yes, I was just picturing the scene."

Lizzie continued. "Somehow, the top button on my blouse had come undone. I don't know why I hadn't noticed, but before I could fix it, Jimmy jammed his hand down the front of my blouse and was trying to get his fingers inside my bra. I definitely noticed *that*. I yanked his hand away. Roping colts and hefting hay bales had given me a strong grip, and I used it."

Interrupting, Wesley said with disgust, "What a jerk."

Lizzie responded with a thin, wistful smile, and then took a deep breath. She blinked a couple times and wiped her eyes, which were beginning to tear.

"I told him to stop it! But he laughed and said he was just trying to see 'what I had underneath my shirt,' and told me there was no reason to be so upset. Upset? I was furious. He said he was sorry, but his voice dripped with sarcasm. I called him an ass and said if I told my dad, he would come after him with his gelding knife."

Wesley's mouth curved into a lopsided grin. "You really said that?"

"I most certainly did. Then I got out and slammed the door and started walking."

"What did he do then?"

"He started the car and pulled up to a slow pace alongside me and said, 'Hey, what's wrong with you? Most girls like it.' I told him to leave me alone or I *would* tell my dad . . . and my brother. He wheeled the car around, squealed his tires on the blacktop, and popped second-gear rubber as he sped away."

Believing that some starch had returned to Lizzie's demeanor, Wesley said, "I know that must have been upsetting, but it sounds as if you handled it like a champ."

"But that's not where it ended. The next day at school Leavitt told a couple of his pals I was easy and that he had gotten to "second base" with me. He also told them that all I had was 'bee stings for boobs.' And before the day was over, that gossip was all over school."

Lizzie exhaled a sigh that sounded weary, yet relieved. "So now you know why I am cautious . . . and, maybe, why my brother Mike is suspicious of strange boys. He nearly got into a fist fight with Jimmy."

When Wesley didn't immediately respond, she said, "You probably think I'm weird."

"No, you're not weird, but you can be a little confusing. I don't want to make you mad, but I feel like I've been getting some mixed signals from you. First, you flirt with me and tell me I can't take a hint. Next, you won't kiss me at the hot springs. I hope you don't think I'm like that Leavitt guy."

"Not even close."

"Then why have you been so hesitant?"

"I guess I get confused, too. Sort of like how I was confused at first with Jimmy. I am not *easy*, but I suppose I do like how it feels for a boy to pay that kind of attention to me. And I know I can be a natural flirt—at least with a nice boy that I think is worthy. But I also wanted to know you better before getting too involved." A muscle in her jaw twitched. "Because if I do get involved with you, I don't know if I am ready for a heartbreak at the end of the summer."

Wesley leaned closer and offered a small smile. "On the way back from the hot springs, you said girls' feelings are different from those of guys. I think I know what you meant now."

Her eyes glistened, and she reached across the table with both hands. "That's the worthiest thing you could have said."

Wesley took her hands in his. "Well, you kept your side of the deal, so now what?"

She squeezed his hands. "I think we are officially dating, and I am declaring you as semi-worthy. But it's late, and one of us has to get up at the crack of dawn tomorrow. With your new semi-worthy status, it is your official duty to walk me to my dorm."

"Then does that mean it's your duty to give me a semi-worthy goodnight kiss?"

"I think that can be arranged, Plowboy."

On the way back to his dorm, Wesley thought how different this night was from the last. He had a warm, joyful feeling that everything would work out fine.

The semi-worthy kiss had been exciting. He had hugged her so tightly he could feel the warmth of her body. And he knew she couldn't help feeling his excitement. He wanted it to last longer, but she had gently pushed him away, saying, "It's getting late. I've got to go in." She pecked his lips with hers again and said, "Sweet dreams."

As he walked down the hall of his dormitory, Wesley saw Hez in the bathroom rinsing his toothbrush.

"Pretty late for you. I guess you got some ass in your pants after all. I've got to meet this mystery girl."

Wesley grinned, and thrust his left arm out like a halfback stiff-arming a tackler. "Don't get any big ideas about my girl."

"*Your girl*. My, how things change in a few hours." His face became more serious. "Don't worry, Cuz, I never bird-dog a friend's chick. But I do want to meet her. I'm having a party Saturday night. A couple girls who work at the lodge rented one of the cabins. A few lodge employees will be there, but they told me to invite whoever I wanted. So I'll pass the word to a chosen few."

Chapter Six

Wesley had the late shift the following day at the fountain. The moment he arrived for duty, Betty and Vivian began peppering him with questions about his new girlfriend. Hez must have ratted him out.

"So, I hear you and this new girl are an item, now," Betty said.

Vivian chimed in. "So I'm not your true love after all?"

The two women could not be ignored, and Wesley struggled for a witty comeback.

"Come on, Wes. Fess up," said Cliff, who had taken a seat at the counter and joined the ambush.

"Et tu, Brutus?" Wesley gave his roommate the stink eye.

Vivian flipped a shop towel at him, which just missed its intended mark—Wesley's butt. "You might as well tell us about her, because you know we won't stop."

Wesley scowled at her in mock anger. "Don't you have a customer to wait on?"

"Not until the geyser blows." The customer side of the counter only had store employees lingering between shifts.

"All right. All right. I give up. She's works at the OFI stables."

"Is she cute?"

Of course, Vivian had to ask that. "Yes," Wesley said.

"How old is she?" Vivian persisted.

"My age. What is this . . . an inquisition?"

Betty came to his rescue. "Back to work, everyone. Customers are arriving."

Undaunted, Vivian said, "What did you say her name was?"

"Elizabeth."

"That's a start. At least she doesn't have a cowgirl name like Buckboard Betty."

With the arrival of customers, the questions ceased, and the remainder of the shift was routine. When the next shift's staff arrived, Betty announced the location of the banana split contest dinner. "Friday night the contest winners will be dining with me at the Wagon Wheel Bar and Grill in West Yellowstone. I'll arrange for shift changes so that Vivian and Wesley can attend."

"Does that include cocktails?" Vivian asked.

"If you are 21, I'll buy one."

"Heck, that puts me on the water wagon with the Mormons," Cliff said.

Margaret elbowed him in the ribs. "Hey, knock off the sarcasm about Mormons, you infidel."

"Sorry, I didn't know you were a Mormon."

"I'm not. Just pimping you, sweetie."

Cliff shook his head. "I can't win around here."

"Back to your duty stations," Betty said.

As Vivian and Wesley walked out, she asked, "Are you excited about going out to dinner, Wesley?"

"I suppose so." They continued to walk to the rear service entrance.

"Wesley, I'm crushed. The opportunity to have dinner with me, and you're not thrilled?"

"That part is exciting." He imagined sitting close to her in the back seat.

She stopped at her dorm entrance. "Be sure and tell Elizabeth 'hello' from your fountain girlfriends." She gave a little wave and stepped inside.

What was that all about?

Later that evening Wesley met Lizzie at the OFI. When he reached the table in "their" alcove, she stood up and said, "Let's go outside." She gazed over Wesley' shoulder. "Don't look now, but this guy across the room has been staring at me. He came over to my table, but I told him I was meeting someone."

Wesley willed himself not to gawk, but as they descended the stairs, he casually glanced over the lobby. The suspect was easy to spot. A college-aged guy in a madras shirt, who defiantly did not avert his stare when their eyes met. A surge of anger engulfed him.

Lizzie tugged his hand like she was reining a horse back on a trail. "Don't cause a scene. My honor is intact."

The fresh air outside calmed him. The acrid smell of the geyser basin was subtler than usual. Wesley wondered if he had simply become immune to it, like residents of a coal mining town ignoring the smoke. But then his thoughts returned to the bird-dogging fellow inside.

"I wonder who that guy was? He seemed like a jerk to me," Wesley said.

"Oh, I don't know. He was kind of cute."

Wesley did a double-take at Lizzie.

"Hey, I was just teasing. Don't be so jealous. He didn't do anything."

"I'm not jealous."

"Come here." Lizzie clutched his hands and pulled him toward her. "Don't be mad. It makes me feel good that you were a little jealous. If you weren't, I would think you didn't care."

She leaned her head and accepted his kiss as they made their way from the inn to her dorm.

"Hey, my friend Hez is having a party at one of the lodge cabins on Saturday. A couple of his girlfriends rented it. Do you want to go with me? We could go after I get off work."

"From what you've said about Hez, it will probably be wild."

"With Hez, it will most likely be interesting. Anyway, he wants me to bring you. Since he's never met you, he says you're my *pretend friend.*"

"Is it a drinking party?"

"Yeah, I imagine it will be."

"I don't like to go to drinking parties."

"I know you're a Mormon, but I'm a Baptist, and I don't drink either. We could still go and not drink."

"No, I'd rather skip it. Saturday will be a long day for me—I have two rides, including the sunset ride. You can certainly go. I wouldn't want you to miss the party on account of me."

Wesley attempted to control the disappointment he felt at the rejection. "I understand, but I can't see you tomorrow night."

"Why? Are you angry because I don't want to go to the party?"

"No. Betty, the fountain manager, is taking a few of us into West Yellowstone for dinner as a reward for winning the banana split contest."

Lizzie displayed a pouting expression. "Then I won't see you until Sunday night, since you are going to the party."

"I guess so."

The euphoric feeling left without excusing itself, leaving Wesley in a state of awkward confusion. Each snippet of a response that came to his mind fell flat and never escaped his lips. The walk back was without conversation. And in the silence, the tension rose.

At her dorm Lizzie gave him a peck for a kiss and simply said goodnight and closed the door.

An evening that had started with such promise soured, leaving Wesley with an uneasy sense about the progress of this new relationship. Or lack of progress. What was the deal with this girl? All that had happened with Lizzie was a few kisses. Maybe it was a religious thing. Or worse, maybe she was stringing him along.

On Friday evening, Betty and the lucky winners piled into her Rambler for the trip to West Yellowstone. To Wesley's chagrin, Vivian called shotgun and sat up front, leaving Margaret between Cliff and him in the back seat.

Betty and Margaret, by park standards at least, had dolled up in evening attire. Betty wore an unfortunate floral print shirtwaist dress that accentuated her midriff rolls. Margaret, a third-grade school teacher with the summer off, wore a simple skirt and blouse suitable for a PTA meeting.

Vivian, the University of Alabama sorority girl, whose "daddy was a friend of Coach Bear Bryant," presented a different picture, with an ivory silk top tucked in black Capri pants. The low-cut blouse revealed the outline of her bra through the sheer fabric. An ensemble designed to show off her shapely figure and draw attention.

Before they got in the car, Cliff whispered to Wesley, "Vivian is all boobs and out for a night on the town." He used the French pronunciation of her name.

Thirty minutes later, Betty parked in the lot adjacent to the Wagon Wheel. The roofline was outlined with neon tubing, and windows on either side of the front door displayed flashing signs for Coors and Olympia beers.

Wesley hurried out, opened the driver's door for Betty, and then darted to the passenger side to open Vivian's door as well. Cliff waited with the back door open as Margaret slid out.

Vivian showed no sign of getting out of the car as Wesley stood next to the open door. "Wesley, when you are assisting a lady out of a car, you don't just open the door and stand there like a bump on a log. You extend your hand so she can take it."

Wesley bowed from the waist with great flair. "M'lady, a thousand pardons. I'm normally pretty suave, but when I get around a Tri Delta, I get all nervous." Vivian laughed, and Wesley extended his hand.

Inside, a lobby and cashier's counter separated the Wagon Wheel into two sections. To the left, batwing swinging doors led to a vintage Western saloon, with an antique wagon wheel hanging behind a 30-

foot bar. Cigarette smoke wafted out, causing Margaret to fan the air with her hand. The dining room was on the right.

Behind the bar, a bartender wearing a cowboy shirt with a bolo string tie tended drink orders for several customers, only men, all in cowboy hats. Maybe women would arrive later; it was only about 5:30. Betty had insisted they arrive early.

A woman about Betty's age, dressed like a cowgirl, including boots with inlaid turquoise bison on the shafts, greeted the group with a cheery welcome. "My name is Sally. I'm the dining hostess at the Wagon Wheel. You must be Betty. I have your table set up."

Betty thanked her, and Sally ushered them through the dining area that continued the Western motif, with mass-produced Western-themed paintings, more wagon wheels, and replica branding irons. Twenty tables of mixed shapes and sizes covered with red-checkered tablecloths provided the seating, and candles burned inside amber-toned votives on each table, filling the room with a warm glow.

Manners being the order of the evening, Cliff and Wesley assisted the women with their chairs as they sat down.

"Thank you, gentlemen," Betty said. Then, as if she were responsible for their courtly behavior, said to Sally, who stood by with menus, "My boys are always polite."

Sally reciprocated with a nod and a smile. "Your waiter will be here shortly to take your orders."

A few minutes after Sally left, a dark-haired man in his early twenties, wearing a white shirt, a clip-on bow tie, and black slacks, approached their table. He stood between Betty and Vivian. Wesley noticed the waiter wasn't wearing socks with his penny loafers. This must be a fashion trend that hadn't hit the Midwest. Apparently, it worked for Vivian, who seemed to be eyeing the waiter with much approval.

"My name is Paul, and I'll be serving you this evening. May I take your drink orders?"

Betty said, "I'd like a Grasshopper."

"I usually have those after dinner," Vivian said, "but it does sound refreshing." She directed her attention to her new interest. "Paul, I'll have one, too."

Margaret peered over the top of her menu. "What is a Grasshopper?" Before the waiter could respond, Vivian said, "It's this divine cocktail of crème de menthe and crème de cocoa mixed with ice cream."

"Well then, I'll have a Grasshopper, too."

Without being asked, Cliff said, "I'll have a bottle of Coors."

"No, you won't," Betty said.

"Oh, all right," Cliff mumbled. "I'll have iced tea."

Wesley followed Cliff's lead and ordered an iced tea.

As soon as Paul left, Vivian said, in a hushed voice, "He's a dreamboat."

"If I were younger . . ." Betty mused, and then added, "but we've got two good-looking guys with us."

"Yes, we do," Margaret said.

When Paul reappeared with the drinks, Vivian asked, "Paul, are you just working here for the summer?"

"That's right." He supplied a big smile and began serving the drinks.

Vivian beamed back a smile. "Are you going back to college in the fall?"

"No, got to get ready for ski season. I'm an instructor at the ski school in Jackson Hole."

The women's eyes locked on Paul as they placed their orders. Cliff gave Wesley a disgruntled look, and Wesley returned a slight nod. Both ordered hamburgers and fries.

After dinner, while the group stood at the cashier's counter, Paul came by and said he hoped to see them again, but his eyes focused on Vivian, who gave him a cute little wave. For sure, Paul would show up at the fountain in the future.

During the drive back, the women seemed delighted with the entire evening. With the cocktails. With the food. And with Paul. Wesley was not so enamored. He'd had no cocktails, he'd tasted better hamburgers at the A&W back home, and although he knew he stood no real chance of getting cozy with Vivian, it didn't stop him from being jealous of the attention she had lavished on Paul. He breathed a quiet sigh and stared at the geyser basin gleaming in the moonlight.

CHAPTER SEVEN

Word had gotten out about Hez's party. Partiers stood elbow to elbow in the rented one-room cabin. The guests, many from Wesley's dorm who didn't work at the soda fountain, took advantage of the opportunity to let off steam.

Some lounged on the double bed. Some sprawled on the linoleum floor. Others hung out by the kitchenette table that served as a bar, stocked with screw-cap wines and several liquor bottles. A guy near the sink, which was full of ice and beer, smoked a pipe reeking of cherry tobacco. He wore an ascot and chatted up a fat girl from the grocery department, who appeared to be hanging on his every word.

Hez held court at the bar, surrounded by several girls, and waved to Wesley when he entered. "C'mon over and get a drink."

Wesley excused himself as he passed between two girls who babbled as they stood in line at the bathroom door. In the far corner, Vivian sat in a chair, with a drink in hand, talking to a guy in a Minnesota sweatshirt. She waved at Wesley as they made eye contact. He waved back and squeezed his way through the crowd toward Hez.

"Quite a party, Hez. Where are the girls who rented the cabin?"

"Over there." Hez nodded toward the bathroom. "Those two girls you just passed—Barb and Wanda. They work at the lodge cleaning rooms. Hey, where's your cowgirl? Thought you had a date."

"She didn't want to come because there would be drinking."

Hez shrugged, as if to say, "Oh, well."

The girls Hez had been flirting with had begun their own conversation when Wesley arrived. So Wesley moved closer to Hez and lowered his voice. "I'm not sure how well it's going with her. She barely lets me kiss her. We were at this secret hot pool with just swimsuits on, and she wouldn't even let me kiss her."

"Son, she's either just a tease or she's testing you."

"Testing me? What do you mean?"

"It's like this. If she isn't just stringing you along, she wants to know if you are a puppy dog—seeing if she can lead you around on a leash."

"I think part of it is her religion. She's a Mormon."

"I don't care if she is a psalm-singing Pentecostal—she's still a woman. Does she have somebody else she's dating?"

"Nobody I'm aware of. She says we are *officially dating.*"

"Well, it doesn't sound very official to me. Grab a beer and join the fun. And follow Cousin Hez's rule: *When I'm not near the girl I love, I love the girl I'm near.*"

From behind Wesley, Vivian said, "Hezekiah, don't corrupt my protégé." She put an arm around Wesley's waist and leaned into him. In her other hand she held a drink.

"I'm just dispensing sound advice," Hez said. "It sounds to me like this cowgirl is trifling with our boy's feelings."

"Well, that little hussy." Vivian's voice had a mocking lilt. "Hezekiah, get him a beer."

"I don't drink beer."

"Then, taste this." She pushed her paper cup toward his mouth.

"What is it?"

"The fancy name is Cuba Libre, but it's rum, Coke, and lime juice. It is a lovely libation."

Wesley swayed as he shifted his weight from one foot to the other. "I don't drink alcohol."

"Wesley, you need to learn to drink socially before you arrive on the college campus. You won't find any sorority girls who don't drink. I know you are Baptist, but let me tell you, if the Baptists and

Methodists in Tuscaloosa quit drinking, all the liquor stores would go out of business."

Wesley certainly understood closet drinking. He swallowed hard as he recalled the admonitions of his grandmother and his vow to himself not to be like his father.

As if reading his thoughts, Vivian said, "Wesley, the boogeyman isn't going to jump out of the shadows and drag you to hell if you have a cocktail. It wasn't grape juice Jesus was drinking."

Vivian radiated her Alabama cheerleader smile—that irresistibly enchanting smile—and then nudged her curvy hip against his thigh. It was the fatal blow to his temperance. With no conscious thought, Wesley took a gulp of the drink as if it were plain Coke.

Vivian waited for his reaction. "Now, was that so bad?"

He licked his lips. The lingering taste of the lime and coke, even with the hint of whiskey, reminded him of a soda fountain drink, not the Apocalypse. He pondered how to respond and finally said, "It wasn't too bad."

"Hez, fix Wesley one of these, and he can tell me about his girlfriend problems."

When Hez handed the drink to Wesley, Vivian put both her hands around Wesley's other arm and led him toward the chair she had vacated but reserved with her cigarette case. "Come and sit with me."

Wesley sat on the cushion and Vivian perched on the wide arm of the mission-style chair.

"So, tell me about this girl who is stealing your heart from me. Elizabeth, is that right?"

"Yes. She leads the horseback rides for tourists."

"Oh, a girl wrangler. Sounds pretty rough to me. Does she smell like horses?"

Wesley reacted with a frown and said, "No."

Vivian poked him on the arm. "I'm just teasing you. I just hate to think little ol' me is being forsaken for a cowgirl."

Halfway through his drink, an unfamiliar warm feeling came over him. Being a first-time drinker, he didn't associate the euphoria with the drink.

He focused on Vivian's lips as she sipped through a straw. He knew she did this so her lipstick wouldn't get smeared, and that she always kept several straws from the soda fountain in her purse. Her lipstick imprinted the straw with a red smudge.

"Have you kissed her? I need to know how serious this is."

"She kissed me on the cheek . . . and then once on the lips, but it was pretty speedy."

"Wesley, you need some help in the kissing department."

"I know how to kiss, Vivian."

"I know a big football star like you didn't get through high school without fogging up the windows of your car with some cutie-pie. What I'm talking about is reading a woman's signals."

She rattled the ice cubes in her drink. "Like this one." She tinkled the ice cubes again. "That's a Southern girl's signal that she would like another libation. It is much more ladylike than saying 'I want some more booze.'" She extended her cup to him.

Wesley got the hint and went back to the table. "Hez, she wants another drink . . . and mix one for me, too."

"You got it. Two rum-Cokes coming up."

Wesley returned with the drinks and sat down.

"Thank you, kind sir. Now, back to *signals*. You said she kissed you one time on the lips, but very quickly. Where were you when this happened?"

"We were at the door to her dorm. I walked her there."

"Ah, the perfunctory goodnight kiss. What did you do?"

"Well, nothing. She pulled away."

"That's the reason she pulled away. Because you did nothing. If a girl initiates the first kiss, she isn't going to hang on if you don't respond."

"She didn't give me a chance." Wesley took long swallow of his drink.

"If a girl puts her lips on yours, she's giving you a signal. And you have to anticipate signals. You knew before her lips touched yours that she was about to kiss you, didn't you?"

"Well, it was *just* before."

Vivian sighed with impatience. "I guess I'll have to show you," she said as she perused the room, apparently surveying the level of privacy. Then she scooted off the chair arm and onto Wesley's lap. She leaned forward and put her lips on Wesley's, then leaned away. "See, you didn't do anything, so I pulled away."

"What was I supposed to do, grab her—you—in a big hug?"

"No, read the signs."

Wesley liked the feeling of Vivian's rounded bottom on him, and the scent of her hair made him want to wrap her in his arms. It felt so natural. He took another swig of his drink. He was oblivious to anyone watching them.

But Hez was watching. And so was a blond girl he hadn't seen walk up to the open doorway of the cabin.

Vivian shifted her weight on Wesley's lap and faced him. "Now, I want you to kiss me—lightly, don't get all Frenchy on me—and I'll show you what to do."

As Wesley's face closed in, Vivian raised one hand to his face and peered into his eyes. She placed her other hand on his cheek and brought her slightly parted lips to his. For a whisper of time, her tongue softly touched his lips, and then she pushed him away.

"See what I did?" Without waiting for a response, Vivian continued, "I read the signal that you were about to kiss me, and then took control by simply planting my hand on your cheek. That way I could initiate the kiss."

"That was so cool. Where did you learn that?"

"I'm a Southern girl. We start learning charm when we're babies."

Beguiled, Wesley said, "Can we do that again? I mean, an actual kiss. You said not to get Frenchy, but you used your tongue." Wesley started to think he might have a chance with Vivian.

"That wasn't Frenchy. It was just part of your edification."

With an imploring tone, he said, "Just one more time."

Still in his lap, she said, "Even though they say they're not, women are always impressed when someone wants them." She put both arms around his neck, her open lips to his, and flicked his lip with her tongue, but pulled away after a couple seconds.

He leaned his head toward her hoping for another kiss.

Vivian eyes twinkled. "Looks like I've still got my power, but the lesson is over. I don't want to mislead you." She slipped off Wesley. "I have to go to the ladies' room."

As Vivian approached the bathroom, she noticed a slender girl with long blond hair and tears in her eyes standing just outside the entrance to the cabin. When their eyes met, the girl turned and walked away.

"Oh my, what have I done, now?" Vivian whispered to herself.

Hez maneuvered to the corner where Wesley was still sitting. "Here, have another one. You may need it." He handed him a refill.

Wesley's scrunched his face, clueless as to what Hez meant.

"If I'm not mistaken, your cowgirl saw your little escapade in the corner with Vivian."

"What are you talking about?" Wesley's voice was loud and a bit slurred.

"She was in the doorway when Vivian was in your lap. She seemed confused at first, but when you started kissing Vivian, it was wide-eyed shock. Looked like she was about to cry."

In spite of Wesley's impaired brain, a regrettably clear picture formed in his mind.

"Cuz, I'm the last one to criticize, and I'm not, but I think you may have your tit in a wringer. Your girl may not be talking to you for a while. And if you think you have shot at Vivian, you're just stepping on your pecker. She looks at you like a little brother and likes teasing you. She's not going to date you. She's dating older guys with cars who can take her to dinner and buy her cocktails—like that ski bum. That ain't you, pal."

Anxiety sobered Wesley's alcohol buzz, with the impact of a red flashing light in his rearview mirror. He no longer felt like a big man.

"Aw, drink up and forget about it, Cuz."

Wesley took a sip of the drink and set it down. "No, I don't think I'll have any more. Everything you say about Vivian is true, and I knew it, but I just shoved it to the back of my mind. I guess it was the booze. It's weird, but I didn't notice that it had affected me. I just thought I felt good."

"You just don't have any experience drinking. That's what people mean when they say let's have some drinks and get to feeling good. Next time you'll recognize the buzz coming on. Meanwhile, don't worry. It will all be funny tomorrow."

Somehow, Wesley doubted it.

CHAPTER EIGHT

The next morning Wesley woke up with a dry mouth and a desperate thirst. His head ached, and as odd as it seemed, he couldn't recall his head ever hurting before.

He raised up on an elbow to see if he was alone. Then he remembered Cliff and Hez had the morning shift at the fountain; he hadn't heard them get up. He shuffled out of the bed and retrieved his watch from the adjacent table. Almost noon—he had to hustle if he wanted lunch before work.

In the shower he let hot water spray on his neck, which helped his headache but didn't remove the image of Lizzie crying in the doorway or the remorse and shame he felt. He was on the verge of crying, when a voice from somewhere in his head yelled, *Well, she wasn't supposed to be there.* Or had he said it out loud?

He sat alone at a corner table in the staff cafeteria and gulped down a half glass of iced tea before trying a rather unappetizing hamburger.

"Mind if I join you?" Wesley looked up to see Sue, who usually worked the early shift at the fountain. Sue, *the sweet one* that Betty kept hinting Wesley should date. Her perpetual optimism and good nature made her likeable, but it was as if she had read a teen magazine about how to be popular. Wesley liked her well enough, and he knew she had a crush on him, but he didn't want to date her.

"Sure," Wesley said, managing a sort-of smile.

"I heard you had quite a time last night." Her sunny face beamed with this juicy information. She leaned forward, with raised eyebrows, apparently eager for the inside skinny.

Wesley bristled inside. It reminded him of boys in a locker room wanting to know if a teammate had "scored."

"Where'd you hear that?"

"At the fountain. I got off early, but it was going around earlier today."

"I suppose I'm the main topic of gossip." He frowned as she bobbed her head with enthusiasm. "So what did you hear?"

"Not too much. Mostly everyone was just laughing because you got tipsy, and because Vivian gave you a kissing lesson." She tried with little success to restrain a smile.

"Did Vivian say anything?"

"She did most of the talking when she stopped in for a Coke." The smile broke thorough followed by a giggle. "I heard her tell Betty that the wrangler girl you've been dating saw you kissing her."

He slowly released the breath that he had been holding.

"Wesley, don't be so upset. You look like you got caught with your hand in the cookie jar—that's what my mother always says. People just think it's funny because you're a Baptist and got loaded. That's all."

"I made a fool of myself."

"Don't make a big deal out of it. If you laugh with everybody else, it will be forgotten in no time."

Easy for you to say. If you knew the rest of the story, that I messed up with someone I liked a lot.

Instead he said, "You're probably right. I'll just have to laugh it off." He glanced at his watch and said, "I gotta go. My shift is about to start." He hurried to the store, but then slowed up as he approached the fountain area, trying his best to appear nonchalant.

Only a handful of customers occupied the five U-shaped counter bays. Betty sat at the back bay talking to Vivian and Hez. Cliff monitored a couple milkshakes on one of the Hamilton Beach mixers. Margaret and the other waitresses waited on customers.

By some uncanny awareness of his arrival, Vivian swiveled on her stool and squealed, "It's my lover boy." It was a high, hard fastball with plenty of hop on it.

Stee-rike one.

The fountain crew gawked, first at Vivian, and then where she was looking. The excitement was not lost on the patrons. Several ignored their ice cream to gawk at Wesley.

Vivian, with a few bouncy steps, made it halfway to Wesley as he opened the gate behind the service bays. It seemed to Wesley she had puffed out her chest—her blouse gapped at the buttons. A banty rooster ready to crow.

Cliff gave him a wicked grin. "The stud cometh. Uh, no pun intended, buddy. I heard you clamoring in last night." More patrons took notice.

Stee-rike two.

Over the din of patrons, "Help Me, Rhonda" by the Beach Boys blared from the jukebox. The lyrics hit home.

Betty moved behind the counters and positioned herself next to Cliff and Wesley. With the command presence from her drill instructor days, she barked, "Leave Wesley alone." And then smirked. "He had a hard night."

Stee-rike three.

Words failed Wesley. No hits or runs. Only errors, and for sure, not cool.

Still in command voice, Betty said, "Wesley, go get an apron. Cliff's already five minutes into your shift."

"Ah, I don't mind, Betty. Anything for a playboy."

Later that morning in the stock room, as Wesley wrestled a carton of Dixie cups down from a storage shelf, Vivian came up behind him and put both hands on his waist. Surprised, he almost dropped the box before setting it down.

"Are we still buddies?" she asked. "You've been awfully quiet."

Without turning and looking at her, he said, "I guess I made a fool out of myself."

"Why do you say that?" With strength surprising for her stature, Vivian twisted Wesley around to face her. Her lips stretched tight and her eyes fixed on his in a beady stare, as if trying to bore sense into a thick skull "It was a party, for goodness sake."

"Everybody's been giving me the business—Cliff calling me a *stud* and—"

"Cliff's just jealous. His face turned green with envy when he heard Betty and me talking. He interrupted us and wanted to know when he could have his kissing lesson."

"He did?"

"Absolutely, but I told him he had to get his own mentor." Then in a softer, concerned tone, she said, "You do know last night was all in fun, don't you?"

"Yeah, I suppose so. I think I may have had one too many of those cocktails."

"Don't feel like the Lone Ranger. I was so thirsty this morning I came over to the fountain for a big glass of Coke—best cure for a hangover. Coke and aspirin."

"Being thirsty is part of a hangover? I never understood exactly what having a hangover meant."

"Yeah, alcohol dehydrates you and . . ." Vivian started to explain but then seemed to drift off in other thoughts. After a lull, she said, "Wesley, there is one other thing I need to talk to you about."

Wesley stiffened in anticipation of hearing something unpleasant, and fear crept into his voice. "What?"

After making sure no one was approaching from the fountain, she said. "When I left for the bathroom last night, a pretty girl with sad eyes was standing just outside the cabin door. I think it must have been Elizabeth, the girl you've been seeing."

"Yeah, I know—Hez told me."

"Didn't you have an earlier date with her?"

"No, she didn't want to go to the party because there would be drinking. I felt bad about her seeing us at first, but then I realized it's not my fault. If she had come with me, or stayed in her dorm like she said she would, everything would be okay."

Her expression hardened. "Wesley, don't make me ashamed of you. Don't be like every other guy and blame the girl for everything . . . it's not like you. Your sweetness is an attractive quality. Don't be a heartbreaker just because you can."

She snagged an apron from a shelf and marched with determined strides to her station at the third bay, leaving him numb. In his heart, he knew she was right.

Just after Vivian left, Betty barged into the storage room. Wesley knew he was about to get more advice. Little got past Betty's radar. As the resident barstool sociologist, insightful sage, and confessor with the local power of absolution, she knew who was dating whom and which couples had broken up, and she was always ready to dispense wisdom to the lovelorn.

She stopped a foot from Wesley with her feet planted in a wide stance and her hands on her waist. "You've been moping around all morning, Wesley. I don't allow 'Soda Fountain Blues' around here. You're on display behind the counter—"

"Not you, too, Betty."

Betty's eyes narrowed in a piercing stare, and Wesley immediately regretted his interruption. "Sorry, Betty."

"Wesley, I'm going to speak to you like a Dutch uncle. I've seen my share of young men come of age over the years, some better, some worse. And you're one of the better ones, but lately, I have noticed some disturbing hints in your behavior."

His head flinched back slightly. "What do you mean?"

"Like how you follow Hez's lead—trying to act cool. And how you are enamored by Vivian and strut around to impress her—it's unbecoming."

He faced away and felt his cheeks burn.

"Why the hangdog face?" Not waiting for an answer, she continued, "You exaggerate your problems. Yeah, your friends are razzing you, but so what? Embrace it."

Her voice had softened, and his ill feeling began to retreat.

Betty wasn't finished. "Quit trying to be Hez—he's an original. Do you know why?"

"I'm not sure."

"It's because he doesn't try to be anybody else. You need to be yourself. Learn from others, but be yourself. And another thing, quit fawning after Vivian. She's a pal, and she's fond of you, but she's not going to date you."

"You're the third person, including Vivian, who has told me that, so I think I get it."

"Why don't you date Sue? Remember, I told you she's a Methodist—that's pretty close to a Baptist—and I've seen how she looks at you. She's a sweet one—"

"Not again, Betty," Wesley moaned.

*   *   *

At dawn the next day, Wesley lay awake on his bunk, staring at the ceiling. Yesterday's anxiety had roosted on his bed overnight, waiting for him to stir. Now it tormented him with the recurring thought that he had no one to blame except himself. Adding to his torment, he recalled how he'd gone over to the OFI after his shift and stood in the lobby for what seemed like ages but never saw Lizzie. He didn't know what he would have done if he'd seen her.

Hez's feet smacked the floor as he hopped off his bunk. With the joy of a schoolboy on Saturday morning, he said, "Top of the morning, fellas."

From across the room, Cliff yelled, "Jesus, Hez, I want to sleep for twenty more minutes."

Not feeling Hez's joie de vivre, Wesley grumbled, "Since I'm already awake, I may as well get up."

Cliff covered his head with his blanket. Wesley and Hez picked up their Dopp kits and padded down the hall to the bathroom.

As they stood shaving side by side, Hez examined Wesley's reflection in the mirror. With a dollop of Gillette Foamy in hand ready to apply it, he said, "Son, you've got a sour-looking mug. You're not still worried about your escapade at the party?"

Wesley shrugged. His mouth opened but nothing came out.

"If that cowgirl likes you, she'll come around. You may spend some time in the woodshed, but meanwhile, you need to have some fun to get out of the funk you're in."

"*Fun* was what got me in trouble in the first place."

"Nah, I mean a distraction. I've got a fire permit."

Wes switched his gaze from the mirror and squared it on Hez. "Really? What's the catch? How'd you manage that?"

Calling on his signature move, Hez tapped his temple with his index finger. "Brains, my friend. Using my brains. And I have a little camping trip planned."

"Who are you taking?"

"Georgia."

"What? Georgia? Really?" He was blown away that Hez had not only obtained a coveted fire permit, but had also asked Georgia, a cutie from the sundries department, to spend the night with him in the woods.

"Doesn't going out with Georgia violate one of your professed rules: not dipping your pen in company ink?"

"There are exceptions to the rule. Technically, it's still kosher since she doesn't work at the fountain."

"You know, this could be serious with you and Georgia. It's one thing to go hitchhiking or hang out at the inn with someone, but in the park, a rock-solid sign of serious couplehood is obtaining a fire permit and going on an overnight camping trip."

"Nah, this is just for fun."

"Wait a minute—she's a Baptist. I'm surprised she agreed to go with you. She's always so quiet."

"She hasn't actually said *yes* . . . that's where you come in." Hez waggled his eyebrows.

"Oh, brother, what have you cooked up, now?"

"You see, she might not go with me alone, but if another Baptist and his girlfriend were also going, then she would."

"You better be careful, Hez. Her dad is a preacher in Memphis. They have shotgun weddings down there."

"Come on, now, this is no time for levity." Hez splashed water on his face and toweled it dry. "I think you should go with us. It'll be a hoot. You could bring your guitar, and we could sing campfire songs under the stars."

"Thanks, but I'll pass." Wesley's voice had become more distant.

"Cuz, I've already told Georgia that you were bringing your guitar."

Wesley did a wide-eyed doubletake. "You've got to be kidding."

"She didn't want to go alone with me. She probably didn't *trust* herself to be alone with me. Or, maybe, she knew about the couplehood rule, too. So I told her that you and your girl were going, and we would be crooning and not spooning around the campfire."

"Well, this is a fine mess you have gotten us into, Ollie." Wesley deadpanned Stan Laurel from Laurel and Hardy, the comedy duo from old-time movies.

Hez gave him a confused look.

"Never mind . . . but back to the matter at hand, it sounds like fun, but I don't think Lizzie is speaking to me after my episode at your party and—"

Hez cut him off. "You know my other rule."

"Yeah, I know. When you're not near the girl you love, you love the girl you're near."

"So why don't you ask Sue? She'd jump at the chance."

Wesley cocked his head to one side and narrowed his eyes on Hez. "Hey, have you been talking to Betty?"

Hez responded with a disingenuous, "Who me?" and without waiting for a response, added, "Besides, I don't have any impure intentions with Georgia—it would just be an outing among friends."

"Why do I suspect there is more than friendship involved?"

"I'm always open to possibilities, but I'm not a hopeless romantic like some people I know. So go ahead and ask Sue."

"I suppose I could," Wesley said, but a sense of guilt crept over him, and he had learned that when he got a "gut" feeling, it was wise to pay attention to it.

His mind went into an analysis of the situation. He wanted to go with Lizzie, but she probably wouldn't go. But if he went with Sue and Lizzie found out, he'd never have another chance with her. Then a thought erupted from another part of his mind and he mumbled, "It's none of Lizzie's business."

"Good thinking," Hez said.

Wesley had spoken out loud without meaning to. He instantly regretted it. Everyone had a stake in his action.

"Wesley, I can tell by the look on your face that you're afraid you're about to step on your pecker again."

"Maybe so, but first I want to see if I can patch things up with Lizzie."

After his shift that night, Wesley zipped over to the Old Faithful Inn hoping to see Lizzie. Maybe she would be in *their* alcove, hoping he would come, and maybe she'd look up as he approached, giving him a welcoming smile. That's what a Baptist would do with a prodigal son. Right? But what would this this Mormon girl do?

Inside, he passed the massive fireplace and climbed the stairs to the second level. His anticipation and hopeful expectations plummeted. Lizzie sat in their alcove. The one where she had shared her story. The one where they had officially started dating. But she sat beside the guy in the madras shirt. The guy who had been hustling her a couple nights before. The guy that she said was cute.

Lizzie peeked away from her conversation and her eyes met Wesley's, widened, and then turned to stone. She held the contemptuous stare for a moment before abruptly refocusing on the madras shirt guy, listening to something he was saying . . . and no doubt deciding if he was worthy.

Wesley did an about-face and scuffed outside. The rotten egg smell of the geyser basin seemed particularly offensive. It matched his mood. When he passed the bench in front of Old Faithful, where he had first put his arm around Lizzie, the resentment he felt at seeing her with someone else became deep sadness. But by the time he reached his dorm, the resentment had boomeranged and found solid footing.

Chapter Nine

Sue glowed with enthusiasm. "Oh, yes, I'd love to go." Then she drew back a bit, and a serious look came to her face. "Of course, this will just be as *friends*." She knew about Lizzie, so she probably wanted to protect herself from hurt feelings and rejection. Combined with her well-deserved reputation of being sweet and smart, her conditional acceptance made Wesley feel better about the situation.

"Yeah, just as friends, and it'll be fun."

Hez switched days off with another fountain guy, and two days later the quartet of Sue, Georgia, Hez, and Wesley gathered outside the boys' dormitory and waited for Ranger Brett. He had agreed to provide transportation to the trailhead five miles north toward Fishing Bridge. They would have to hitch rides home the following day.

Brett had been Hez's resource in obtaining the permit, and the ranger spent the entire ride recounting tales of accidents caused by careless campers. As they unloaded the car, he said, "Be sure to hang any food up in a tree away from the tent. A bear can smell food several miles away."

After the four were out of the car, Ranger Brett leaned across the front seat and rolled down the passenger window. With a devilish gleam in his eye, said, "And, just so you know, bears only ate three people last season."

After Brett had nosed the cruiser back onto the highway, Georgia, in a plaintive Southern drawl, said, "There probably won't be any bears bothering us—will there?"

"Don't worry, Georgia," Hez said, "Wesley can fend them off with his guitar."

The dirt trail, smooth and hard from countless hikers, ran along a ridgeline through a forest, heavy with the scent of evergreens. After a half-mile it forked, with one leg leading upward to a lookout point, and the other descending to a mountain glade.

Sue gushed when the panoramic clearing came into view. "It looks just like a postcard—a mountain meadow with wildflowers and a stream. I've never seen any place so beautiful."

Through the middle of the grassy meadow, a crystal-clear stream meandered, about twenty feet wide and, as Hez later said, "Ass-deep to a tall Indian."

Hez hoofed out first, toting the tent, a sleeping bag, and his army blanket. Georgia tagged a step behind carrying a canvas shopping bag filled with bread, chocolate chip cookies, catsup and mustard packets (all compliments of the fountain), paper towels, and cups. Sue toted two rolled-up blankets tied with a rope. And Wesley brought up the rear with his guitar, a borrowed beach bag with a plastic sack of ice, also scrounged from the fountain, which cooled a six-pack of Cokes, a pound of hamburger wrapped in foil, and six hotdogs.

Based on his Kansas wheat field experience, Wesley reckoned that the glade must be about forty acres, as it would take two days to plow it. A few groves of trees bordered the stream, but tall, native grass ideal for grazing elk and deer carpeted the rest.

As they neared the edge, Hez, in a loud whisper said, "Stop. There's a moose with a calf drinking from the stream."

The girls moved to the front. "Ooh, they're so cute," Sue said.

"They may be cute, but that mama moose isn't Bullwinkle. If she feels threatened, she can be meaner and more dangerous than a biting sow," Wesley said.

"Yeah," Hez said, "Ranger Brett told me a moose charged onto

Fishing Bridge and tourists jumped off into the Yellowstone River fearing for their lives."

"She's looking around and sniffing the air. She's a football field away. Can she smell us?" Georgia asked.

"With her big ol' nose, if she were downwind from us, she could. But the wind is blowing toward us, so I doubt she can," Wesley said.

"She must smell something because she's hightailing it off, with the calf right behind," Hez said. "Maybe it was a bear."

"Oh, great," Georgia moaned.

"In a couple hours it will be dark. We need to get a fire going and the tent pitched," Wesley said.

Within an hour a camping site had been selected, the tent pitched, and a group effort commenced to get a fire started. They gathered pine cones, dried branches, and a couple of dead logs.

Hez set the flame of his Zippo lighter to the tinder, which just smoldered until the pine cones ignited and burst into flame. In a short time, the fire blazed with flames two feet high.

Wesley said, "We can't cook the burgers until the fire dies down to coals."

"Coals are a long way off," Georgia said. "We'll starve before then."

"But we can have a weenie roast," Sue said. "Hot dogs can be our hors d'oeuvres. We just need some sticks."

"That's a good idea," Hez said. "I'll cut some limbs for skewers. Here's another idea."

"What's that?" Wesley asked.

"We can cook the hamburger like they cook a pig in the ground in Texas. The hamburger is covered in foil, so we spread the fire apart a bit, dig out a shallow hole, throw it in, and cover it with some dirt and ashes. In an hour, we'll have a meatloaf."

"Brilliant idea," Georgia said, as she and Sue began moving the logs and Wesley looked for something to dig with.

Hez beamed at the compliment. "I have another idea. We can have a cocktail with our hors d'oeuvres."

Hez reached in his sleeping roll and pulled out a pint of Jim Beam. "The single thing they don't make good in Texas is whiskey. For that, I'll tip my hat to Kentucky . . . or maybe Tennessee."

Hez had everyone's attention as he poured Coke into a paper cup and topped it off with slug of the Jim Bean. "Anyone else care for a libation?"

To Wesley's surprise, Sue said, "I'd like one."

"Coming right up." He passed the mixed drink to Sue. After Georgia and Wesley declined, he raised his cup to Sue's and toasted, "Here's to good friends and good whiskey."

Sue said, "Amen," and looped her arm through Wesley's after taking a sip.

Georgia stole a glance at Wesley. He sensed her exception to the mundane use of *Amen,* as if it were a sacrilegious act. Her eyes shifted to the bottle and back to him. Wesley responded to her concern with a shrug that said, *Well, that's just Hezekiah,* as Georgia had been calling him. He thought it remarkable that Hez had not yet corrected her.

Waiting for the hamburger to cook, Wesley broke out his guitar for some of the promised campfire songs. At first only Wesley and Georgia sang. Georgia remarked it was easy to tell who had sung in the church choir.

After another round of drinks, Sue and Hez joined in. It impressed Wesley that Sue could sing harmony, and he didn't mind that she leaned into him while she sang. Hez couldn't sing a lick, but no one in the group was more enthusiastic.

An hour later, Hez stood up. "The hamburger ought to be done, so I'll pull it out."

Wesley said, "I'll bet it's burned up."

Hez grappled the foil package from the fire with the forked hotdog sticks and opened it. A savory aroma, steeped in smoke, steamed out. "Wow! That smells great."

The rest of the group gathered around and took turns sniffing. Wasting no time, they hacked off chunks of the moist meat and made sandwiches. Without regard to manners or rules of etiquette, they gulped the food, washed it down with Cokes, licked their fingers, and wiped their chins with paper towels. Only after several bites did anyone speak, and then, they just uttered short compliments of satisfaction.

After a dessert of the purloined cookies, Hez pulled the Jim Beam from his blanket for an after-dinner nip and raised the bottle. "Sue, how about you?"

"Well, maybe just a small one, but first I need to find the girl's bush." At that, Hez and Wesley burst out laughing. Sue turned red but then began giggling as well. "That didn't come out right," she said. "I meant that I need to find a bush to pee behind!"

Georgia, who hadn't laughed at the faux pas, said, "I'll go with you."

"Take the flashlight . . . and watch out for snakes," Hez said.

"Snakes?" gasped Georgia.

"They're just messing with us now," Sue added, shaking her head, but still giggling a bit.

Hez threw another log on the fire. Sparks flew upward, glowing in the darkening sky. Once the girls were out of sight, he said, "You ever notice that girls never go to the restroom by themselves. They always take a buddy with them."

"Yeah, now that you mention it, I have. Why do you suppose they do that?

"It's like a huddle in football. That's where they call their plays."

"What are you boys laughing about?" Georgia said, as she and Sue returned to the fire.

"Just that girls always go to the restroom in pairs."

"For your information, Mr. Hezekiah Smarty Pants," she replied, "that's not true. But out here, someone has to hold the flashlight."

Wesley couldn't see her, but she sounded as if she might be smiling.

Georgia sat by Hez, and Sue nestled next to Wesley. Was it just the chill in the air, or was this the play they had called? In either case, Wesley liked the closeness.

With a cloudless sky and only a fingernail clipping of a moon, thousands of stars blazed in the sky. Wesley gazed up and said to no one in particular, "I could never really see the whole Milky Way until I came out here to Yellowstone. Back home trees or street lights get in the way. And to think that Earth is part of all that."

"That *is* amazing," Sue said, as if it were the wisest statement she had ever heard.

"Look!" Georgia said. "A shooting star."

"Technically, it's a meteor," Wesley said, buoyed by Sue's comment.

"I don't care." Georgia said. "Star light, star bright, first star I see tonight. I wish I may, I wish I might, have this wish I wish tonight."

Hez put his arm around Georgia's waist. "What'd you wish for?"

"I can't tell you or it won't come true."

"There's another one." Sue stood up and pointed in the air. "Look, it's still there."

Wesley stood beside her and followed her line of sight. "That's no meteor. Must be a satellite. Telstar or Sputnik, maybe."

"Or a UFO," Hez said.

Sue and Wesley sat down. Sue scooted close to him and locked both her arms around his. "Wesley, do you believe there are such things as flying saucers?"

Wesley didn't respond.

Hez said, "Hey, Mr. Knows-All-About-Meteors, what do you say about UFOs? Flying saucers, that is."

"I've never seen one, but this lawyer back home told my stepdad and me about one that his client saw. He saw it, too."

Sue squeezed his arm harder.

"Ah, heck, you know how windy lawyers are," Hez said.

"Not this one, not J. Bob. And I know the client, too—an ol' boy named Ethan Collier. Anyway, never mind."

"I'll take your word for it. Don't stop now."

"Yeah, we want to hear." Sue jostled his arm, and her grip on his arm was compelling.

"Okay, but you need to understand that Ethan is a strange bird. A definite backwoods hillbilly. Heck, *he* might be from another planet. One time he was standing by the railroad tracks when a train with over thirty boxcars came through town, and afterwards, he recited the names on all of them—forwards and backwards."

"That's pretty remarkable, but get on with the story," Hez said.

"I will, but first you need to know a little about this guy for the story to make sense. Ethan Collier is a skinny man, in his forties, with a bushy beard. He cuts his own hair with sheep shears and wears threadbare bib overalls. And you ought to see the way he walks. His joints must be loose, or somehow not properly hinged, because when he walks, even though he's moving forward, it looks like his body is trying to go in two different directions because his feet point outward."

Sue laughed at Wesley's description, and then said, "Go on."

"Most folks think Ethan is scary and not too bright, but his teachers have all said he might be plain-spoken, but he's not dumb. When he was still in the sixth grade, he could calculate high school algebra problems in his head.-

"We get the picture," Hez said.

"All right," said Wesley. "So there's this river, the Jack's Fork, a spring-fed stream of rapids and deep swimming holes. It meanders through some of the most remote parts of the Ozark Mountains.

"Well, Ethan is a trapper, and one day he was down by the Jack's Fork checking his illegal traps, and he heard splashing near one of his traps about thirty yards downstream. A lot of splashing. He thrashed through the brush, and a noise stopped him short. It sounded like a hurt rabbit.

"So he crouched down, crept up further, and pulled back a willow branch. That's when he saw it. In one of the snares he'd set the day before, he'd caught this creature, no bigger than a child. But it was gray, and it wasn't a child. J. Bob, the lawyer who saw it later, said its eyes were big and black, and its head was huge and out of proportion to its body."

"Oh, this is scary," Georgia said.

"But the next part is funny," Wesley said. "Ethan pointed his rifle at the creature and said, 'You ain't from around here, are you?' He thought it was a demon that had come to fetch him down to hell."

When everyone quit laughing, Wesley continued. "So Ethan took the creature home with him and called J. Bob to come over and see it. J. Bob was the only person Ethan trusted. To this day, J. Bob swears the thing was the real deal. He describes it as … *unexplainable*. The only thing he could think to do was to get law enforcement involved. So J. Bob took off to find the sheriff, but while he was gone, a complication arose. You see, Ethan had this no-good brother. And while Ethan was back out checking the rest of his snares, the brother came home and discovered the creature. Well, he thought the creature was some kind of monkey—figured maybe it had gotten loose from the circus that was in a nearby town. So he 'kidnapped the monkey,' thinking he could return it to a circus and collect a reward."

"This is getting a little dubious," Hez said.

"Don't interrupt, Hez. I want to hear how it ends," Sue said.

"Well, the sheriff and J. Bob hightailed it after the brother. And when they got to the circus, J. Bob swears that he saw a flying saucer come down from the sky. He says it hovered over Ethan's brother and the creature for a long time. And then it shot down a beam of light that sucked them both up in the spacecraft."

It became eerily quiet. Nobody responded. Only the gentle flow of the creek and the crackling of the fire could be heard. The fire had burned down considerably while everyone's attention had been focused on Wesley.

With a tentative voice, Wesley said, "Well, there you have the story. Believe it or not."

Hez stood up and stretched his back. "That was some tale."

"I know, but nobody has seen the brother since—he's just disappeared. Some folks say he must have left with the circus since that was the last place anyone saw him."

"Did this lawyer say anything else?" Hez asked.

"He said it was like Enoch, one of two men in the Bible who went to heaven without dying."

"Wesley, do you think it's possible that's what happened to Enoch in the Bible?" Georgia asked.

"I don't know, Georgia. You can ask him when you get to heaven."

Hez laughed. "What if Enoch isn't there?"

"Then, we'll let *you* ask him, Hez."

"Hey, hold on, Cuz. I'll be in heaven, too."

"It's a joke, son, it's a joke, I say," Wesley said, mimicking the cartoon character, Foghorn Leghorn, which got laughs from everyone.

When the laughter and back-and-forth banter settled down, Sue unclenched Wesley's arm and stretched both of hers. "I don't know about the rest of you, but I'm tired. Are we all going to sleep in the tent?"

"It will be snug, but we all should fit," Hez said.

"Like sardines," Georgia added.

"It'll be cozy, and we can listen to the stream rippling." Sue stood up and added in a cheery voice, "We'll be snug as bugs in a rug."

"I better tie our supplies up in that tree over there." Hez pointed to a pine near the stream and began gathering up the supplies.

Getting situated in the tent was a close-order drill that ended with boys on the outer edges and girls in the middle. Georgia next to Hez and Sue next to Wesley.

After they were in their respective positions, Georgia said, "Goodnight, everyone." She had become a camp counselor, calling "lights out," implying no talking . . . or anything else. It generated a collective goodnight from her tentmates, followed by silence.

Sue rested her head against Wesley's shoulder. She was lying on her side, and he could feel her breast against his chest. He had never spent the night sleeping next to a girl. And he found himself thinking about Lizzie. He could have been sleeping next to her.

Sue moved her lips to his ear and whispered. "If you want to kiss me goodnight, you can," and nudged her lips against his ear.

Her breath had the scent of bourbon, and for some odd reason, he wondered if kissing her would be like kissing Vivian. Sue's mouth against his ear excited him, and he rolled to his side and met her lips with his. Her mouth opened and her tongue shot into his with pent-up energy, as if she had been waiting to do this all night. Maybe it was the whiskey, but this was definitely not her first kiss, and it felt great.

"What's that noise?" Georgia whispered.

Wesley jerked his head away.

Georgia must have heard us. Crap.

"What noise?" Hez was now alert.

"Outside," Georgia said.

Hez sat upright and opened the tent flaps. With the flashlight he scanned the perimeter. "Hell, it's a bear climbing the tree where our supplies are."

Huddled together, they peaked out from the tent, watching the bear. It was a black bear, typical in Yellowstone, the type that caused "bear jams" because tourists stopped their cars to photograph them and feed them cookies, in spite of park rangers' admonitions and large signs prohibiting bear feeding. As a result, the bears had become mooching panhandlers.

This particular bear, an apparent forest-dwelling kind, which could have smelled the hamburger cooking a mile away, had now succeeded in knocking down the bundle and was about to eat the remaining cookies and hotdogs.

Hez bolted from the tent and began flapping his arms and yelling "Yee-hah" like a West Texas bronco buster.

"Be quiet, Hezekiah, or it will come over here."

"Nah, it's running away now," Hez said as the startled bear loped along the riverbank. "Maybe we should build the fire back up and one of us keep a lookout. We don't want it to come back looking for dessert."

Suspecting that any hope for romance was over, Wesley agreed and said he would take the first watch.

"I'll sit outside with you," Sue said.

After the fire was stoked and blazing, Wesley and Sue sat covered with a blanket and stared at the fire, with Sue, again, clinging to his arm.

Georgia and Hez retreated to the tent, and Wesley thought, *out of sight and hidden from God*. He wondered what kind of activity might be going on inside and chuckled at the old joke about why Baptists would not make love standing up . . . because God might see them and think they were dancing.

"What are you thinking about, Wesley?"

"Oh, nothing."

She gripped his arm tighter and nudged his shoulder. "Come on. I saw you laughing." He told her the joke and they both began laughing.

In the firelight and shadows, Sue was alluring. And as if moved by gravity, he leaned over and kissed her. She responded as before. As he put his arms around her, his hand grazed her breasts. She tensed and squeezed him closer.

Encouraged, his hand found its way under her sweatshirt. She intercepted it and moved it to her side, but they continued kissing for a moment before she pulled away.

After taking a deep breath and exhaling, she said, "We need to slow down."

"I'm sorry, but from the way you kissed me, I thought you wanted to make out."

"I did . . . but suddenly it doesn't feel right. I know I agreed to come on a friendship basis, but it felt so good being next to you, I got a little carried away. Maybe because I was drinking."

Wesley thought of Hez's motto about loving the girl that was near, but it was overridden by what Betty had said. No, he wasn't Hez.

"I guess I got a little carried away, too, but I know what you mean about booze." They both laughed.

"Still friends?" Sue asked.

Wesley nodded and said, "Let's lie down."

Lying together under the blanket, Sue snuggled close to him and rested her head next to his shoulder. "Goodnight, Wesley."

"Goodnight, Sue." And his thoughts floated to Lizzie.

CHAPTER TEN

By dawn, the last log on the fire smoldered but produced little heat, and Sue and Wesley had curled up together to keep warm.

Semi-awake, in and out of a dream state, Wesley thought about getting up but didn't want to leave Sue's warmth. He heard a cracking sound, as if someone had stepped on a twig. Startled, he held his breath and listened.

A man's voice said, "Well, now, don't you two look cozy."

Wesley rolled over, propped himself up on one elbow, and turned his head toward the sound of the voice. Ranger Brett, in his Smoky Bear hat and full uniform.

"Are Hez and his girl in the tent?"

"Yes, sir."

"Knock on the tent and wake them up."

Wesley laughed. "How do you knock on a tent?"

Although fully clothed, Sue sat up and clutched the blanket around herself. With a nervous laugh, she said, "Good morning,"

Brett tipped his hat.

Hez poked his head through the tent flaps. "Hey, Ranger Brett. What's up?"

Betty asked me to check on you hoot owls and give you a ride back. She wanted to make sure you all would be on time for the afternoon shift . . . and one of you got a phone call from back home that must be important."

"Who got the call?" Wesley asked.

"I don't know. You'll find out soon enough, so get your gear packed up."

After a quiet ride back, the campers unloaded themselves from Brett's car, bedraggled and unwashed. Saying goodbye to Georgia, the other three went into the soda fountain and walked toward the empty back bay, where Betty sat.

"I need to talk to Wesley. The rest of you, go get cleaned up."

With confused facial expressions, they all left except Wesley. A sense of foreboding settled on him. "What's going on, Betty?"

"A person-to-person, long-distance call came for you early this morning at the office in West Yellowstone. The personnel office gave them the number for our store."

"Do you know who it was from?"

"The person on the other end said she was your grandmother."

A jolt of panic struck him. His grandma would never call long distance unless it was an emergency. With his stepfather in the middle of the Atlantic steaming to India, it must be about his mom. His throat felt dry and his voice faltered. "I need to call her back."

Betty pivoted on the barstool and patted Wesley's shoulder. "She said she would call back at noon. That gives you time to get cleaned up and have lunch—you are still on duty for second shift. If you don't hear back, then you call her collect."

Back in his dorm, Wesley inhaled the steam from the hot shower. Some of the tension left as the stream of hot water rushed over his neck. Massaging shampoo on his hair reminded him of the times his mother had shampooed his head in her beauty shop. At first his friends teased him, but soon they all started lining up at his mom's shop to get haircuts that didn't look like the bowl-cuts from Ridgeview's aging barber. The reverie of a happier time helped his mood.

As he was putting on his jeans, Cliff stuck his head in the bathroom. "Hey, Wes, there's a long-distance call for you. They will only wait a minute. Get your ass moving, pal."

Wesley threw on his shirt and raced to the phone. Betty stood waiting with the receiver in her hand. He took it and brought it to his ear.

Out of breath, he said, "Hello. Grandma?"

Because of the poor connection, he cupped his hand over his other ear as he listened, and then said, "Fitzsimmons Army Hospital in Denver?" As he continued to listen, he closed his eyes to stop the tears that were forming. He blinked several times and gripped the phone so tightly that his knuckles turned white.

To be heard on the other end, he spoke in a loud voice. "No, I'm not going to stay here. Give me the address, Grandma."

He looked at Betty and made a writing motion with his hand. She handed him a ballpoint pen and a guest check pad, and he scribbled the address and telephone number.

"Now, you call me collect if you hear anything," his grandmother said.

"I'll call if I learn anything. Goodbye, Grandma."

Vivian had about finished lunch, when she noticed Wesley, stooped-shouldered and staring at the floor, as he stood in line at the employee's cafeteria. When he sat down by himself, she picked up her tray and made a beeline to his table.

"How are you doing?" Seeing his dismal eyes, she didn't wait for a response. "Betty told me you got an urgent call from home."

Wesley slumped and stared at his tray, still not speaking.

She placed her tray opposite his and sat down. "Wesley, you might as well tell me because I will find out sooner or later, one way or another." She fixed her eyes on him in a determined stare, which implied she would wait as long as necessary for a response, and that she was used to getting what she wanted.

Wesley raised his head and in a flat monotone said, "My mom has cancer and she's in an Army hospital in Denver."

Vivian's eyes softened. "I'm so sorry, Wesley," she said as she grabbed his closest hand with her own. She said nothing else for a moment, just holding his hand as if she hoped to absorb some of his pain.

She released his hand but stayed focused on his eyes. "I don't mean to be blunt, but what kind of cancer? I mean, where is it?"

"My grandma said it was her cervix . . . but I'm not exactly sure what that is."

Vivian wagged her head back and forth, and in a pedantic manner, said, "I sometimes forget how naïve you are. The cervix is part of her female organs. It's the opening to the uterus."

Wesley clenched his teeth and felt a muscle in his jaw twitch.

Vivian squinted her eyes. "You do know what a *uterus* is?"

"It's part of the female anatomy."

"Oh, for goodness sakes, Wesley, you've heard about a *womb* in the Bible, haven't you?"

"Of course. I'm not a complete moron. It's where a baby is conceived."

"Finally," Vivian said with mild exasperation. "Yes, *womb* is also the old-fashioned name for uterus, and it is a reproductive organ. The cervix is the opening to that organ."

"Thanks, I get it," Wesley said, in a tone that didn't indicate gratitude.

"Wesley, I didn't mean to offend you. I just wanted to make sure you understood."

"I'm sorry. You didn't offend me. I'm just worried, I guess."

"It's understandable. Why is she in an Army hospital?"

"My stepdad is retired military, so she can go to the hospital for free."

"So what are you going to do?"

"I'm going to hitchhike to Denver."

"Not a good idea."

"Why? We hitchhike here all the time."

"Maybe so, but up here it's mostly tourists. Outside the park, you don't know who could pick you up—weirdoes or criminals."

Wesley sat taller and drew back his shoulders. "I can take care of myself."

"What about your job here? You've got two months left on your contract."

Wesley swallowed and took a sip of water before answering. "Betty said she would give me a week."

"Why don't you take a bus? It will be a lot safer and speedier. If you get stuck between rides this time of year in the mountains, you could freeze."

"If you want to know the truth," he paused and searched around for eavesdroppers, "I need to travel as cheaply as possible."

Vivian nodded to the employees standing in line for food. "Look over there."

Wesley gazed across the room. "What are you talking about?" When he turned his head back, a twenty-dollar bill lay next to his plate. "Vivian, I can't take this."

"It's a loan, not a gift. Pay me back out of your next paycheck. And don't run out on me. I expect more than that from my protégé."

"I don't know what to say."

"I swear, Wesley, sometimes I think you haven't learned anything at all. What have I said about—"

"I know, I know …" He paused, then repeated the words she'd taught him, "Why, thank you. How nice of you." And then he smiled.

"That's better."

Vivian didn't know for sure if Wesley would return to Yellowstone, but one thing she knew for certain: She needed to clear up a misunderstanding. Although she had laughed off the episode at Hez's party, a speck of low-level guilt lurked in her mind, and it surfaced every time she thought of the pretty girl crying outside the cabin that night.

After lunch, without changing to off-duty clothes, she left the cafeteria for the wrangler's barn. Vivian's psyche had little room for spilled milk or guilty feelings, and such notions would always take a back seat to her moxie. Even so, she felt a bit nervous as she approached the horse barn.

After she rounded the Old Faithful Inn, the smell of horse manure assaulted her nose before the barn came into sight. Not much of a barn in her mind. Actually, not impressive at all, just a two-story shed with a pitched roof and wooden shingles. A baby barn, maybe.

Two guys in Wrangler jeans and Western shirts straddled the corral fence talking to a group of tourists waiting for a trail ride. One, a rather handsome blond boy she'd seen strumming his guitar at the OFI, caught her eye.

Both guys averted their attention from the tourists when Vivian strolled over, cool and slow, as if it were girls' choice at a dance.

"Do you boys know where I can find Elizabeth?" Vivian focused on the blond boy and appraised how well he filled out his jeans.

The blond boy's face sobered. He tipped his cowboy hat upwards and said, "Who wants to know?"

Vivian shielded her eyes from the sun with her hand, and after flashing her signature smile, simply said, "Me."

"And just who is *me*?"

Vivian's uniform dress, without the apron, was cinched at the waist with a narrow belt and hemmed above her knees, showing off her curves. The boys, from their vantage point on the corral fence, undoubtedly saw her cleavage exposed by the unfastened top button.

Ever the coquette, Vivian glanced down toward the ground, as if she were shy or at a loss for words. Then she slowly lifted her head, and with big eyes met the blond boy's gaze. In her formidable Southern accent, she said, "Where I come from, a gentleman introduces himself first."

Mike hopped off the fence and eased over to her. By now, all the tourists' eyes were on Vivian.

"I guess I forgot my manners, Miss. My name is Mike Smith. I'm the head wrangler."

Vivian stepped forward and extended her hand. When Mike took her hand, Vivian squeezed his. She expanded her chest, ever so slightly, and said, "Well, I have the right man then. My name is Vivian."

"Lizzie is still at her dorm." He gestured toward the building fifty yards to his right. "She's got a trail ride in 20 minutes, so you can find her there."

"Thanks, Mike." She squeezed his hand again and let go. "Maybe I'll see you around."

As Vivian neared the dorm, she saw Lizzie coming out the front door. Jeans, Western shirt, and cowboy boots. A rare shot of envy rose in Vivian. Long legs always made her jealous. *That girl could be a model,* she thought.

Their eyes met and Lizzie froze on the top step. Her face at first appeared confused, and then turned suspicious. Vivian marched forward, continuing to size up Lizzie. Not an ingénue. A no-nonsense girl next door. Diplomacy, that's the key, just like rush week at the Tri Delta house.

Vivian halted at the bottom of the steps. "My name is—"

"I know who you are," Lizzie said, feigning indifference with a cool voice. "My question is, *why* are you here?"

"I've come to clear up a misunderstanding. Something I should have done before."

"I'm listening." Lizzie crossed her arms across her chest, keeping a three-step distance.

Vivian inhaled through her nose and slowly exhaled. "I saw you standing outside the cabin crying the night of Hez's party and thought you probably saw me sitting on Wesley's lap and—"

"And kissing." Lizzie interrupted.

"That's right," Vivian admitted, "but we were both drinking . . . a bit too much. What you don't understand is we had been talking about you . . . about Wesley's fondness of you and his uncertainty if you felt the same way. I decided to give him some pointers about women, and one thing led to another, and finally a kissing lesson."

"Oh, really?" Lizzie's previous indifference turned sarcastic.

As Vivian repressed her usual smile, her lips spread to a thin line and she jutted her chin upward. She knew how to set a course, and also how to change the tack and maneuver around any obstacles. But she would have been appalled if someone accused her of being manipulative—such an ugly word.

"You see, Elizabeth, I have been Wesley's mentor to help him become worldlier. The boy is so unsophisticated. Frankly, I'm not sure what you saw in him. He's rather backward."

"You didn't seem to mind that night when you sat in his lap." Lizzie's eyebrows shot upward as she unfolded her arms and planted both hands on her waist.

"Like I said, we had been drinking. Don't get me wrong, he's a pleasant boy, but it was *amitié pas romance amour.*"

"Friendship, not love. I speak French, too. But as a wrangler might say, quit pussyfooting around and get to your point."

"Of course. Since I was partly the cause of your breakup with Wesley, I thought I owed you an explanation . . . and some information. First, as I've already said, there's nothing serious between us. Secondly, did you know Wesley went over to the OFI a few nights later to apologize to you?"

"No, I didn't." Lizzie's tone softened.

"And he found you sitting in the corner making eyes at some college guy."

"That was because—"

"Hold on, I'm not through," Vivian interrupted. "Wesley also just got news that his mother has cancer and is in a hospital in Denver. He says he's leaving to go there right away. I don't know if he's coming back. I thought you would want to know. Maybe, say goodbye."

The suspicion left Lizzie's face. A shadow of sadness replaced it, and her eyes became teary. She gazed off in the distance, wiped her eyes with her shirtsleeve, and then brought her full attention to Vivian.

With a tempered voice, she said, "I think I may have misjudged you. A lesser person wouldn't have made this effort. Thank you for telling me."

With sorority girl poise, Vivian moved up the steps and extended her hand. "I think we both want the same thing."

Lizzie accepted Vivian's hand with a firm grip. "When is he leaving?"

"Later today or tomorrow. After lunch he went to his dorm to pack. He said he planned to hitchhike, but I tried to convince him to take a bus."

Lizzie's face turned ashen. Barely audible, she said, "He could get stuck in the mountains at night, shivering in the rain waiting for a ride." With hopeful eyes, she stared at Vivian. "I have a trail ride in a few minutes . . . would you do me another favor?"

"If I can. What is it?"

"If I don't see him before he leaves, tell him goodbye for me."

Vivian extended her arm and touched Lizzie's shoulder. "I will."

Chapter Eleven

After Vivian was out of sight, Lizzie sat down on the porch steps. She nibbled at her lower lip but made herself quit when she realized she was doing it. It had always been a nervous habit of hers. If only she could talk to her mother—she'd know what to do. Lizzie knew she couldn't call her now, so she imagined what her mom would say. She would ask whether Lizzie had a part in the problem. Remind her that every story had two sides. Tell her to listen to her head and not just her heart. And, of course, she'd ask about the boy's worthiness.

I thought I was over him.

She glimpsed at her watch. Better get moving. It would be bad enough telling Mike she couldn't go on the trail ride, but worse if they left without her. He'd send someone to look for her, and she would never hear the end of it.

When Lizzie approached the corral, Mike had begun his usual, cautionary safety spiel for the riders. Tourists were already mounted on their horses, and someone had saddled her horse.

Mike scowled when he saw her. "Here's our lost wrangler," he announced to the group. All eyes focused on her. She tipped her hat.

"Mike, I need to talk to you in the shed." Without waiting for an answer, she scooted into the tack shed, leaving the door open behind her.

Mike entered and wasted no time showing his impatience. "What's going on? Something wrong with you?"

"Nothing is wrong, I just can't make this ride. I'll do the sundown ride."

"It's awfully generous of you to make up your own schedule. Do you mind telling me why?"

"I just got word that a friend's mother has cancer, and he's leaving the park this afternoon. I want to say goodbye."

Showing little regard, Mike said, "I suppose it's that soda jerk. I thought you were through with him."

"Soon enough, Mike."

"With your head where it is, you wouldn't be much good on the ride anyway. So you might as well go." On his way out, he called back, "And forget about the sundown ride—it's covered. By someone more responsible than you."

She had never in her life considered giving the finger to anyone, until now. She almost had her hand up, but then she thought better of it. Thinking about what her mother would say, she had to admit that she had a part in this problem. The image she had of herself—being dependable on the job—did not match her action. She had always prided herself on not taking advantage of the fact that she worked for her brother. Now, she felt like a shirker, something her mom abhorred.

She took a deep breath and exhaled it very slowly. And then another. She followed Mike out the door without speaking to him and tramped to the Hamilton Store men's dormitory.

She hesitated at the entrance, but then decided it would be mostly deserted in the middle of the afternoon and opened the door. Although she had never been inside, she knew the location of Wesley's room on the far end of the first floor.

Through the open door of Wesley's room, she saw him standing in front of a suitcase holding a jacket. The Samsonite two-suiter overflowed with unfolded clothes.

"It looks like you're going someplace, Hillbilly."

Wesley jerked his head toward the door. "Lizzie! What are you doing here?"

"I heard about your mother and wanted to see you before you left . . . in case you didn't come back and . . . .." Her voice broke and she swallowed hard, "and I didn't see you again." She couldn't stop her eyes from flowing.

And neither could Wesley. His eyes filled as he rushed to her and put his arms around her. "I'm so sorry, Lizzie."

They held each other for a long time without speaking. Words seemed unnecessary. Lizzie's mind went to someplace far off, beyond thought, where only feelings resided. But then a thought crashed in. *Head over heart.* She pushed Wesley to arm's length. "We need to talk."

But instead of talking more, she grasped Wesley's face with her hands, and her open lips found his in a deep, but short-lived, kiss before she pushed him away and pointed at his suitcase.

"That's a lot of stuff for a trip to Denver."

"How did you know about Denver?"

"Never mind. Are you coming back, or were you just going to leave without saying goodbye?"

Wesley opened his mouth to speak, but then hesitated and looked away. "I thought about telling you . . . but I didn't know if you would care."

Lizzie put her hands on her hips. "You think that I wouldn't have been concerned that your mother was sick?"

"Of course not, but everything got so confused."

"For your information, I do care. And what's this I hear that you're considering hitchhiking to Denver? That's over 500 miles."

"I know how far it is. I rode the bus up here."

"Then you ought to know better than to hitchhike. If you get stuck in the mountains at night, you'll freeze. If you are committed to the trip, at least take a bus."

"You're the second person to tell me that today, and after I thought about it, it made more sense. I called the bus depot in West Yellowstone. I can get a ride there on a YP bus tomorrow morning at 7 o'clock and then catch a Mountain Express bus to Ogden. I'll have to change buses there and hook up with Greyhound to get to Denver."

"Good, that's a better plan," she said, her voice softening. "Do you know how long your mother will be in the hospital?"

"Not exactly. But my grandmother said she'd be there quite a while. Some kind of experimental treatment."

"Have you called your mother?"

"No."

"Why not?"

"She'd tell me not to come."

"That would be like a mom." Lizzie hesitated. "You never answered whether you were coming back?"

"I'm not sure."

"If you pack everything, you won't be back. Leave something to come back for."

Wesley dug through clothes in his suitcase, and from the bottom of the pile, grabbed his Mizzou sweatshirt. The one that caused locals to ask if he went to school in Missoula. He held it out for her.

"Here, keep this until I get back."

"You better keep it. You'll need it for the trip. What you don't need is to be lugging a suitcase full of clothes from bus to bus. You need a backpack. My brother Mike spent two years in Europe for his Mormon missionary commitment. He traveled all over France with just a backpack."

"I don't have one."

"We have them for trail rides. I'll get one for you to use. Meanwhile, fold up everything that won't fit in a backpack and put it back in the dresser."

Lizzie pecked Wesley on the lips. "I'll be back with the backpack." She gave him a skeptical squint. "On second thought, give me the Mizzou sweatshirt. I'll keep it as collateral."

On the way back to the wrangler area, a new plan occupied Lizzie's head. The idea had actually started as soon as she'd walked in and seen Wesley packing, but she didn't want to say anything to him yet. She worried that the plan was crazy, that it threw logic out the window—just an emotional whim that came from the heart instead of her brain.

Is the head always smarter than the heart?

The rule, wherever it came from, seemed too rigid to apply to every situation. Was she being foolish in what she was thinking? What would Mike think . . . or do?

By the time she willed away the mind chatter, to her surprise, she had made it all the way back to the tack shed. Inside, she rummaged for two backpacks. Then she waited for Mike to return from the sunset ride. He would be tired and not in a good mood, and it would only get worse when she told him her plans.

After the returning trail ride tourists dispersed, wranglers pulled saddles and blankets off the horses to wipe them down before corralling them for feed and water. Mike plodded toward the shed, carrying his saddle and blanket on his shoulder. He held the bridle in his other hand, with the reins dragging on the ground. He glared when he saw Lizzie but kept walking without speaking.

As he entered, Lizzie said, "We need to talk."

"Yes, we do."

The muscles in her midsection tensed and her mouth went dry. Drawing herself to her full height, she went straight to the point. "I need to take a few days off work."

Mike slammed the shed door behind him. "You *what?* What is wrong with you? And the answer is *no.*"

"Mike, will you hold on a second? I'll be back by Tuesday."

"Back? And just where do you think you are going?"

"To Denver with a friend to visit his mother in the hospital. She has cancer."

"Who's the friend—that soda jerk?" Mike's voice dripped with sarcasm. "And just how were you planning on getting there?"

"On the bus. It's basically just going there and back. A quick turnaround. Sunday is a light day, and Monday is my day off. I'll be back on Tuesday. I'd just miss tomorrow and Saturday."

"You're not running off on a bus trip with some guy we barely know. Not while I'm in charge."

Lizzie bristled. "Yeah, the big man in charge."

"Like I said, the answer is *no*. I need all my hands here to do their jobs." Mike took a long stride past her and threw the saddle and bridle on a bench. "I'm going to the bunkhouse."

Before he was out the door, Lizzie grabbed his sleeve. "You took off two days to go to Salt Lake City to hear the Mormon Tabernacle Choir practice. And as I recall, you went with some girl I didn't know."

"No!"

"Then I quit." Lizzie's voice had become calm and measured, the same as her father's whenever he was angry.

Mike spun around to face her. "You can't quit."

"I just did."

"I'm calling Mom."

"Then, I'm calling Dad and having a conversation about what you did on your mission trip in France." Lizzie had seen his threat and raised it—put up or shut up.

"And just what do you think you know about France?"

"Little sisters have big ears." Lizzie strode off.

"Come back here."

Lizzie kept walking and called back over her shoulder, "You're not my boss anymore. Remember?"

Chapter Twelve

At 6:45 the next morning the yellow YP bus, with an image of Old Faithful painted on the side, sat with its diesel engine idling. The driver wore an olive-green uniform and loaded luggage into the storage compartment below.

An OFI bellboy assisted the ladies up the bus steps, while a handful of men and women waited to board. A few men took last drags off cigarettes, tossed them on the sidewalk, and crushed them with their shoes.

Lizzie frowned at the litter bugs as she sat on a bench next to her a backpack, wearing the gold Mizzou sweatshirt and waiting to surprise Wesley.

Where is he? The bus will leave for West Yellowstone in a few minutes.

At the soda fountain, Wesley fended off last-minute advice and concerns about his safety. He reassured his friends and promised to return as soon as possible. Hez and Cliff wished him luck and pledged to take turns working his shift to protect his job.

Cliff added, "You'd better come back. I wasn't planning on heading home to Missouri by myself at the end of the summer."

When Vivian hugged him, she said, "I expect to see you again. There are still some lessons you need to learn, my young protege." She pinched his butt and pushed him away into the waiting arms of Sue.

"Be careful. I'll pray for your mother." The sentiment touched

Wesley. Sue was a sweet girl, and now she seemed like a dear friend.

"All right, girls, break it up." Betty, who had been oddly missing, waltzed in from the back entrance. "I need to get some things squared away with Wesley. She motioned for him to follow her.

Inside the storage room, Wesley said, "Betty, I have to hurry, or I'll miss the bus. It leaves in fifteen minutes."

Betty folded her arms across her chest. "Don't worry, I'm gonna drive you to West Yellowstone."

Wesley stiffened. He had hoped Lizzie might show up at the inn to say goodbye. He wanted to hold her one more time, in case he didn't come back because his mother . . . He wouldn't allow his thoughts to complete the scenario that had played over and over in his mind through the sleepless night before.

"That's okay, Betty. I can just take the bus."

"Just listen. I need you to come back here after your trip. I'm going out on a limb for you. Company management has a strict policy about summer employees—when they leave, no second chances. They have a list of kids wanting jobs here. Can I count on you to get your ass back here?"

Thoughts swirled in Wesley's head. He knew she loved her boys, and he didn't want to let her down. She was everyone's tough mom away from home. And he knew in his heart what he wanted. "Betty, unless the worst happens, I'll be back."

"That's all I can ask. Give me a few minutes, and I'll drive you to West."

"Thanks just the same, but if I run, I may still be able to catch the YP bus. I'd rather just split now."

"Suit yourself." Betty crushed him in one of her famous body hugs. Her breasts smashed against his chest and the scent of baby powder invaded his nose. "Now be careful." As they separated, she reached into her apron pocket and then palmed his hand. "Take this."

"Betty, I can't accept this." He tried to hand the folded twenty-dollar bill back to her."

"Put it in your pocket and get moving or you'll miss your bus . . . and your chance to say goodbye to that Mormon girl."

He smiled at her comment. *Is there anything she doesn't know?* "Thank you, Betty. I'll pay you back."

"Damned straight, you will."

Lizzie's watch indicated 7 o'clock. She stared in the direction of the upper Hamilton Store, but no Wesley. Had he left earlier? When they said goodbye yesterday afternoon, he planned to catch the 7 a.m. bus. She checked her watch again.

She hadn't told him about quitting her job, because she hadn't decided until this morning what to do. All night, she kept equivocating between saving her job and going with Wesley. If she went back now, she could apologize to Mike. He would forgive her as a prodigal sister, and things would go back to normal. But each time she thought about his self-righteous attitude, it upset her all over again.

In the lonely predawn hours, lying in bed thinking, she had concluded that although she understood her mom's advice about listening to her head, the mind could also sabotage the heart. Her mother had told her many times that a woman's intuition was a type of intelligence—an inner-knower. A gut feeling that comes from someplace beyond the head and heart. But its voice is often small and still, and you have to be quiet to hear it, or the noise in your head will drown it out. Finally, she had decided. She would go with Wesley and then come back to Yellowstone to make peace with her brother. But now, in the sunlight of the morning, waiting for a boy who was either late or already gone, those plans that had seemed so perfect began to seem perfectly foolish.

"All aboard!" The bus driver stood next to the bus door. The last few passengers had boarded except Lizzie. "Miss, are you getting on?"

Lizzie met the driver's stare wondering if Wesley had gotten another ride. "Sir, do you know when the Mountain Express bus leaves West Yellowstone for Pocatello?"

"Nine o'clock, and this is the only YP bus that can make the connection. So if you want to make it, you need to get on or get another ride."

If he's not there, I'll come back.

Lizzie boarded and took a seat at the rear and stared out the window. In the distance she could see the corral and the wranglers saddling up another batch of dudes for the next trail ride. She heard the *wumpth* sound of the bus door closing and pushing out air.

Lizzie settled back against the seat and closed her eyes, clutching at her backpack as if it were a ragdoll. Then loud pounding on the bus door startled her from her reverie. Her eyes followed the sound, as the bus door opened. "Young man, you barely made it. Hurry up," the bus driver said.

"Thanks, Mister."

The wariness that had numbed Lizzie vanished at the sight of Wesley, but then rebounded in full force. *What if he doesn't want me to go with him?* That thought evaporated when she saw his eyes widen in surprise and his face break into a happy smile.

Wesley grappled an overhead handrail to steady himself as the bus rolled forward, and with several long strides he plopped in the aisle seat next to Lizzie. "I didn't expect to see you here." The joy was still on his face.

"Why are you late? I thought you might have gotten another ride."

"Betty offered to drive me to West Yellowstone, but I thought you might be here to say goodbye. By the time, I told her 'No thanks,' I had to race to get here. I didn't know you would be on the bus." He pointed at her backpack. "Are . . . are you going to Denver?"

"That's the plan unless my brother claims you kidnapped me and has the bus stopped and you arrested."

"What?"

Lizzie started laughing.

"Phew, you had me worried for a second. Speaking of Mike, how did you manage to get off work?"

She back pulled a strand of hair away from her eye. "I didn't."

"I'm confused. Did you tell him you were going with me to Denver?"

"Yes, and I told him I needed a few days off."

"What did he say?"

"He said I couldn't go. So I quit." As she spit out the words, the gravity of the situation became real. She took a deep breath and sighed.

"Are you serious?"

"Yep, and he is hopping mad. He threatened to call my mother. And I double-dog dared him to do it."

"Gee, Lizzie, do you think that was a smart move?"

"Maybe not, but he was being his 'I'm in charge of you' annoying self, and he made me really mad. I told him if he called Mom, then I would tell Dad about something that happened when he was in France. He nearly blew a gasket, and now he's not speaking to me. But if I'm back by Tuesday, I'm betting he won't do anything."

He put his arm around her and nestled his face in her hair near her ear. "You risked a lot on account of me, and I appreciate it."

Lizzie twisted toward him, oblivious to anyone else on the bus, and brought her lips to his for a brief kiss. In a soft, quiet voice she said, "You're on your way back to being worthy." She pecked him with another kiss.

He placed his hand on hers, and she intertwined her fingers with his and turned her head to the window, as gentle tears filled her eyes.

She smiled at her last thought and blinked away her tears.

CHAPTER THIRTEEN

The forty-minute ride to West Yellowstone passed in silence. The hum of the big tires and the droning diesel engine lulled them both to sleep. Wesley first, and Lizzie not long afterwards.

As the bus slowed and pulled to a stop at the depot, Lizzie awakened with her head on his shoulder. Wesley, who hadn't slept at all the night before, remained asleep. She raised her head, kissed his cheek, and nudged him with her shoulder.

"Wake up, sleepyhead, we're at West Yellowstone."

Wesley blinked his eyes and jerked his head upwards. Disoriented at first, his lips formed a smile when he realized he was next to Lizzie. "Hey, I guess I *was* sleepy. How do you feel?"

"Fine."

"You look worried. Are you having second thoughts about going? It's okay if you want to change your mind."

"No, I haven't changed my mind." She examined his eyes trying to read his mind. "You're not trying to get rid of me, are you?"

Wesley met her stare. "No way." He shook his head, underscoring the statement.

The bus stopped and the driver announced, "West Yellowstone. Connections from here to Pocatello, Ogden, and Salt Lake City."

The bus depot, converted from a gingerbread cottage with an ornamental ridge turret, sat between a filling station and the Branding Iron restaurant. An open-air porch with a backless park bench provided a boarding area. Lizzie remarked that the depot reminded her of a fairytale house where elves might have lived.

Inside, a cluster of men and women stood in line at the only ticket counter, where a man wearing a green visor punched holes in tickets. Other customers sat in wooden folding chairs set against the walls. Three florescent ceiling fixtures illuminated the 15- by 30-foot room and reflected light from a white ceiling to a gray tile floor.

Lizzie and Wesley moved to the back of the line. Lizzie wore her backpack like a girl scout on a hike. Wesley's hung by one strap from his shoulder. He shifted his weight from one foot to the other and leaned to whisper to Lizzie.

"I want to pay for your ticket. I borrowed a few bucks before I left, just in case something came up."

"Save your money. I will buy my own ticket."

Her comment spurred Wesley's memory of a circus in his home town. "You buy your ticket and you take your chances," he said, attempting to imitate the sideshow barker.

Lizzie leveled a suspicious look at him. "What's that supposed to mean?"

"Oh, nothing. When you said you were buying your ticket, it made me think of a circus back home and a girl that reminds me a little of you.

"A hometown honey?"

"No, not unless the summer after the seventh grade counts. Frankly, after grade school she was never that interested in me. I played football, and she was president of the debate club."

"Sounds interesting. So tell me about the circus."

"It's a long story."

"We have a long bus ride, and since I'm going across several states with you, I need to know these things," she said with mock importance in her voice.

"I'll tell you after we get on the bus."

Without speaking, the ticket agent crooked his finger for Lizzie to come forward. His wrinkled face formed the grimace of a man bored with his job. Lizzie thought he resembled the cartoon character Deputy Dawg, but she smiled at him. He sneered back at her.

Grumpy.

"Where to, Miss?"

"Denver."

"One-way or roundtrip?"

She looked at Wesley for an answer, but he shrugged and gave her the palms-up "Who knows?" gesture. She turned back to the agent and said, "One-way."

What did I just say? For sure, I'm coming back.

Grumpy licked his finger for traction before flipping through the pages of an inch-thick schedule book. He used a ruler to line up the correct rate. Then he filled in the tickets and endorsed them with a rubber stamp.

"That'll be $28. You'll have a layover in Ogden, Utah, where you'll have to change buses. Times are on the tickets. Are you traveling alone?"

"Why are you asking?" *What a nosey old man,* she thought.

"If you are, I can arrange for you to sit near the driver. A pretty girl like you might draw unwanted attention from some unsavory characters that ride busses."

"She's with me." Wesley stepped forward. "I need the same tickets that she got."

"I see." Grumpy's perpetual frown changed to a lecherous grin. Wesley drew a bead on him with a hard glare.

The leer had left Grumpy's face by the time he finished writing the tickets.

Since the Mountain Express bus would not arrive for another hour, they roamed over to the Branding Iron and sat at a booth with a window view of the driveway. Outside, angry gray clouds threatened rain, making it feel chilly inside.

When a waitress appeared, they both ordered scrambled eggs and bacon with toast and glasses of milk. Wesley ordered a cup of coffee.

As she buttered her toast, Lizzie said, "That ticket agent—what a creep. I thought about giving him a piece of my mind. I guess my life has been sheltered, but I'm not used to men behaving like that. My father would have told him off."

"My stepfather would have knocked him on his butt."

Lizzie said, "I guess since your stepfather is a sailor, he's a pretty tough guy."

"Yeah, he trained the heavyweight boxing champion of the Navy in World War II."

"That's impressive. Did he ever give you any tips about boxing?"

"He did, but it's a long story—"

"Another long story? Speaking of that, since we have some time before the bus arrives, I want to hear about your girlfriend and the circus.

"Let's see. I'm not sure where to begin. The story actually starts before the circus and involves some crazy stuff."

"Oh, good. I love crazy stuff."

Wesley adjusted his sitting position and told Lizzie the same story about Ethan Collier and the UFO that he'd told Hez and the others at the camping trip. It took a while to recount, but he knew it was worth it by her reaction.

"Wow," Lizzie said, "that's an amazing story. Do you think it really happened?"

"I don't know. Folks in the Ozarks tell a lot of tall tales, but with this one, nobody is sure what to think. Heck, J. Bob, the lawyer, was supposedly there when it happened, and he's not even sure *he* believes it! But if you press him, he swears he saw it with his own eyes. J. Bob has been known to drink a bit, but he says he was stone-cold sober the day it happened.

"Gee, and I thought Mormons were complicated."

"And here's the kicker. The sheriff later confirmed the story to my stepfather. What do *you* think?"

"I don't know, but some Mormons believe that God created other worlds inhabited by people. So maybe. But how does the story about Ethan fit with the circus story?"

"It was the same circus I went to, and that's where the girl comes into the picture."

"Oh, good, I get to hear about your *girlfriend*," Lizzie teased.

Wesley sighed. "She wasn't my girlfriend."

"Just get on with the story, Monsieur Standish."

"Okay, okay, hold your horses," Wesley said, smiling at her impatience and her use of the pet name she'd given him. He thought, *I'd better make this a good story after it's been built up so much.* He gathered his memories and started the tale.

"The circus came to Ridgeview in the summer of 1960, and my best buddy Truman and I were dying to go. Weeks before, advertising posters had started popping up around town. The posters featured a scantily clad woman sitting on top of an elephant. As you can probably imagine, that prompted strict warnings from the local pulpits. According to the preachers, nickels and dimes wasted on sinful games of chance would pay better rewards if deposited in the offering plates. But their cautionary sermons didn't keep me from hoarding my allowance."

"Boys will be boys," Lizzie said. Wesley pursed his lips, and she said, "Go on."

"Truman and I were so excited that we arrived an hour before the performances under the single Big Top were scheduled to start. Our first hint that this wasn't Barnum & Bailey's came when we got a whiff of the air—it smelled like sawdust, cotton candy, and manure. This circus wasn't as grand as I had imagined."

"Not *The Greatest Show on Earth*?" Lizzie joked.

"No, how about *Cecil Harding's Circus of Thrills?* But it was better than *no* circus, and definitely a welcome change from the usual

Friday night movies at the Star Theater in Ridgeview."

Lizzie stretched her arms as she settled into a listening mode.

"The first thing we saw after we got inside was a sideshow tent behind a painted plywood poster. It pictured a python-like snake that had the head of a fanged woman with flowing red hair."

Wesley could still picture the scene in his mind, but he wanted to make the story more fun for Lizzie, so he used a coarser voice and imitated the sideshow barker. "Come inside and see the incredible snake woman! She walks. She talks. She crawls on her belly like a slimy reptile!"

Lizzie laughed and Wesley continued to paint the picture for her. "The pitchman had a wheezy smoker's voice. His face drooped like wax that had gotten too warm, and he had thin, splotchy skin and watery eyes that squinted through half-closed eyelids. He asked how old we were. We told him we were thirteen."

Again, Wesley changed his voice to play the barker. "Well, that's too bad, *boys*." He placed extra emphasis on *boys*. "You have to be fourteen to see the snake woman. She has some things to show that's only for adults to see. Things I expect you boys have never seen—or will likely never see."

"Oh, I can picture that guy," Lizzie interrupted.

"Yeah, he was memorable, for sure. He told us if he broke the rule and let us inside, he could lose his job. So we started to leave, but then he told us to hold up. He said, 'Boys, I feel sorry for you, I really do. I'll tell you what I'll do. If you make it worth my risk, say, each of you give me an extra fifty cents, I'll let you in.'"

Lizzie's eyes became spellbound as she listened. "What a con man! But this is getting good."

Wesley continued, "Inside, the tent was dark, except for a single hanging bulb near the rear. In the corner behind a spectator rope, we saw a woman who appeared to be coming from the waist up out of the center of a coiled snake. She was wearing a dingy yellow bikini top, snake bracelets and rings, and a red wig. Dark eyeliner and shadow made her eyes look really exotic, and she had curved fangs coming out of her dark red lips."

"We crept toward the spectator rope for a better look. Then the snake woman hissed and said, 'Come closer, boys, so I can kiss your necks-ssss.'" Wesley uttered a menacing hiss with this last word. At the same time, he jabbed his hand, like a snake, at Lizzie's waist.

Lizzie flinched and jumped a bit from her seat. "Oh my gosh, stop it!" she cried. She relaxed as they both began laughing hard. "Don't scare me like that, mister," she chided him. "What happened next?"

"The barker stuck his head through the tent flaps and said, 'Show's over, boys' and told us to get moving. That's all we got to see. And the snake woman's body odor was so strong that it made the whole tent smell like a locker room. Basically, he rooked us each out of fifty cents."

Lizzie smirked. "That's what you boys get for going to a naughty show. But wait a minute. I still haven't heard a thing about the girl."

"Hold on, that's coming next. So we were on our way to the rides when we saw Brenda Richards getting on the Ferris wheel with her mom and dad. Just so you know, I sat behind Brenda in the seventh grade. And I guess I thought she was the smartest and cutest girl in the class. She never seemed to get any grade below an A.

"She also seemed more mature and surer of herself than the other girls in my class. I could usually get the more timid girls to giggle or at least get angry with my awkward attempts at flirting. But Brenda didn't pay any attention to me. She was a tough cookie. For instance, once I passed her a note during class to tell her that her bra strap had fallen off her shoulder."

Lizzie arched an eyebrow.

"I was sure it would make her blush, but she just handed me back her own note that said, 'I know, it keeps falling down.' I could never rattle or impress her."

"I think I would like that girl," Lizzie said.

"I told you that she reminded me of you."

"Nicely done. That was very worthy. Get on with the story."

"When the Ferris wheel ride ended, we walked over to Brenda and her parents. Mr. Richards was an officer at Ridgeview Bank, and one of the few men in town who wore a coat and tie, other than on Sundays. That night, even without a tie, his sport jacket and white Arrow shirt made him stand out from the other men in the crowd.

"Anyway, I said hello to Mr. Richards and his wife, but I couldn't keep my eyes off of Brenda. She was wearing powder blue Bermuda shorts and a matching striped blouse. I swear, she could have been a child model for a clothing catalogue, the way she always dressed."

"She must have made quite an impression if you still remember what she was wearing," said Lizzie.

"I told you she was cute. So I asked her if she wanted to come along with us to throw baseballs and try to win one of the big teddy bears.

"She turned to her dad and batted her eyes at him and asked, 'May I, Daddy?' With her pleading look and the lilt in her voice, she seemed like a little girl asking to stop for ice cream. Not at all the aloof, confident Brenda we knew. She had transformed into an Oscar-worthy actress to get what she wanted.

"And it worked. Mr. Richards changed from the stern banker to an indulgent daddy. He said yes, but that she had to meet them at the Big Top before the show started. Then the stern banker reappeared and said, 'You boys take good care of Brenda.' His eyes narrowed and got our attention.

"After we were out of her parents' sight, she grabbed both our hands and said, 'Let's go. You guys had better win a teddy bear for me.' Real Brenda had returned."

"I definitely like her," Lizzie said. "Sorry for the interruption. Proceed."

"At the baseball stand, the pitchman yelled, 'Step right up, boys. Knock over the milk bottles and win your girl a teddy bear. Three throws for a quarter.' He was about six feet tall and skinny, with tattoos on both forearms. And he wore a grease-stained, sleeveless T-shirt that needed washing. We called him Tattoo Man.

"Tattoo Man snatched a lavender teddy bear from a shelf that had at least a dozen more pastel-colored, teddy bears, each about two feet tall, and he held it above his head. Then he pointed at Truman and challenged him to win one for his girlfriend and nodded at Brenda.

"Truman was my best friend, but it annoyed me that Tattoo thought Brenda was his girl. And I got even more irritated when Brenda squeezed Truman's arm like he was some kind of he-man. Truman's big grin didn't help.

"Tattoo said, 'Watch, I'll show you how easy it is.' He walked over to the pyramid of three metal milk bottles on the ground and nudged them over with his foot, like it was easy.

"Truman, who was the best pitcher in summer baseball, stepped forward ready to demonstrate his skill. As he held the first ball, he said, 'How old are these things?' and showed us how the ball squished in when he gripped it. And the bottles, about thirty feet away, appeared to be made of solid lead, despite how easily Tattoo Man had knocked them over with his foot.

"But Truman was game. With a confident and determined look, he wound up, kicked his leg high, and fired a strike, but it only knocked off the top bottle. He tried two more times with no better luck and gave up, but Brenda cheered each of his throws.

"So I forked over a quarter and took my turn. Without Truman's smoothness, I hurled the mushy baseball at the bottles and missed them all. Embarrassing, to say the least. My second attempt was no better. On the third try, I only managed to knock off the top bottle.

"Without waiting to be asked, I handed over another quarter. I connected with each throw but still never knocked over more than one bottle. Another quarter and three more throws produced no better results. After four quarters, I gave up.

"Deciding that the game was rigged, the three of us left and just moseyed from one area to another, and bought some pink cotton candy. A clown on stilts passed by and tossed three plastic flowers to us. Brenda put hers in the top buttonhole of her blouse and said she had a souvenir for the evening, even if it wasn't a teddy bear.

"I told them we needed to head for the Big Top or we'd be late meeting her parents. But then I made up an excuse about going to the restroom and said I would catch up with them.

"I trotted back to the baseball booth. Without any other suckers throwing baseballs when I arrived, Tattoo was passing his time trying to juggle three baseballs. I got straight to the point. I told him I had spent a dollar there trying to win a teddy bear, and that I could probably spend two more and still not win one.

"Tattoo stopped juggling, and his face got defensive. 'It's a game of chance. You pays your quarter and you takes your chances.'"

"Ahh," Lizzie said, "now, I know what you meant at the bus depot, about paying for a ticket and taking your chances. Sorry, keep going."

"I told him I already took my chances and wanted to know how much it would cost to buy one. He said they weren't for sale, and I asked what my *chances* would be if I paid four dollars in advance. He sneered, showing a decayed front tooth, and said they would be pretty good if I paid five dollars up front.

"I told him I only had four dollars left, but I'd already paid one dollar, so that *was* five dollars. Without speaking, Tattoo shuffled over to the milk bottles. He knelt and adjusted them, maneuvering one of the lower bottles back by an inch. On the way back, he scanned the midway, as if searching for a possible problem, and eased over next to me. Keeping his gaze on the crowd, he muttered, 'Give me the cash,' and extended his hand. I slipped him the four bucks. On my third try, I knocked over all three milk bottles.

"As people passed by, Tattoo yelled, 'Look, folks, we have another winner. See how easy it is? Even a child can do it!' He handed me a lavender teddy bear.

"With the teddy bear under my arm, I jogged back to the main tent, hoping Brenda and the others had not already gone inside.

They hadn't. Brenda, her family, and Truman were peering over the crowd looking for me. Brenda saw me first, and her lips spread into a broad smile.

"She said, 'Look, there's Wesley. And look what he has.' Truman grabbed my free arm and wanted to know how many throws it took me. I fudged a bit and said I got it on the third try, which was more or less true.

"I handed the teddy bear to Brenda and told her that, now, she had a real souvenir. She thanked me and said she would keep him in her bedroom. I felt proud, until she said what she was going to name him."

"What was she going to name him?" Lizzie asked.

"She said since he was a *teddy* bear, and *teddy* started with a *t*, she would name him *Truman*. It flabbergasted me. I didn't know what to say.

"Mr. Richards cleared his throat in a distinct signal to his daughter, and Mrs. Richards pursed her lips. A mischievous smile came across Brenda's face and she said, "But since Wesley won him, his last name shall be *Sanders*. Meet Truman Sanders.' So now you know the story."

"It was a great story, Wesley. I'm sure I would have liked Brenda Richards."

"I liked her, too, but she had an implied superiority about her. Whenever I talked to her, it always seemed she knew what I was about to say and wished I would hurry up and finish. If I hesitated, she would finish the sentence for me."

Lizzie frowned at him. "And that's how she reminds you of me?"

"No, not that part. The confident part. You probably would have been her best friend."

"That's better. So what happened to Brenda?"

"She got a scholarship to some fancy school back East. Brown or Villanova—one of those you see on College Bowl. That was her favorite TV show, so maybe that's why she applied."

Lizzie's face became thoughtful, as if an idea had just occurred. "You tell the best stories. You should write a book."

"Maybe I will someday."

CHAPTER FOURTEEN

The Mountain Express bus arrived ahead of schedule. After the passengers unloaded, the driver shut the door and marched to the station. He stopped in front of the new passengers, who had gathered outside the building.

"Good afternoon, folks. It will be twenty minutes before departure, so I suggest you use the restroom before we leave. The next stop isn't until Pocatello, and the bus doesn't have a restroom."

Later, when the driver opened the bus door, Lizzie and Wesley boarded first and took the rear seats on the driver's side. Lizzie sat by the window, and Wesley took the aisle seat. With the small number of passengers, they had the back third of the bus to themselves.

After a few more chuckles about Wesley's story, Lizzie's voice took a serious tone. "Wesley, what if your mother is in isolation? You said she was in an experimental treatment program."

Wesley grimaced as he peered across the aisle through the window at the tree-covered mountains. "I hadn't thought about that . . . but I'll find a way to see her."

Lizzie took his hand in hers. "*We'll* find a way." Lizzie cuddled next to him and held his hand. Soon, they were both asleep.

Through the microphone, the driver announced, "Pocatello. We'll have a thirty-minute rest stop."

They had slept for most of two hours. Wesley's sleep had mostly been fitful dreams of hospitals full of strange mechanical devices.

Lizzie raised her head from Wesley's shoulder and stretched her arms toward the ceiling. "I can't believe we slept all the way to Pocatello," she said while yawning, "but since neither of us slept last night, I guess it's not surprising."

Wesley rotated his neck to get the kinks out. "All I know is I'm hungry."

"You just ate breakfast."

He checked his watch. "That was ages ago."

"Waaaah, baby needs his twelve o'clock feeding."

Wesley produced a cranky frown. Lizzie restrained a burst of laughter and gave him a sock on the arm. Wesley grinned, at first with reluctance, and then couldn't stop a full belly laugh. Finally, Lizzie laughed, too.

"I'm a growing boy. What can I say?"

After eating a couple mealy apples and splitting a bag of potato chips at the lunch counter, they hustled back to join the line that was forming to board the bus. As they left, Lizzie picked up an abandoned copy of *Newsweek* from a chair. The cover featured a photograph of U.S. Marines in Vietnam.

Some of the new passengers gravitated to the rear of the bus, including a man wearing wireframe sunglasses, the kind truck drivers and pilots wore. This man now sat in their previous seat.

Fashionably dressed, but rumpled, the man wore a gray chalk-stripe suit with a modern, narrow lapel and a white shirt. His thin black tie had a Windsor knot and hung loosely from his unbuttoned collar. He hadn't shaved in a day, maybe two.

"Great," Wesley said under his breath.

"What's wrong?" Lizzie asked.

"The only seat in the rear is across from that hoodlum-looking guy in the suit."

Apparently undaunted by the change in seating arrangements, Lizzie said, "It'll be fine."

Still irked, Wesley said, "Well, I didn't like the way he watched you while we were waiting in line. Take the window seat again."

Lizzie leveled a glare at him that could only be interpreted as "Don't be so bossy." Wesley cringed as he got the message.

With a softer expression, she mouthed, "It's okay."

They sat down opposite the stranger, with Lizzie by the window. The smell of booze wafted across the aisle. The reason for the rumpled suit became obvious. The man had been drinking. Or still smelled from the night before. Wesley's stomach tightened. He'd seen plenty of drunks in his stepdad's tavern.

Once the bus moved forward, Wesley situated his back toward the stranger. Lizzie leafed through her magazine but had the uncanny feeling of being watched. She shifted her view across the aisle, and the man averted his gaze and focused on the seatback in front of him. Wesley had already closed his eyes.

The stranger appeared to be in his mid-forties. Slim, maybe six feet tall. Not bad-looking for an older man, but as Lizzie's dad might have said, he had been ridden hard and put up wet. His suit needed pressing, but the quality was not inexpensive. And the gold cufflinks securing the French cuffs had not come cheap either.

Lizzie refocused on her magazine to avoid staring, but her mind began playing a mental detective game: *Who is he?* She imagined bloodshot eyes behind the shades, and the paper cup he held was surely filled with coffee—the morning-after antidote of a drinker. Yet his straight nose and high forehead made him appear intelligent.

She peeked over again. He still stared trancelike at the seatback and steadied the paper cup with long interlaced fingers, which would be great for playing a guitar—Mike would be envious of those fingers.

She flipped the pages of *Newsweek*, pretending to be interested but continued her speculation. The man's pale complexion indicated he hadn't spent much time in the sun. Maybe he was a pool player like Paul Newman in *The Hustler*. Then a humorous thought came to her. *Unless he has a suitcase stowed below, where's his pool cue?* The black leather satchel next to him looked like a doctor's bag, but she doubted he'd been on a house call.

Then it dawned on her. He must be a gambler … like Bret Maverick in the TV series. Gambling offended her Mormon sensibilities of thrift and honesty, but another part of her found it exotic and fascinating.

She rubbernecked again, and this time the stranger looked directly back at her with those dark glasses. Caught. She willed herself not to snap her head away. Embarrassed, she bit the inside of her lip. She felt like a rabbit hypnotized by the black eyes of a snake. Had she just peered into the eyes of the Devil? Her lips pursed into an ill-at-ease pout.

He took a sip from his cup, not taking his eyes off her. "Are you interested in some conversation?"

"No, thank you."

"The way you've been looking over at me, I inferred you might be. You're curious about who I am, what I do, and why I'm on this bus."

His analysis gave her a start that she hoped didn't show.

Wesley opened his eyes when he heard the conversation. He glanced at Lizzie and then at the stranger. "What's going on?"

"Nothing much," the man said, "your companion and I just started a conversation. I didn't mean to disturb you."

Wesley jerked his head toward Lizzie and gave her a bewildered look. In a whisper, he said, "I thought we agreed to avoid this guy."

Lizzie tilted her head back and raised her eyebrows as she thought, *One bossy brother is enough.*

"Well, don't let me interrupt." Wesley said, with a peevish edge to his voice.

Resting her hand on Wesley's arm the way she might calm a skittish horse, Lizzie said, "Wesley, this man was about to introduce himself."

Wesley harrumphed under his breath.

"My name is Caraway David—"

"That sounds made up," Wesley said. "Like you flipped around

'Dave Garraway' from the *Today Show*." The stranger's half-smile suggested he understood the reference or had heard the observation before. "You know," Wesley continued, "like the *Rocky and Bullwinkle Show* had the 'Kirwood Derby,' which spoofed TV announcer Durward Kirby."

Lizzie rolled her eyes.

"I'm afraid I haven't watched a lot of *Rocky and Bullwinkle*," replied the man. "As for my name, it's actually a junior, so you'll have to blame my father for the moniker."

"Oh," Wesley mumbled.

"When I was a boy, kids called me Caraway Seed so often that they eventually just nicknamed me Seed. Now, my friends call me Carry .. . and you can too if you like. What are your names, if you don't mind me asking?"

"I'm Lizzie and he's Wesley."

"Are you two married?"

"No," they both said at the same time.

"Brother and sister?"

"No, she's my girlfriend." Wesley spouted and then added in a more restrained tone, "We're going to see my mother." He cleared his throat and glanced at Lizzie.

Lizzie smiled. The current status of their relationship had not been ironed out, but his spontaneous utterance reconfirmed it in her mind.

"That's right," Lizzie said, "she's in the hospital in Denver."

"Denver … you don't say. That's where I'm headed. Well, a bit east of Denver."

Lizzie's intuition activated. The turn of the conversation had become a little too familiar. Wesley nudged her with his elbow. His protective side had resurfaced.

Taking the unsubtle hint, Lizzie said, "Well, that *is* a coincidence," and began flipping pages of her magazine.

Wesley joined her apparent interest in the magazine and asked, "Anything interesting?"

"The Marines, I suppose."

Carry wadded up his paper cup. His lips tightened and the space between his eyebrows formed a tight crevice forming a picture of a man with something on his mind, or a conversation unfinished. He twisted in his seat toward the couple.

"Excuse me," he said. After he had their attention, he continued. "I assume you two will change buses in Ogden." His voice had a Western accent, a bit nasal, like some of the Wyoming wranglers at the park. Or like Chester on *Gunsmoke* when he said "Mr. Dillon," hammering the first syllable.

With little enthusiasm, Wesley said, "I believe so."

Carry continued. "If I recall correctly, there's a four-hour layover before you can take the bus to Denver."

Wesley, vigilant again, remembered an incident his stepfather had told him about hustlers on the waterfront. Responding, he said, "Are you just making conversation or trying to make a point?" It came out brusquer than he intended. Lizzie whipped her head up from the magazine.

An easy, relaxed smile spread over Carry's face. His teeth were straight and even. Perfect, in fact. It was disarming how friendly he seemed.

Wesley instantly regretted being so abrupt, but he still felt the need to be cautious and thought of an aphorism his grandmother often spouted: *Rarely does the Devil appear patently evil. More likely, he comes silver-tongued and reasonable, appealing to the vain natures of the unsuspecting.* "I didn't mean to sound rude . . . Carry." It felt awkward being so familiar—on a first-name basis—with a stranger.

Still smiling, Carry said, "Your parents obviously taught you well to be suspicious of strangers, but I do have a point, or rather, a proposition to make."

Lizzie's eyes locked on Carry. Wesley remained silent but kept a beady focus on Carry.

"I assume you both would like to get to Denver as soon as possible and save some time and money." He waited for them to reply, and when they didn't, he continued.

"You see, I didn't take the bus all the way from Denver to Pocatello. I flew from Denver to Ogden—I own my own plane."

"Like Sky King on TV?" Wesley's interest perked up. He had never been on an airplane before.

"No, Sky King had a Cessna T-50, and later a Cessna 310. Both twin engines. I own a single-engine Piper Cherokee. And I don't have a ranch."

Touché, thought Wesley. *He knows his planes and his Sky King.*

"Why didn't you fly all the way to Pocatello?" Lizzie asked. "Doesn't it have an airport?"

"It does, but because of the weather report, I had to take the bus from Ogden. I'm a licensed pilot, and IFR—instrument rated—but nobody with any sense would have flown into the turbulent front that had locked in. And I couldn't wait. I had a . . . meeting I needed to attend."

Wesley's guard lowered. A man who owned his own plane—if he did—couldn't be a complete bum. "That's interesting, but what does that have to do with us?"

"I don't much like flying alone on a cross-country trip. If you two would fly with me, you could save twelve hours and the cost of bus fare."

"How do you figure it would save twelve hours?" Wesley asked.

Lizzie answered. "A four-hour layover and twelve-hour bus ride. I'm guessing we could fly in four hours."

"That's pretty good figuring, young lady, and you're right. Cruising at 120 knots, that is, about 140 miles an hour, less with three passengers, say 130, we could be there in four hours."

Math wasn't Wesley's strong suit, but saving most of a day and half the bus fare struck a favorable chord. Lizzie seemed interested—even excited—but he still had doubts.

He leaned his head to Lizzie's, ignoring Carry's presence, and whispered, "What do you think?"

With her lips to Wesley's ear, Lizzie said, "I'm in favor of saving time, if it seems safe. I need to get back as soon as possible, or Mike will call my parents. Tell him we need to think it over."

After Wesley explained that they needed to think over the proposition, Carry nodded agreeably and retrieved a Ralph Compton paperback from his satchel and began reading.

Lizzie and Wesley murmured to each other, weighing the pros and cons. Saving time versus traveling with a pilot they barely knew. He seemed to know about planes, but they needed to determine whether he was a good pilot and get more information about his plane. After all, this stranger with an odd name could be full of baloney or up to no good.

Wesley pursued the inquiry. "Carry, how long have you been a pilot? Is your plane big enough to carry three people?"

Carry looked up from his book and answered, "Been a pilot since World War II, and a Piper Cherokee will seat four. You don't appear to have much baggage, so weight won't be a problem."

"Were you a pilot in the war?"

"Yes, I wanted to be a fighter pilot, but with my size I was better suited to B-17 bombers. Still better than being on the ground . . . or so I thought. Don't worry, the Air Corps trained me well, and I fly regularly."

Lizzie's mouth twitched. "What do you mean, *or so you thought?*"

Carry removed his sunglasses revealing the roadmap eyes Lizzie had imagined and began cleaning the shades with a white handkerchief from his suit coat. As he wiped the lenses, he said, "I don't usually like to talk about my experience in the war, but since you asked, it seems the Germans didn't like me bombing them."

Lizzie leaned forward to see around Wesley. Her eyes fixed on Carry. He had Wesley's full attention, too.

Carry's eyes had a faraway look, as if he were recalling a distant memory, long suppressed. "I was shot down over Germany in March of 1944."

"Where?" Wesley asked.

Somewhere near Frankfort. I co-piloted a B-17 and had a mission to bomb a ball bearing factory."

"You crash landed?" Lizzie asked.

"Yeah. The captain took some anti-aircraft flak in his shoulder, so I had to try and land it. Fortunately, we had already dropped our bombs, and I dumped as much fuel as I could. The tail gunner and bombardier bailed out on my orders, but the rest of us rode it in. It was daylight, and I was able to see some kind of clearing—a potato field maybe—and I skid in on a wing and a prayer, as they say."

"What happened next?" Lizzie asked, with no disguise of her interest. "Did the other crewmembers make it out?"

"We all survived, and other than the captain, nobody had serious injuries. Fire engulfed the plane, and it started filling with smoke. We scrambled out, and then from out of a tree line a hundred yards away, a squad of German soldiers charged toward us, spraying machine gun fire all around us, and yelling words we didn't understand. But we got their meaning and put our hands behind our heads."

"That must have been terrifying," Lizzie said.

"Numb describes it better. Everything seemed to move in slow motion." His eyes became glassier. "I can't recall every detail, but I thought the entire crew would be killed on the spot. I remember thinking my mother wouldn't know where I died."

"Oh, that's so sad." Lizzie eyes welled.

Wesley, with postured manliness, said, "Well, they obviously didn't kill you. What happened?"

"The Germans loaded us on trucks and hauled us to a POW camp. Stalag Luft 3."

Wesley's face lit up as if he had special insight. "I saw the movie *Stalag 13*. Was it like that?"

"Not exactly, but speaking of movies, did you see *The Great Escape?*"

"Yeah, that was a cool movie," Wesley said, nodding his head.

"Oh, yeah, Steve McQueen. Ooh." Lizzie said, with dreamy eyes.

Carry finished his point. "That movie was based on Stalag Luft 3."

"Were you part of the escape?" Wesley asked.

"No, that was the Brits. My understanding is the escape involved no Americans. Some may have helped tunnel. You've got to realize there were 5,000 prisoners there."

"Wow! How long were you there?" Wesley asked.

"Seventeen long months that I really don't like to think about. It brings up painful memories."

"Oh, we're sorry, "Lizzie said, apologizing for them both.

"No problem," Carry said flatly, as his vacant stare returned.

Sensing the subject needed to be changed, Lizzie said, "Just what is it that you do for a living? If you don't mind me asking."

"I'm in marketing."

His answer did not satisfy her speculations. "What kind of marketing?"

"Oh, different things. Enough about me. Are you going to see Wesley's mother for a special occasion?"

"My mom is in Fitzsimmons Army Hospital."

"I know exactly where that is." Carry's voice inflected upwards but then became more concerned, "I hope it's nothing too serious."

"It is. She has cancer."

"Oh my. I'm sorry to hear that. No doubt, you want to get there on the double. How do you plan to get from the bus station in Denver to Fitzsimmons?"

"We hadn't thought of that yet," Wesley said.

"You know, Fitzsimmons is in Aurora, Colorado, which is about twenty miles east of Denver. And that just happens to be where my plane is hangared."

Wesley and Lizzie eyed each other with their mouths gaped. Was this a little too fortunate to be believed?

Carry pushed the forelock of his hair back in place. "Friends, I don't believe in coincidences. I think the reason I'm here is to meet you two and fly you to Denver."

Wesley and Lizzie whispered between themselves about Carry's proposition. Even considering the negative possibilities and the odd coincidence, they agreed that they both had a good feeling about Carry. They decided to cast their fate literally to the wind and fly with him.

Chapter Fifteen

At the Ogden depot, Carry insisted on paying for a taxi to the airport on the outskirts of town. He directed the driver to an open-front, T-shaped structure made of corrugated aluminum, which housed the red and white Piper Cherokee he had described.

Carry paid the cabdriver with cash from a thick wallet, loaded with currency. It reminded Wesley of his stepfather's billfold after a weekend of gambling and the phrase he often used. *You could burn a wet elephant with all that green.*

Lizzie's eyes narrowed on the wallet, and then her face relaxed in a knowing smile—more evidence for her that Carry was probably a gambler and not a marketer. She was now more intrigued than worried, though, and eager to learn more about this mystery man.

They exited the cab, and Carry pointed at the plane. "Here's my baby. I call her *Miss Leeta*, after my wife. Her name is actually Carmelita."

Carry stepped to the plane, opened the pilot-side door, and said, "C'mon and stow your gear. I need to go to the flight office to check the weather report and file my flight plan. I won't be long." He removed his tie and exchanged his suit coat for a tan jacket from behind the seat and strode away carrying his satchel.

The gray sky and drizzle overwhelmed the euphoria Wesley felt about his first ride in an airplane. It troubled him that they would be flying over mountains. Hearing Carry talk about his WWII adventures made him seem like some kind of a hero—and maybe he was—but now fear rose up to sabotage the logic of the plan.

Maybe it was fear of fear, but when fear stepped up to the plate, Wesley could always count on his mind to race through a parade of imaginary horrible things, which took on the strength of prophesy. Currently, it was the airplane crashing in the mountains, with Carry and Lizzie the only survivors, stuck in the snow in Donner Pass.

Lizzie apparently had similar misgivings. He saw the apprehension in her eyes and touched her shoulder. "Are you getting cold feet about flying? We've still got time to get back to the bus station."

Lizzie shook her head, but the look in her eyes didn't change. "We need to save the time." Then looking more hopeful, she said, "He must be a pretty good pilot since he flew B-17s. And this one only has one propeller."

Returning from the office, Carry wore the tan jacket, a red baseball cap, and his aviator sunglasses, which reflected the sun, now peeking through the clouds.

He had shaved while inside and appeared confident with an easy stride, but the growing apprehension of his two young passengers would have been hard for him to miss. Their conversations in the back seat of the cab had been reduced to whispers by the time they got to the airport. Lizzie had scoped the surroundings like a lioness gazing across the savannah searching out potential danger and a way to escape.

"You two have the look of rookie tail gunners on their first mission." Carry gestured toward the aircraft and with a confident voice said, "The Piper Cherokee is one of the safest small planes you can fly. It cruises at 140 miles per hour at 7,000 feet and can climb over 17,000 feet—we'll probably fly at half that and closer to a 120 miles per hour. We can make it to Denver without refueling. Plus this weather is predicted to break shortly, and we'll be VFR."

"What's that?" Wesley asked.

"VFR stands for *visual flight rules*. That means we can see the ground and where other aircraft might be. I think I mentioned that

IFR stands for *instrument flight rules,* which and means visibility is poor—like flying in clouds—and you have to rely on instruments and not sight. Not a problem either way because I am instrument-rated."

It all sounded professional and matter of fact. No cause for concern, Wesley rationalized, but then thought, *I hope I'm not just whistling past a graveyard.*

Lizzie's and Wesley's eyes met. Her face was expectant, as if she hoped he would have an answer to the ultimate decision.

"I'm game if you are," Wesley said.

Before she could answer, Carry intervened. "Tell you what, let's mosey over to the café by the flight office. I could use a cup of coffee. And we ought to use the restrooms before we take off. Four hours is a long time at 7,000 feet."

Wesley held back a smile as he pictured what going to the bathroom might look like at that altitude.

Carry drank the last of his coffee as they returned to the plane and tossed the paper cup in a trash can at the hangar. His matter-of-fact confidence in the café was that of a commander leading a crew to battle. He delegated flight assignments for Wesley and Lizzie. He gave Lizzie a navigational map and the job of locating landmarks. Wesley would provide a second pair of eyes and keep a lookout for other aircraft. By the time they'd left the café, they were invested in the flight.

Before they boarded, Carry circled the plane for a pre-flight check. He kicked the tires, moved wing flaps, and made checkmarks on a preprinted form attached to a clipboard. "Everything looks shipshape. Who's going to sit in the co-pilot seat?"

"You go ahead, Wesley," Lizzie said, "I'd just as soon sit in the back seat."

After they boarded, Carry started the engine and continued to mark items on the list, muttering "check" at each one. "Fuel level, check. Oil pressure, check . . . ."

When he finished, he said, "Fasten your seatbelts."

He eased the plane from the hangar and called the flight office. "Piper N Five Niner . . ." he completed the tail numbers and continued, "requests clearance for takeoff."

In short order, the tower replied. "You are cleared for takeoff, Piper Cherokee N Five Niner."

Carry taxied onto the runway and built up speed. As they left the ground, Wesley and Lizzie held the sides of their seats as if they were on a roller coaster ride. Neither said a word—and both held their breath.

In his red baseball cap and aviator sunglasses, Carry could pass for a movie aviator. His whole persona seemed to change. From a tentative, hung-over suspected gambler to Jimmy Stewart in *Strategic Air Command*. When they reached cruising altitude, Lizzie and Wesley exhibited a new level of comfort and began chatting about the marvels below.

"Look over there, Wesley," Lizzie said. "That must be the Great Salt Lake."

"That's right, Lizzie," Carry said.

"How big is it?"

"I think it is about 75 miles long and 35 or so miles wide. It's not very deep—probably averages about 12 feet. Of course, some parts are deeper."

Wesley joined the conversation. "I didn't know it had islands."

"Yeah, it has eight or ten. Some are peninsulas depending on the varying water level. The largest is Antelope Island, which has bison on it, ironically. If we didn't have a tight schedule, we could zoom over and dip down to see them."

Wesley watched as Carry operated the controls with comfort and ease. "Why do you only have one hand on the steering wheel?"

"In an airplane, it isn't a *steering wheel*. It's the yoke. To answer your question, it's a tradition—and how I was trained—but the practical reason is that it leaves the other hand free to operate other controls such as the throttle. And another reason is, you don't want to oversteer the aircraft."

"That makes sense."

"You want to fly the plane, Wesley?"

"Nah, I better not."

"Yes, I agree," Lizzie chimed in.

"Don't worry, I'm right here. Besides, if something happened to me, the co-pilot ought to know something about operating the airplane. Otherwise, we might make a large airplane-shaped hole in the ground."

"Don't say that!" Lizzie said. "Don't even think it. I'm just starting to get un-nervous."

"Sorry, it's an old pilot's joke."

After waiting a few moments to let Lizzie recover, Carry said, "Wes, go ahead and put your right hand on the yoke. No need to strangle it. Just kind of rest it there."

Carry demonstrated how pushing forward on the yoke made the nose dive and pulling back raised it. He showed how pushing either of the two peddles on the floor of the cockpit directed the aircraft to the left or right without turning the yoke.

At first, Wesley used the yoke as if it were an automobile steering wheel and banked the airplane steep to the right.

Carry leveled the plane and reminded him to use the peddles if he wanted to direct the plane left or right. "Try it again, and watch the artificial horizon gauge—it will tell you if the aircraft is flying level."

After fifteen minutes of following Carry's instructions, Wesley had gotten the hang of it and managed to keep the aircraft level.

Lizzie, feeling more relaxed now, tapped Wesley's shoulder and said with a laugh, "You fly an airplane better than you ride a horse."

Wesley focused on flying and didn't respond.

"Good job, Wesley. You'd better let me take over now. We're getting into an area where we may experience some turbulence, so make sure your seatbelts are tight."

Moments later, with no warning, the plane dropped straight down, as if it had dropped off the edge of a cliff. Lizzie's head came within inches of hitting the ceiling.

"Wow! What was that?" She said. "It felt like the bottom dropped out of the sky."

"Just a little bumpy. Are you okay?" Carry said, looking over his shoulder.

"I'm fine, but if I hadn't tightened my seatbelt, I would have hit my head."

"Sorry about that. Even on a clear day you can hit a pocket of warm air that is less dense, and that can cause a loss of altitude. But it's nothing to worry about."

The Piper Cherokee withstood the turbulence and flew on an even keel thereafter. During the remainder of the flight, wide-ranging and relaxed conversation ensued. However, Carry continued to avoid any specific details about his occupation, and he skillfully redirected Lizzie's queries to more general topics or back to questions about her and Wesley.

As the Piper Cherokee descended for landing at the small airport in Aurora, Lizzie braced in anticipation of a crash and "a large airplane-shaped hole" on the runway. But other than one slight bounce as the tires contacted the pavement, Carry executed a smooth landing.

They taxied to another T-shaped hangar that had an automobile, covered with a form-fitting canvas shroud, parked next to it.

Carry killed the engine and said, with some pride in his voice, "Another mission accomplished. Welcome to Aurora."

After they disembarked, two airport workers jogged to the plane and pushed it into the hangar. Carry thanked them and pulled cash out of his overstuffed wallet for a tip.

The wallet shifted Lizzie's imagination back into high gear. She tried to guess how much it contained. It was at least an inch thick. No wonder he kept it in his jacket pocket; it would be uncomfortable to sit on. She sneaked a glance at Wesley.

He edged beside her and whispered. "What do you think? A thousand?"

Under her breath, she said, "Maybe. The mark of a gambler, for sure."

The two workers left, and Carry gestured to the covered car. "Wes, give me a hand uncovering my car."

The unveiling revealed a blue 1958 Cadillac Eldorado Seville. With mirror-perfect paint, the two-door coupe could have just come off the assembly line in Detroit.

"Man, what a creampuff, Carry."

"Thanks." Carry opened the trunk and stashed the cover and his satchel inside. Lizzie and Wesley held on to their backpacks.

"Lizzie, I'll sit in the back this time," Wesley said, as he opened the door and slipped onto the rear passenger-side seat.

The leather seats gave the car a luxurious smell, and the engine produced a resonant rumble—not the usual whisper-quiet sound of a luxury car.

As if he needed to explain, Carry said, "I couldn't resist installing a couple of Hollywood glass-pack mufflers. A friend of mine in Texas has a Seville with steer horns, and I didn't want to be outdone."

"Boys and their cars," Lizzie said. "My brother put those little round hubcaps on his '48 Ford. What are they called?"

"Baby moons," Wesley said.

"You're right about boys, Lizzie," Carry said. "They just keep getting bigger toys."

Carry nosed the Caddy onto a main street and glanced at the gold watch strapped to his wrist with a black leather band. "We made good time—it's only 6 o'clock. We'll be at the hospital in twenty minutes."

"That's a handsome watch you're wearing, Carry. I'm surprised I didn't notice it before."

"I wasn't wearing it before. I don't want to risk losing it when I travel on a bus or train, so I keep it packed. But I always wear it when I'm flying."

With a sudden awareness, she said, "I know why I didn't see it. You steer the plane with your left hand. From the backseat where I was sitting, no wonder I didn't see it."

"You are certainly observant, Lizzie."

She beamed, taking the comment as a compliment. Still looking at the watch, she said, "So, do you wear it when you fly because it has those little wings on the dial?"

"Yes and no. The wings are the winged hourglass logo of Longines watches. This one is the flagship model. Longines watches have been associated with aviation for years. Charles Lindbergh helped make them famous. But the other thing, it's my talisman—my good luck piece."

"Why is it good luck?"

"Let's just say it has come in handy a time or two . . . and Leeta gave it to me."

Wesley faked a cough. She shifted her eyes to him, and the questioning stopped.

As they motored to the hospital, Carry asked, "Wes, if you don't mind my asking, why is your mother in an Army hospital?"

"My stepfather is a retired navy warrant officer. He's a merchant seaman now, on his way to India. As dependents, my mom and I get free military medical care."

"With your card, you'll be able to get in the PX," Carry said. "Do either of you know anything about Fitzsimmons?"

Lizzie and Wesley shook their heads.

"One thing that might be of interest, President Eisenhower stayed in Fitzsimmons when he recovered from the heart attack he suffered while on vacation in Colorado."

"If the President was a patient there, it must be good," Lizzie said.

"Yes, it is. He stayed there for about two months, on the eighth floor."

Fitzsimmons Army Hospital came into view at the end of a tree-lined lane a quarter-mile long. The hospital stood immense and foreboding like a citadel, eight stories tall, etched against the snow-capped Rocky Mountains. The Cadillac came to a stop in the parking lot, which appeared to cover a couple acres in front of the entrance.

"Wesley, do you want me to go in with you and Lizzie? I could possibly be of some assistance in getting you directed to the right place. Sometimes, adults are taken more seriously—not that you two are kids—but some grizzled old top sergeant or head nurse might try to give you the business."

"No, Carry, you've done enough. And we are grateful."

"Boys never want to ask for help," Lizzie said, with a hint of exasperation," Looking at Carry, she said, "Since we don't know where we are going, a little help getting us started would be appreciated."

Carry parked the car, and the three advanced to the hospital. Inside, they approached a counter, identified by an overhead sign that read "Admissions." A stern-looking woman behind the counter wearing a nurse's cap eyed them. Her name tag indicated she was *D. Jenkins, RN.*

"Hello, Captain David, I haven't seen you in a while. What brings you in today?" It struck Wesley they had become so familiar with Carry that he had forgotten his full name was Caraway David. "And who are these two civilians with you?" Her voice was professional, but pleasant.

"Hello, Nurse Jenkins. These two are here to visit the young man's mother, who is receiving cancer treatment. How do they find her? By the way, I'm just their chauffeur."

Jenkins exhibited no sign, other than a slight twitch of her lips, of what she was thinking. Her face suggested she didn't suffer nonsense. The countenance of a by-the-book military lifer, one with which Wesley was familiar. Although he sometimes had difficulty judging the age of adults, Nurse Jenkins seemed older than his mom, but younger than his grandma. He calculated she must be in her early fifties.

"You say they are *family*?" Jenkins asked.

"Wesley, show her your ID card" Carry said and then gestured at Lizzie. "And this young lady is a friend of the family."

"It's in my bag. I'll dig it out." Wesley rifled through his belongings and finally found it. He handed it to Nurse Jenkins.

"This indicates your sponsor is named Rockwell, but your surname is Sanders."

"Sam Rockwell is my stepfather."

"Where is he?"

"On his way to India—he's a merchant seaman."

"I see." Jenkins shifted her attention to Carry. "Captain, are you vouching for these two?"

"Yes, ma'am."

Looking at Wesley, she said, "What's your mother's name?"

"Rita Rockwell."

Jenkins opened a ledger book and thumbed through the tabbed pages. "Here she is. Room 432. I'll have an orderly escort them, Captain."

"Thank you, Nurse Jenkins."

The nurse's face softened, and she made strong eye contact with Carry. "How's Carmelita?"

"Thank you for asking. She's doing well. We think she is in remission."

Lizzie's face turned toward Wesley. His jaw dropped.

This man is as inscrutable as the Sphinx, he thought.

They all thanked Nurse Jenkins, and in a short time, an orderly arrived and handed them pocket-sized, clip-on visitor tags. "Follow me, please."

Carry said, "Friends, I have to be going. You've got passes and Orderly Jones will get you to your mom's room. Pay attention so you don't get lost."

He handed them a business card. "This has my address and home phone—I only give it to friends. But if you need my assistance, call me. Meanwhile, good luck. It has been my pleasure meeting you."

He extended his hand to Wesley.

Shaking his hand, Wesley said, "I can't thank you enough."

Lizzie stepped forward and extended her hand, too. "Thank you, Carry. You are a gentleman and a man of mystery."

With a glint in his eye, Carry said, "Me? I'm an open book." He gave her a half-salute and pivoted toward a long hallway.

Chapter Sixteen

Toting their backpacks, Lizzie and Wesley followed Orderly Jones. After a short walk from the elevator, he left them standing next to the open door of Room 432. Wesley walked to the edge of the doorway and craned his neck to see inside.

The highly polished asphalt tile floor in the hallway continued inside the room, which was painted a pale green. Two beds, separated by a privacy curtain, which had been drawn open, covered most of the floor, leaving only enough room for side tables, personal lockers, and two visitor chairs.

The front bed was empty but covered with sheets stretched tight and anchored by military/hospital-tucked corners. A sleeping Rita Rockwell occupied the back bed, and a man in civilian clothes dozed in a corner chair.

Wesley stepped back from the threshold and froze.

"What's wrong?" Lizzie asked.

"It's my dad." His voice was a whisper.

"I thought he was in route to India."

"No, not my stepdad, my *real* father—Ray Sanders—the one I haven't seen in eight years. Not since I got locked in an old bank safe when he tried to kidnap me."

"What?" Lizzie exclaimed. She shook her head, clearly confused. "You said your real father was dead." Her face became granite and her voice stern. "What is going on? And I want the truth."

Caught in a bold-faced lie, Wesley knew judgment day had arrived. In a dull tone and not facing her, he said, "To me, he was dead." What a hollow response. He knew it dodged the question and left him dangling like a caught fish. Unable to think of a stalling tactic, he turned his head and faced her. "But that was no excuse to lie to you. The truth is, he had gone to prison, and I was ashamed to tell you."

Her eyes bulged and her lips puckered as if to say "what," but the word never sounded. She closed her eyes and sucked in a deep breath. Her cheeks ballooned full of air before she blew it out and opened her eyes. Wesley remained silent, but he tensed in anticipation of what she would say. And what she would do. In a few seconds, which felt much longer to Wesley, her lips started to move, then stopped before she finally spoke.

In a measured, hushed tone, she said, "Wesley, I am very angry— no, disappointed—that you didn't trust me enough to tell me the truth."

Wesley flinched. Disappointed stung more than angry.

She sighed and slowly closed, then opened her eyes to meet his. She placed a hand on his cheek and squared his face to hers. "I can understand why you didn't . . . it was early in our relationship, and for a while we were star-crossed. But you need to understand that the sins of your father are not yours."

Wesley nodded.

With a penetrating stare, she said, "But don't ever lie to me again."

He tensed again. The scolding hurt, but he stood at a turning point. He recalled the words of his grandmother. *Look 'em in the eye and tell them what you know.* "As I said before, it was no excuse to lie to you . . . and I won't do it again."

She touched his arm. "It's all right, Wesley." She glimpsed over his shoulder to see Ray Sanders, and then back at Wesley. "You were locked in a safe?"

This was a matter Wesley had never told anyone. So far as he knew, the only outsiders who knew about this were the sheriff and J. Bob, the lawyer. But since he had disclosed the most shameful secret—his dad being an ex-con—he now spoke with no hesitation.

"It's a long story …" He paused to see if Lizzie would rib him for using that phrase yet again. Apparently, she was too shocked to joke, so he continued. "My mom and dad were fighting a lot before they got divorced, and he planned to haul me off to Iowa outside the jurisdiction of the court, as a bargaining chip."

"That's terrible," Lizzie said, slowly shaking her head with disbelief. "But how in the world did you get locked in a safe?"

"I don't want to lurk outside the door here and have him wake up and hear me. Let's walk back to the visitor's lounge. We passed it about halfway back to the elevator." Lizzie nodded in agreement, and they walked to the lounge where they found a quiet corner and Wesley returned to his story.

"Anyway, my grandfather got wise to Dad's plan, so he took me out of school and drove to the beauty shop in a nearby town where my mom worked. With Dad hot on our trail, Grandpa, Mom, and I hightailed it to J. Bob's—he's the town lawyer I told you about. But he was in court, so they left me with his secretary and took off to find him.

The secretary didn't know what to do, so she put me in J. Bob's office with some magazines. But before long, I heard my dad in the reception area yelling at her. He thought she'd hidden me and threatened to search the place. I was really afraid—"

"I'm sure you were, you poor thing."

"J. Bob's office was in an old bank building that had a walk-in vault he used for his law books. When I heard Dad coming into the office, I hid in the vault and closed the door. I didn't realize the combination to the lock had been lost years before."

"Oh my! How did you get out?"

"Ethan Collier—the one who saw the flying saucer—"

"What? That weird hermit?"

"That's a good way to put it. Ethan is something else, all right. My stepfather always said he didn't have a lick of sense. Ethan had been held back in school so many years that he had to be excused from class for a day in the eighth grade to register with the Selective Service Board. But he can do all kinds of complicated mathematic calculations in his head. J. Bob said he could solve problems it would normally take an engineer with a ten-foot slide rule to calculate. Anyway, when J. Bob found out I was locked in the safe, he got Ethan and rushed him over there. Ethan was able to figure out the four numbers of the combination to the safe in no time."

"Wow. He's quite a guy. So what happened to your real father?"

"That's the mystery. After the gunfight—"

"Gunfight?" Lizzie said with undisguised shock.

"That's another story . . ." and he winked at her. She rolled her eyes, but he could see that she wanted to know. "I'll have to tell you the rest of that one later. But the sheriff and my stepfather said my dad hopped a westbound train. And nobody has heard from him since."

"This is crazy—I mean, I believe you, but it's so fantastic."

"A few years ago, somebody sent a newspaper clipping to my mom that said Ray Sanders had drowned in the Mississippi River in Iowa. Later, we learned it was a different Ray Sanders, but I originally believed the article and felt no remorse. So I just went on half believing he was dead. Isn't that weird?"

"No, it's very sad. And I am sorry for you, but I am beginning to see why you are so guarded."

Wesley turned his head turned downward, avoiding eye contact.

"Get your chin off the floor, Wesley. I just made an observation, not a criticism."

Wesley faced her. "I know. I guess I wouldn't have told you all this if I didn't trust you."

"I appreciate that, but back to the subject at hand. Somebody had to know where your real father ended up or he wouldn't be here. Your mom?"

"I don't think so. Probably my grandmother. She would never allow me to be critical of him. My mom suspected Grandma knew more than she admitted. Despite all the problems in our family, Grandma and my dad were close. He always called her *Mom*, and Grandma always said he was the son she always wanted but wasn't able to have."

"That's interesting." The corners of her eyes crinkled—her detective face had returned. "Your dad must not have always been so ornery for your grandmother to have been so fond of him."

"Not always, but when he started drinking, things could get bad."

"Tell me about it."

"Someday, maybe, but not now."

"You mean, someday if I am *worthy*."

Wesley smiled. Their special word had just become more defined.

Lizzie smiled, but shortly, her face was serious, again. "Back to business. Should we head back to the room or wait until we're sure they are awake before going in?"

Wesley's lips set in a hard line. "We came a long way to see my mom, and I don't give a damn whether we wake up my ol' man or not. I may not even speak to the son of a bitch."

"I've never heard you use that kind of language, Wesley. It does not become you. Remember that b-i-t-c-h is your grandmother."

"I'm sorry." Wesley regretted the vulgarity as soon as the words leaped out of his mouth, but his contrition didn't linger. "It's just that he doesn't have any right to be here. He left us for another woman."

Lizzie clinched his hand, covered it with her other hand, and peered into his eyes, as if she were trying to enter hallowed ground and feel his spirit. The look of pity on Lizzie's face twisted his stomach in a knot.

In a gentle voice, she said, "It will be okay. And you are okay. You don't have to feel disgraced about anything." She continued to hold his hand in hers, and after a moment of respectful silence, jutted her chin. "I agree with you—heck with him. We have come a long way, and it's time to go in—without your tail between your legs."

Once they'd walked back from the lounge, Lizzie stayed outside the doorway as Wesley padded past Ray Sanders with the silence of a stalking Indian. Ray continued to snore.

The snoring brought instant memories of Wesley's childhood and, surprisingly, calmed him. Snoring had meant his parents were asleep and no longer fighting. Snoring was a peaceful bell, the end of Round 12 of an all-night event.

Wesley stood next to his mother's bed in silent contemplation. Not yet forty, still with her black Irish hair, Rita resembled her aunt and namesake, the tall woman in the old family albums, the one his grandma said showed their Indian heritage. The 1920s flapper his mom lived with for a year as a child, who carried a revolver and a whiskey flask in her purse.

Lizzie attracted his attention in the doorway as she flicked her wrist outward, giving him a *get moving* signal.

He gently placed his hand on his mother's shoulder and whispered, "Mom." When she didn't respond, he tapped her arm.

Her eyes blinked several times before she opened them and turned her head toward him. She blinked again, confused, or maybe trying to determine if she was dreaming.

"Wesley, what are you doing here? You're supposed to be in Yellowstone."

"I took a few days off to see you." He jerked his thumb at Ray. "What's he doing here?" Their voices woke Ray.

Ray stretched his arms over his head, shaking the kinks out from his nap. "I see we have a visitor, Rita."

What's this WE baloney? Even though it was only a thought, Wesley's couldn't hide his contempt.

Always the perceptive interceder, Rita said, "Your father heard I was in the hospital and came to see me. He's driving over the road again and happened to have a Denver run."

Ray rose from his chair, hitched up his wrinkled khaki trousers, and gave a half-hearted attempt at tucking in his shirt. Trimmer, with much of his sizeable paunch was gone, his belly still protruded enough to keep his shirt from draping properly. His hairline had receded, leaving only a few wiry sprigs on top, and the remainder that curved around his head from ear to ear was now mostly gray. But he still had the smile. Yeah, *Smiling Ray*, that was his handle.

"Hey, Sport, it's been sometime since we've seen each other."

Wesley recoiled and stared blankly at this man he now considered a stranger. He resented being called *Sport*. What would Ray do next? Tussle his hair?

Ray stepped to the foot of Rita's bed and continued his familiarity. "You've surely grown. How tall are you now? Six-foot?"

"Six-two. A boy grows a lot in eight years."

Again, Rita jumped in. "If you give your father a chance, I think you will find he has changed."

"I came to see you—not him."

Ray said, "I'll go get some coffee and leave you two alone to visit," and shuffled to the door.

From the hallway, Wesley could hear Ray talking to Lizzie and didn't like it. His resentment came out in his voice as he spoke to Rita. "So did he just show up out of the blue?"

"No, your grandmother called him."

"Why would she do that?"

"Because she thinks I'm dying, and that he would want to say goodbye."

In a barely audible voice he said, "Dying? How bad is your cancer?"

"It's bad, Son. The doctors said the tumor is as big as a baseball and has legs on it."

Wesley gasped. His mother's description conjured a horrible image, both menacing and evil.

"I am in an experimental program with five other women diagnosed as terminal. There were six, but my roommate, who was in the next bed, died three days ago. She was so sweet. Little Miko. A Japanese war bride." Rita's eyes filled with tears that did not fall.

Wesley's own tears were for his mother. He wiped his eyes with the back of his hand. Just like that, fear had replaced his anger at Ray's presence. Jumbled thoughts scattered through his mind.

This can't be happening. This kind of stuff happens to other people.

"Don't worry, Killer," Rita said, using the nickname that her husband Sam had hung on Wesley. "I've made peace with my Maker. And I made a bargain with Him. I told him I had a little ol' boy that still needed me, and I think He's going to take care of me. Plus, I'm a tough old bird. It will be the hardest thing I've ever done, but I will make it."

His mother seemed to have a glow about her as she spoke. Although he knew she believed in God and Jesus, her admission that she prayed surprised him. She'd never talked about that before.

"What kind of medical treatments are you getting? Are they going to operate?"

"No, it's too late for surgery. The doctors said if they cut into the tumor it would likely spread. They have to kill it in place with radiation. I've already had many hours of cobalt radiation. It didn't hurt at the time, but afterwards, it felt like someone had taken a blowtorch to my belly. I'll show you."

Rita slid her pajama top up just a bit and pushed the sheet down to expose her stomach.

Wesley winced. Her entire abdomen was red and angry-looking, except where scabs were forming, as if she had been scorched in a house fire. It reminded him of his arm, when he had bumped against a wood-burning stove as a child. He remembered the pain and couldn't fathom the agony such a large burn would cause.

"That's horrible, Mom."

It's much better now. Before, it resembled a piece of raw steak. They gave me this to put on the area." She pointed to a metal canister labeled *Aquaphor*.

"Is the radiation treatment finished?"

"No, there's more to come. That's not the worst of it."

His eyes rounded. "Criminy, what else?"

"Live radium implants. They stick live radium up inside you. One of the other women had that procedure and said it was like having a hot coal shoved up her ass."

His expression hardened as he imagined the image. "Good Lord! How awful."

Rita wasn't finished. "The live radium implants killed Miko. The radium burned her internal organs. She was so thin, and she didn't have any fat to absorb the radium. Because I have a lot of fat, the doctors hope it will insulate me."

Rita sat upright. "Sorry to upset you, Wesley. Give your mama a hug." After they embraced, she said, "Sit down, and tell me some lies," borrowing a familiar phrase his stepfather had often used.

Outside the room, Ray and Lizzie had their own conversation going. Wesley could hear their muttering, and it interrupted his thoughts. Smiling Ray, no doubt, was using his charm to impress Lizzie. But she was nobody's fool.

"Son, a penny for your thoughts."

Wesley refocused. "Sorry, Mom. I guess my mind wandered."

"I wonder who Ray is talking to."

Wesley weighed how to respond. "It's a friend who came along with me. Her name—"

"A girlfriend?"

"Yes, and Ray is probably filling her head with a bunch of BS."

"Son, you might be surprised, but he has changed."

Wesley's lips puckered and he made a dry spitting sound. "Yeah, right."

"He's quit drinking."

"I've heard that before . . . like the morning he staggered into my bedroom after he fell into the Christmas tree and smashed the presents."

"This time seems different."

"So, how long has he been on the wagon?"

"He says eighteen months. Says he joined some organization in Texas. A and A, I think he called it. And part of their rules is they have to make amends to people they have harmed. In fact, he apologized to me for what he did."

Wesley remained mute and stone-faced.

"At least give him a chance. You're a Christian, aren't you?"

"You know I am, but what does that have to do with him?

"Remember the prodigal son?"

Warily, Wesley said, "Yes."

"I believe the same principle applies to prodigal fathers."

"Are you sure he's not just trying to horn his way back into Sam's place?"

"No." Her voice was emphatic. "That would never happen—in fact, he's remarried."

"What?"

"And there's one more thing," Rita said, leaving the comment hanging.

"What?"

"He has a little boy."

Wesley exploded. "Jesus H. Christ! That's just what I need—a half-brother."

"Take it easy, Wesley. And watch your language, or you'll be talking just like Sam."

Shamed, Wesley's eyes went heavenward, and he said, "Sorry, Jesus."

An orderly in hospital scrubs came through the door pushing an empty wheelchair. Rita introduced the twenty-something man with red hair as her "favorite orderly, Joe Thornton."

Thornton extended his hand to Wesley and said, "Nice to meet you, Wesley," He stepped beside Rita's bed. "I would like to stay and talk, but you have a test scheduled up on the sixth floor."

"Son, can you come back this evening after supper? I want to meet your girlfriend."

"We'll be back."

"Do you need any money?"

"No, I'm fine."

"Where are you staying?"

"We just got in, but we'll find a place. Maybe a YMCA or YWCA. Don't worry." He and Lizzie had only discussed the subject in general terms. The focus had been on getting to Denver. Then Carry showed up, and their attention had shifted.

After Thornton assisted Rita into the wheelchair, Wesley hugged her, and said, "We'll see you later, Mom."

Wesley walked out of the room, following his mom and the orderly. Ray had gone and Lizzie sat waiting on a chair. Her face brightened, as if she hadn't seen him in a long time. It buoyed his spirit and he walked over to her.

Lizzie stood up, and Wesley put his hands on her shoulders. Before he turned back around, Rita cleared her throat. "Son, aren't you going to introduce me to your gal?"

In a synchronized movement, with his hand on Lizzie's back, they twirled around to face his mother. "Mom, this is Lizzie."

With no hesitation Lizzie approached Rita and extended her hand. "Actually, Mrs. Rockwell, my name is Elizabeth, but most folks that know me call me Lizzie. I am happy to meet you and hope you are getting better. Wesley has been awfully troubled about your illness."

The whole time Lizzie was speaking, Rita seemed delighted. She had always taken a keen interest in Wesley's girlfriends but hadn't always been pleased and would tell him bluntly whether or not she liked the girl. He would, no doubt, get her full opinion later.

"Lizzie, you are about the cutest thing I have seen in a month of Sundays. I hope we can chat later, but now I have to go let them poke around on me some more." Rita turned her head to the orderly and said, "Okay, Thornton, let's go."

Chapter Seventeen

When Rita was out of earshot, Wesley said, "I think she likes you."

"Your mother is very pretty. I like her, but I can tell she is very sick and trying to put up a brave front."

"I know," Wesley said.

"Your father may be a different matter, but I am withholding judgment."

"What did you and Ray talk about?"

"At first, he didn't associate me with you, so when I said, "Hello, Mr. Sanders," he was surprised and asked how I knew him. So I told him, and then he gave me this big smile, and—" "That's what they call him—*Smiling Ray*. He's always—"

"Do you want me to tell you or not?" Lizzie said and put a finger to her lips in the universal sign of shushing.

"Sorry."

"At first it was just pleasantries, and then he got all apologetic and said I had probably heard a lot of bad things about him, even after I fibbed and told him we had never talked about him."

"I didn't intend for you to get drawn into my family soap opera. Frankly, it's embarrassing."

"I find it fascinating because I have so little drama like that in mine. He asked me where we were staying. I told him we hadn't decided. By the way, where are we staying?"

"I don't know. It seems our logistical planning, as my stepfather would say, got sidetracked after we met Carry. Right now, we just need to eat. Mom says there is a cafeteria and a coffee shop that serves meals on the first floor. I've got my PX card, so I bet if I flash that, they'll let us in. I don't think we resemble spies like Boris and Natasha."

On the first floor, Nurse Jenkins remained on duty and watched as they approached.

"Hi, Nurse Jenkins, Wesley said. "Which way is the cafeteria?"

"Keep walking and follow the signs. You can't miss it. Oh, and Captain David asked me to have you call him before you leave the hospital."

"Thanks."

As they entered the cafeteria, Wesley showed his card to the hostess sitting behind a cash register. The wrinkles in her yellow uniform dress suggested she had been there since breakfast, and her tired eyes would benefit from a cup of coffee. Rita would have said the poor thing needed to get rid of the hair bun. Although it served as a makeshift pencil holder, it made her middle-aged face look drawn.

"You don't need that ID, young man. You both have visitor badges— that's all you need."

Distinctly utilitarian, the cafeteria had little decorative ambience. The design facilitated getting personnel fed and back to their duty stations. Food entrees languished in stainless steel pans on a steamtable behind a glass sneeze guard, waiting for the next victim.

They picked up food trays and slid them along the tubular slide of the serving line, passing opportunities for liver and onions, macaroni and cheese, mashed potatoes, and green Jell-O. Instead, they opted for pre-cooked hamburgers, soggy fries, a Coke, and a 7-Up. They selected a table near a window with a view of the mountains.

After several bites of their burgers, Lizzie said, "The case of Captain Carry gets curiouser and curiouser."

"I know what you mean. He's like a most unforgettable character from *Reader's Digest.* Nurse Jenkins seems to hold him in some esteem."

"I agree," Lizzie said, "he is a most unforgettable character, maybe a real war hero. But that doesn't account for his apparent wealth. The airplane. The Cadillac. The Longines watch. I still think he is a gambler. It's sort of romantic."

"I didn't think Mormons approved of gambling."

"That doesn't mean we can't imagine things that are more exciting than our mundane lives."

"My stepfather is a gambler, and it's not romantic. He and his cousin Big John used to have high-stakes games, and one resulted in a gunfight."

"Really?" Her pitch inflected. "You seem to have a lot of unforgettable characters in your life. Maybe you attract them, and that's why Captain Carry showed up?"

"No, it was just a coincidence that we were on the same bus."

"My dad says there are no coincidences; it's just God's way of remaining anonymous."

"Maybe so, but should we call him?"

"It would be the polite thing to do."

In the lobby, Wesley deposited a dime in one of the pay phones on the wall across from the reception desk Nurse Jenkins had occupied. Another RN had replaced her.

Lizzie held the card with Carry's number for Wesley to see as he dialed.

"Hello," Carry answered.

"Carry, this is Wesley. Nurse Jenkins said you wanted me to call."

"Hello, Wesley. Yes, that's right. Carmelita and I want you and Lizzie to come over for dinner."

"We just ate in the cafeteria, and we are going back to visit my mom."

"That's fine. Do you have a place to stay?"

"We haven't decided yet. Maybe the YMCA."

"Wesley, the YMCA is way back in Denver. You both are staying with us, and *no* is an unacceptable answer. Call me when you get through visiting, and I will come pick you up."

"We wouldn't want to impose."

"Look, Wesley, you have no idea about this area. You don't know the good parts from the bad, and for the sake of Lizzie, be smart and play it safe."

The logic couldn't be denied. "Thanks . . . it's awfully nice of you to invite us." He hung up the receiver.

"I take it we are staying at Carry's," Lizzie said.

"He's says it is the safest thing for us to do."

"I'm glad. Let's go see if your mom is back."

When they entered her room, Rita hushed her conversation with Ray.

Ray cracked a smile. "We were just talking about you . . . how when you were little you couldn't talk plain—you used *p*'s for *f*'s and would say, 'I never have any *pun*.' He began laughing at his own humor.

Wesley seethed, and his stomach churned. Memories of childhood taunting and embarrassment flooded over him. Rita shot a hard glare at Ray. Lizzie grimaced in sympathetic pain.

Rita tried to salvage the tactless remark. "Now, Ray, that was a long time ago. Wesley no longer has any speech impediments."

Her efforts failed. Wesley's embarrassment turned to anger. He spoke no words, but every negative thought he felt ignited in a blistering glare aimed at his runaway pappy.

"Mom, we'll just come back tomorrow."

Ray stood up. "Son, I'm sorry. I didn't mean any harm. Can we go out in the hall and talk, and let the girls get to know each other? I know your mom would like that, and I have something to tell you."

Lizzie didn't wait for an answer. She slipped to the bedside and covered Rita's hand with both hers. "You two men go out in the hall. Mrs. Rockwell and I can get to know each other better."

Wesley delivered a sullen look to Lizzie, but she met his stare and pointed toward the doorway, sending an unmistakable message for him to get moving. Wesley turned and clomped through the door, with Ray at his heels.

Rita touched Lizzie's arm. "Let me tell you, Honey, you are a breath of fresh air for this sick old lady. For the past couple weeks, all I've had is a bunch of men—doctors, male nurses, and orderlies—poking at me and sticking me with needles."

The comment tickled Lizzie and made her feel welcome, but as she thought about what she planned to say, her facial expression turned more pressing. "Mrs. Rockwell—"

"Just call me Rita, Honey,"

"Okay . . . Rita. I hope you don't think I'm some kind of tawdry delinquent traveling here with Wesley. He's my friend, and I just couldn't let him come here alone."

The corners of Rita's mouth turned up in a smile that showed appreciation for Lizzie's emotional uncertainty. "As we say in the country, darling, I've attended a rodeo and a county fair, and I'm also a pretty good judge of character. I'm proud Wesley has such a good friend."

Lizzie emitted a sigh of relief. "Oh, good. I feel much better. I was worried about what you might think."

Out in the hallway, Wesley stood closemouthed, with his arms folded across his chest, several feet from Ray. Ray began the conversation by reiterating the apology for his earlier comment. When Wesley didn't respond, his tone became even more somber.

"Son, I know—"

"Just call me *Wesley.*"

"Well, all right . . . Wesley. I was just going to say, I know you have the right to be angry at me, and I don't blame you, but I want you to know from the bottom of my heart that I am truly sorry for the way things turned out."

Wesley didn't respond, and he peered toward the elevator, as if he had someplace else he needed to be. He rotated his wrist to see his watch, adding emphasis to his attitude.

Ray picked up on the unspoken message. "I won't take much of your time, but I want you to know that I have changed. I know there is no way I can make up for the harm I've caused, but I hope you can find it in your heart to forgive me."

Wesley broke eye contact and exhaled slowly through his nose. His mind drifted back to the years of poverty, before Sam, when there were no child support payments and neighbors brought food to their house.

Ray broke into Wesley's thoughts. "I've stopped drinking." He sounded desperate—making a final plea, hoping for a breakthrough.

Wesley glowered at Ray. "I've heard that before."

Ray winced as if he were in physical pain. He blinked, as his eyes moistened. "Maybe we can talk again. I'm leaving tomorrow afternoon." He waited for a response, and getting none, he said, "I'm going for some coffee and to get your mom a cookie."

His father lumbered down the hallway, with a purposeful but labored stride. Wesley took the slight hitch in his gait as a sign the hard miles were catching up with his old man. He thought of what his mother had said about prodigal fathers and wondered if he should feel remorseful for not being more sympathetic.

Laughter from inside Rita's room diverted Wesley's attention. He followed the sound. Lizzie sat on the edge of his mom's bed holding one side of a magazine. Rita held the other. They both switched their attention to Wesley as he entered.

"We were just saying that Liz Taylor could do a lot better than Richard Burton," Rita said.

"I'm glad to see you two are getting along famously—at least someone is."

Rita's eyes narrowed, as she read the face of her son. "What did he say that has you so upset?"

"I'm not upset."

"Well, your face didn't get the news, because it looks upset."

Looking at them, he felt outnumbered, and a sense of abandonment lurked below the surface.

"Don't look so sad," Rita said. "We're your two best girls."

He waited for Lizzie to deny she was "his girl," but she didn't. He searched his mind for the right thing to say. As it turned out, he didn't have to.

With her growing understanding of Wesley, Lizzie tried to lighten the mood. "Come on, Miles Standish. Has the cat got your tongue?"

Wesley's face relaxed, but not his attitude. "No, Priscilla, it's just that I've seen all I want of Ray Sanders today. I'd like to go before he gets back. We'll be back tomorrow morning, Mom."

"Where are you two going to stay tonight?" Without waiting for a response, she said, "The hospital has rooms for dependents, but that might not include Lizzie."

"We've been invited to stay with the friend who flew us here from Utah. He invited us for dinner and insisted we stay with him and his wife. He is an interesting fellow. He reminds me of Sam in some ways. Lizzie is convinced he is a gambler."

Rita's face became pensive.

Reading her reaction, Wesley said, "What?"

"Now, I know you've been on your own this summer, and you two managed to get to Denver by yourselves, but my motherly instinct makes me wish I could meet this man before you spend the night at his house."

"Rita," Lizzie said, "we had that same concern before we got on the plane with him in Ogden."

"What plane?" Rita asked, apparently missing Wesley's previous comment.

"His plane, Mom. He flew us to Aurora in his personal airplane. He was a pilot in World War II, got shot down, and was a prisoner in a Nazi POW camp."

Lizzie added, "If it weren't for his generosity, we would still be on the bus. He was concerned we didn't know the safe parts of town. Plus, he is married and his wife will be there, too."

To seal the deal, Wesley added, "The head nurse here knew him by name. Called him Captain David and said that his OK was all we needed to get in."

"Well, I feel better, now," Rita said. "He sounds like a good man. When do you two have to leave for Yellowstone?"

"Tomorrow afternoon, so we'll be back in the morning."

"Good. Give your mama another hug. You, too, Lizzie."

When they got off the elevator on the ground floor, Ray was waiting to get on.

"Are you two leaving?" Disappointment clouded his face.

"Hi, Ray," Lizzie said. Then, as though she were speaking for Wesley, who was avoiding eye contact, added, "We'd love to chat, but we have to meet a friend and we're running late."

Ray held the elevator door open and turned his attention to Wesley. "I had hoped to talk with you some more."

"Maybe tomorrow."

The elevator buzzed an annoying sound. "I'll be here until noon," Ray said and stepped inside.

CHAPTER EIGHTEEN

Lizzie and Wesley got inside the Cadillac for the ride to Carry's home. Lizzie insisted that Wesley take the front seat. After they exchanged greetings, Lizzie got in the back, scooted to the center, and began telling Carry about meeting Wesley's mom.

To Wesley's surprise, the subject of Ray's appearance came up. When Lizzie referred to him as Wesley's dad, he interrupted to point out that his parents were divorced and that his stepfather Sam had essentially taken the place of his natural father.

Carry seemed content to just listen, as they headed west, and his aviator sunglasses hid whatever he might be thinking. Wearing a green polo shirt with an alligator on the front, Carry appeared markedly different from their first meeting. Chemise Lacoste—straight out of *Playboy* magazine. His clean hair, thick and dark, with a hint of gray and parted on the side, smelled of a light finish of Brylcreem. Wesley thought of a magazine photo he'd seen of President Kennedy on a sailboat.

Twenty minutes into the trip, Carry said, "In a moment, you'll see the house on the right."

As they rounded a curve, a striking two-story house came into view: two stories of mahogany-colored bricks accented by white-framed windows. In the front, a round porch with Doric columns ascended to the second story. A porte-cochere on the side covered a '64 or '65 Mustang convertible. Wesley was dazzled. Carry turned the Cadillac onto a crushed-stone circular driveway and stopped in front of the house.

"What a beautiful house." Lizzie said, as she gave the home a panoramic gaze. "It looks like it could be in *Better Homes and Gardens*." Then in a lighter tone she added, "Or as we say in Wyoming, *Better Barns and Gardens*."

"Thank you. It's interesting that you would say that. A Colorado magazine featured an article Carmelita wrote about it."

"You wife is a writer?" Wesley asked.

"She does freelance articles about contemporary life in the *Old West*. A famous miner owned this house before Carmelita's father bought it."

"Wow, that's pretty cool," Wesley said.

"You see," Carry continued, "the house belonged to Leeta's parents. Her father did quite well in the mining business. After her mother and father died, we moved here. You'll like Leeta—she loves young people. Because she was an only child, I sometimes think she is still looking for new playmates." He hesitated and his voice became wistful. "We haven't been blessed with children of our own."

With sympathetic softness in her eyes, Lizzie said, "I'm sorry."

"Thank you, Lizzie, but don't worry. Leeta and I have a good life."

One half of the double front door opened, and a gray-haired lady who appeared to be in her sixties emerged.

"That's Rosie. She's our live-in house manager. She keeps us organized and fed. We think of her as family."

A huge poodle also poked his head outside. Seeing Carry, the black standard poodle bounded to the car and assumed a sitting position.

"This is Buster, also known as the Wild Man from Borneo."

"Like in the Little Rascals?" Wesley asked.

"That's where he got his nickname. Yum, yum eat'm up." Carry mimicked the catch-phrase of the film character.

They got out of the car and surrounded Buster. With a hand

signal from Carry, the dog went into a prone position. "You can pet him if you like."

"His hair is so soft," Lizzie said, as she stroked Buster's back.

A woman appeared next to Rosie, and called out, "Carry, bring our guests inside." The voice, no doubt, belonged to Leeta, tall and slender, with dark eyes, and skin the color of rich cream and smooth as porcelain. Her lips spread in a generous and inviting smile.

As the trio entered the doorway, she extended her hand to Lizzie. "I'm Carmelita, and you must be the delightful Lizzie that Carry has talked about."

"Yes, ma'am." Lizzie shook Carmelita's hand.

Carmelita offered her hand to Wesley, and said, "You are, of course, Wesley."

"Yes, ma'am."

"I must say the two of you have impressed my husband. But Wesley, I am so sorry to hear that your mother is ill."

"Thanks, ma'am."

"There's no need to be so formal. Just call me Carmelita, or better, Leeta, which is what Carry calls me. Let's go inside. Rosie has prepared a delicious snack for us."

A wide foyer separated a formal dining room on the left from a parlor on the right and led to a stairway. Paved with marble tile polished to a high shine, it reflected light from a crystal chandelier hanging above. Matching gold-framed mirrors on opposing walls had a widening effect, before it narrowed and formed a hallway past the staircase to the kitchen.

"I know Carry said you had eaten at the hospital, but I suspect you won't turn down what Rosie has prepared. I hope you like Mexican food."

"Whatever it is, it smells wonderful." The hospital cafeteria had not quelled Lizzie's appetite.

"It's Rosie's quail tacos."

Turning to her husband, Leeta said, "Dear, take their bags and show them their rooms so they can freshen up before dinner if they want to."

"Leeta . . . do I have time for a shower?" Lizzie asked. She pushed a strand of hair away from her face. "I won't take long."

"Of course," Leeta said.

Carry guided them upstairs and showed them their rooms, which were separated by a bathroom. "Lizzie, everything you need for your shower is in there," he said, nodding at the bathroom.

After her shower Lizzie emerged in the hallway. Wesley saw her through the open door of his own room as he unfolded a clean shirt in front of the dresser mirror. He took in her reflection. She wore clean jeans and a red and white gingham-check blouse, with pearl snap buttons on the front and cuffs. Tucked in, it accented her trim waist and hips. A knowing smile on her face acknowledged the appraisal he had given her.

He walked into the hallway and hugged her. They held each other without speaking. Tension and anxiety of the trip drained like a huge sigh. Their lips joined in a deep kiss.

In less than a minute, Lizzie pulled away, flushed. She extended her lower lip and blew her breath upward over her face. "We don't want to be bad guests and be late for dinner."

"Yeah, you're right, but I want to tell you something, and I'm not sure how to put it, other than to say, thank you for coming with me."

Lizzie smiled at him and then added with a wink, "Well, as I've heard you say before, 'Thank you, how nice of you to say so.'"

Downstairs, Leeta and Carry lounged on barstools at one end of a bi-level breakfast bar. A serving platter with chips and salsa dominated the center, and a savory aroma of cumin hung in the air.

"I hope you are hungry," Leeta said, as Lizzie and Wesley approached.

"We are," they said simultaneously.

Behind the counter, at the lower level, Rosie stirred the contents of a huge iron skillet on the stovetop. She watched the younger couple with a big smile.

"The tacos will be ready in a few minutes, so have some of the appetizers," Rosie said, and pointed to the food displayed on the counter. "Dip the taco chips in the salsa."

Carry held a can of Coors, and a stemmed glass of white wine sat next to Leeta.

"Would either of you like something to drink?"

Wesley said, "Water will be fine."

"For me, too, please," Lizzie said.

"There's a pitcher and glasses on the counter. Help yourselves."

After sampling the chips and salsa, Wesley said. "I've had potato chips and Fritos before, but these taco chips are better, and this tomato dip is super."

"It's salsa, not tomato dip, Mr. Wesley," Rosie said.

Leeta gestured toward a round table with a mosaic top in a cozy corner of the kitchen illuminated by a green, leaded-glass Tiffany shade that hung from the ceiling. Two colorful prints of dancing senoritas decorated the corner walls.

"We can serve ourselves from the buffet and sit at the little table. Carry and I have breakfast here. It's more intimate than the dining room."

After her first bite of the quail taco, Lizzie, with her mouth still full, said, "Mmmm." She swallowed and took a sip of water. "This is so good."

From behind the counter, Rosie said, "Gracias, senorita."

"The two women who live in this house are the best cooks in the world," Carry said.

"Well, I don't know about that," Leeta said, "but we try."

When they finished eating, Lizzie helped Leeta clear away the dishes, while Rosie cut squares of chocolate cake from a sheet pan.

"We have Mexican chocolate cake and coffee for dessert," Leta said. "Let's have it on the veranda. It's such a nice night. Oh, I should have asked whether you two drink coffee."

"I don't, but Wesley does."

"Then how about some strawberry leaf tea? It goes well with chocolate cake."

"That sounds nice."

Leeta indicated the patio door. "You two go on outside. Carry and I will bring out the dessert."

Colored lights strung along a wrought-iron railing defined the terrazzo patio and cast a festive glow. The lights of Denver in the distance contrasted against the black sky and the mountains beyond.

They plopped down on a cushioned love seat, which was part of a patio set, and then scooted closer to each other. Wesley put his arm around Lizzie and pulled her closer. She rested her hand on his knee.

When the patio door slid open, Lizzie scooted away from Wesley, as Leeta and Carry emerged. Carry set a dessert tray on the bistro-style table, and he and Leeta sat on two matching chairs across from them.

"I think I have some good news for you two," Carry said. Lizzie and Wesley looked expectantly at him. "I have to fly back to Pocatello tomorrow, and you're welcome to fly with me. It would save you a bunch of time and some of the bus fare."

"That's great," Wesley said. "What time are you leaving?"

"If we take off at one o'clock, that will get us to Pocatello around five, in time for you two to catch the six o'clock bus to West Yellowstone. And it will give you time to see your mother tomorrow, while I get the plane ready."

Lizzie said, "That will get me back in time for an afternoon trail ride . . . that is, if my brother hasn't fired me." A blushing half-smile emerged, as if family laundry had just been displayed.

Leeta leaned forward to enter the conversation. "The bus from Pocatello actually departs at ten after six—I checked the schedules."

Carry nodded toward his wife. "Leeta is my dispatcher."

"Gee, thanks. That was awfully nice of you," Lizzie said.

"Then it's settled," Carry said. "We'll fly back together."

Wesley and Lizzie raved about the Mexican chocolate cake,

and Leeta explained that the recipe came from Old Mexico. After everyone finished eating, the conversation lulled, allowing them to appreciate the sound of the wind blowing through the aspens that surrounded the house.

Carry slid his chair forward and adjusted his sitting position. "Wesley, since you've graduated from high school, I assume you have registered for the draft."

"Yes, when I turned eighteen this year, I went to the local Selective Service Board." It had been a perfunctory action on his part. Every boy did it at eighteen, not unlike getting a driver's license at sixteen.

"Because you'll be in college, you won't have to worry about being drafted, and that's good. I'm worried that this conflict in Vietnam is going to get worse."

Until recently, Vietnam had been of no immediate concern to Wesley. Girls and sports had occupied most of his interest and time. Now, wanting to appear knowledgeable, he said, "In my Contemporary Issues class, we discussed American involvement in Vietnam. My teacher said we had to be there to stop the spread of communism. He said if Vietnam fell to the Communists, all the other countries in the area would fall in the Communist quest for world domination."

In an academic tone, Carry said, "It's called the 'Domino Theory.' Intervention proponents say the Asian countries are like a row of dominos. When one falls, it will set off a chain reaction and the rest will fall."

Lizzie, somewhat abruptly, said, "My feeling is we shouldn't go to war over some itty-bitty country on the other side of the world."

"But we have to stop the spread of communism," Wesley said.

Carry responded. "Some very smart people have differing views on that theory, Wesley. Senators Goldwater and Fulbright to name a couple—they wrote books on the subject. And the military is concerned about the shipping routes that could be compromised, but let me ask you this. Do you think President Eisenhower knew anything about warfare?"

"He commanded the D-Day invasion, so I would say that he does."

"Did you know he said that we shouldn't commit ground forces in Southeast Asia?"

"No . . . I never heard that."

"Why do you suppose he said that?"

Anticipating he was heading into a rhetorical trap, Wesley searched for a reasonable response but came up blank. "I'm not sure."

"Jungles, rice paddies, and no roads. Why do you suppose he was the force behind the interstate highway system?"

"Better transportation?"

"Sure, but what motivated him?" When Wesley didn't answer immediately, Carry continued. "His experience with the poor roads in Europe during World War II impacted his strategic thinking. He wanted to be able to move troops and machinery efficiently from one coast to the other."

Tilting her head so she faced Wesley, Lizzie said, "Well, I hope you don't get drafted."

Wesley sat up straighter and was swift with his response. "I heard about a 2-year Marine Corps officer candidate program. After my sophomore year I would go to summer camp at Quantico, Virginia. After my junior year, I'd go to summer camp at Camp Pendleton. And after graduation, I would automatically be commissioned as a second lieutenant."

Carry didn't respond, but he displayed the facial expression of a man experiencing a painful spasm.

Wesley added, "I'm thinking about doing that, rather than getting drafted."

"I think you should discuss that with your stepfather. People who have experienced war have a different view than those who have a romantic notion gained from movies. Being a second lieutenant in the Marine Corps in the time of war equals a short life expectancy."

Leeta reached over to Carry and touched his forearm. "He gets upset with the talk of war. Anyway, Carry, it's time for us to go to bed."

"You're right as usual, dear. I'm sorry for my bluntness." Looking at his guests, he said, "Don't let me put a damper on the evening. You two are welcome to enjoy this beautiful evening a while longer."

After their hosts said goodnight and retired for the evening, Lizzie skootched closer to Wesley, and they sat holding hands.

Wesley pondered Carry's observations and war experience and hoped he hadn't sounded like a punk. In his mind, he pictured the scene from *Gone with the Wind,* where the young Southern men cheered with the prospect of war and the glory it held. It made him wince.

With Wesley apparently lost in his thoughts, Lizzie broached a subject that had obviously been on her mind since the hospital. "Why didn't you want to talk to your father?" From her frame of reference, a world with a loving father and an intact family, she found it hard to understand. His shoulder tensed up and his grip tightened.

A bit of time passed before he responded. "I've always thought if I ever saw him again, I'd unload a bunch of stuff at him, but when I saw him, I couldn't remember any of it. Now, I can."

"Like what?"

"I'd rather not talk about it."

"Maybe you should. My mother says a problem shared is half-repaired."

"What do you want to know?" The memories gave a sarcastic edge to his voice.

Lizzie didn't respond, and her stillness had a way of making him reflect on what he had said, and how he had said it. His grandmother had that same effect on him, but he could trust his grandmother. An intuitive thought struck him. By now, he should know he could trust Lizzie.

Lizzie leaned away and squared her face with his. "I get it that you're angry at your dad, but don't take it out on me."

"I'm sorry."

"It's okay."

In a tone devoid of emotion, Wesley said, "Okay, try this on for size. I was in the second grade, it was Christmas Eve and my parents were both home, which wasn't always the case, since Dad was a trucker. Presents were under an eight-foot pine tree—it went all the way to the ceiling.

"We were going to open gifts at midnight. I was excited I could stay up that late. My dad was drinking Seagram's 7 whiskey, and my mom was drinking gin out of a stemmed glass. I remember it as clearly as a photograph.

"As the night went on, the fighting started, and soon they were yelling at each other. My mother had left a roast in the oven too long and it burned. He said she wasn't the cook her mother was. Then my dad stumbled over a footstool and fell into the Christmas tree and knocked it over. Water from the tree stand spilled all over the presents. That just made my mom yell more."

Wesley paused to see how she was taking the revelation. Her eyes were doleful, but unwavering as she listened.

"Go on, Wesley."

"Dad stomped off and said he was going to bed, but a few minutes later came out of the bedroom in his underwear. He was trying to hide a .38 revolver underneath his boxer shorts, but I could see it. He was blubbering that he was going to kill himself. Mom started yelling again, telling him to stop scaring me.

"I slid off the couch crying and asking what I had done. I thought everything was my fault. Mom told me to go to my room. I cried until I finally feel asleep, even though I could still hear them arguing. The next morning Mom woke me up and said that Santa Claus had come. The tree was back up and I could smell bacon frying. They were both drinking beer and acting as if nothing had happened."

Lizzie put her arms around him and said, "It wasn't your fault." She felt his body go limp as he started to cry.

After a moment, Wesley regained his composure and turned his head to her. "I feel like an idiot."

"Don't ever think or say that again. You shouldn't feel ashamed. It's your mother and father who should be—not you—but it's hard for me to imagine your mom like that."

"I know. She's changed a lot since she married Sam." A faraway look came to his face, and he chuckled.

Lizzie squinted her eyes. "Why are you laughing?

Wesley smiled. "After they were married, Sam used to say, 'Rita, when you die, come Saturday night, there'll be a mole trail from your grave where you've burrowed out to go to the honky-tonks.' He's been good for her."

"And for you, too, it seems."

A peaceful feeling came over Wesley, as if a burden he had been carrying was lifted. Maybe that "problem shared is half-repaired" thing was true. His mind drifted back in time again, and wrinkles formed around his eyes.

"What are you thinking now?"

"After that big fight they had, I wrote a letter to God asking Him to please make Mom and Dad quit fighting." Wesley laughed. "And Mom found it. I thought I was in trouble. As usual, she said they weren't fighting. Yeah, like I was too dumb to know what I saw. It was like the punchline to that old joke. Who are you going to believe—me or your lying eyes?"

"Except it's not funny, Wesley. No disrespect to your mom—she may not have intended it—but she was teaching you not to trust your own judgment."

"I never thought about it like that." He stared off into the distance.

With the pause in the conversation, Lizzie squeezed his hand, and in a voice barely above a whisper said, "You don't have to answer, but why did Ray go to prison?"

Wesley turned his head to face her. "He wrote a bad check."

"Really? That's all? That doesn't seem like all that big of a deal."

"The amount was large enough that it was a felony. There's more to it—"

"I know, it's another long story." She patted his hand several times the way she might calm a horse.

Wesley, with a grin on his face now, said, "You seem to be having a lot of fun with my troubled childhood."

"I know. It's great. Nothing interesting like this ever happened in my family."

Holding his gaze on Lizzie's eyes, he said, "Well, what do you think of your traveling partner, now? Some character out of *Peyton Place*?"

"First, I am your *girlfriend*—you haven't changed your mind, have you?" She didn't give him time to respond. "And second, I'll show you." She placed both hands on his face and delivered a deep kiss. She moved her lips to his ear. "Does that answer your question?"

Still feeling some of the weight of what he had shared, Wesley simply said, "Yes." He put both arms around Lizzie and held her in silence. He knew what she would say if he spoke: *leave a tender moment alone*.

"I think we should go upstairs and get some sleep," Lizzie said. "Tomorrow will be a long day."

At the top of the stairs they embraced and kissed a simple goodnight kiss before going to their separate bedrooms.

In his room, Wesley stripped down to his shorts and folded his shirt and jeans before pulling back the covers and crawling between the soft sheets on the double bed. He turned off the bedside light and lay there thinking about his mom, and Ray, and especially Lizzie, wondering if she had fallen asleep yet. He dozed into a half-asleep stream of floating thoughts and images.

Sometime later, he felt the other side of the mattress depress and realized Lizzie had slid next to him, fully clothed, on top the covers.

"Are you awake?"

"Yes." Wesley turned and put his arm around her. She nuzzled her face on his chest under his chin.

The softness of her body against his side seemed so natural. He had never been in a bed, nearly naked, with a girl before. He turned his head downward and her lips met his.

He slipped his hand to her breast. As if by reflex, she caught his hand with a firm grip, but after a few seconds, relaxed her hand and cupped it around his and held it.

"Wait a minute." Lizzie sat up, unbuttoned her shirt, and draped it over the adjacent night stand. "I have to wear it tomorrow and I don't want it to look like I slept in it all night." She lay back down and brought her lips to his.

Her breast beneath the soft cotton of her bra pressed against his chest. His hand drifted downward again, and she whispered, "Just hold me."

He swiveled to his side and pulled her closer. "I know. Leave a tender moment alone."

She kissed him and said, "Goodnight, Plowboy."

In a moment they both fell asleep.

CHAPTER NINETEEN

Sometime in the night Wesley thought Lizzie had slipped out of her jeans, but now, as he was beginning to wake up, he thought it may have been a dream. He felt a tap on his arm and opened his eyes.

Lizzie stood next to the bed, in yesterday's clean jeans and the same long-sleeved shirt rolled up to just below her elbows. The morning sunlight beaming through the window gave her recently shampooed hair a lustrous shine. She bent over and kissed him on the forehead.

"Good morning. You better get up. I went downstairs, and Rosie said breakfast would be ready in thirty minutes."

Wesley started to pull back the covers but felt oddly shy because he was in his undershorts, despite the fact that he'd just spent the whole night next to her.

Lizzie interrupted his thoughts. "Don't worry. I've already seen you in your underwear."

His eyes crinkled at the corners. She had read his mind again. "I was surprised when you came in here last night."

"I just didn't want to sleep alone."

"I wanted to sleep with you, too, but I didn't think you would want to."

"I'm glad you were thinking the same thing."

Wesley raised his head and sniffed audibly. "Hmmm, I smell bacon, and boy, am I hungry."

"I'm hungry, too. You know I don't drink coffee, but it smelled temptingly good. I've become such a worldly woman. The next thing you know, I'll be drinking coffee." She grinned. "I'm going back downstairs. You need to hop in the shower."

After breakfast, expressions of gratitude, and goodbyes, Carry drove them to the hospital. It was 10 a.m. when they arrived at Fitzsimmons.

"I'll pick you up at noon. I hope that gives you enough time to visit."

"It's much longer than we would have had if we were catching a bus back," Wesley said.

From inside Rita's room, Ray's voice filtered into the hallway. Wesley paused at the door, unexcited about another family reunion. Lizzie latched onto his hand. Wesley squeezed back, and they entered.

Ray shifted his attention from Rita. "Good morning, you two." He winked at Lizzie. Smiling Ray had resurfaced.

Wesley only nodded at Ray and said, "Hi, Mom."

She motioned them over and patted her bed. "You and Lizzie come over and give me a hug. Ray is just getting ready to leave to take care of some business."

Ray stood up. "That's right. You two want anything from downstairs?"

"Not me. We just finished breakfast," Lizzie said.

Wesley shook his head.

"I'll be back in thirty minutes," Ray said. "I have some phone calls to make." He touched Lizzie on the shoulder as he was leaving and said, "Nice to see you again."

"You, too," Lizzie said. After he left, she added, "I'll excuse myself for a few minutes, too, and give you two some time alone. I'll be back before Ray returns."

"You don't have to go," Wesley said.

"That's okay. I'll be back in fifteen minutes."

After Lizzie left, Wesley sat on the side of the bed near the bottom.

Rita said, "Son, that's one heck of a girl you've got there. Fresh-faced as a scrubbed child, sensitive, and mature. I hope you know she's one in a thousand."

"Yeah, Mom, I know. She sacrificed a lot to come here with me—her brother's temper and maybe her summer job. Plus, there'd be problems with her mom and dad if they found out. They're Mormon."

"Mormons can't be any stricter than foot-washing Baptists," Rita said.

Wesley laughed. "The odd thing about Mormons is they'll dance but won't drink coffee or Cokes. The foot-washers, on the other hand, wouldn't be caught dead on a dance floor, but can drink coffee like truck drivers. Speaking of truck drivers, when is *ours* leaving?"

"He's leaving this afternoon. You know, he really wants to talk to you."

"Everybody wants me to talk to him."

"Everybody?"

"Well, you and Lizzie. But I'm here to visit with you—not him. How are you doing?" He wanted to ask what her chances of living were but couldn't summon the courage to bring up the subject.

"Look, son, don't worry about me. As I told you, I have made peace with my Maker."

"But what do the doctors say?"

"One says I've got a fifty-fifty chance of full recovery—that I will have a full life expectancy. Another says, better than that. For a change, it's good that I have some excess fat to absorb the radiation and insulate my organs."

After a while, their conversation became lighter, and they were laughing by the time Lizzie returned. "What's so funny?" she asked, genuinely curious.

"Mom told me a story about my grandma's little neighbor kid."

"Ooh, tell me. I love your stories." She sat on the side of the bed across from Wesley.

"Mom's a better storyteller." He turned to Rita. "You tell it. It's your story, and I just heard it."

"If you insist, but first crank my bed up a tad higher." She pointed toward the foot of her bed. Wesley found the handle and cranked it to her satisfaction. Refocusing on her audience, she began. "Well, as Wesley mentioned, there was this neighbor kid, Darrell, who lived a few houses away from Wesley's grandma. A fat little fart, about eight or nine years old."

"This is going to be good," Lizzie said, as Wesley sat back down on the bed.

"Grandma's house is one of, maybe, twenty houses in Tremont, a little Ozark town with one country store and a one-room post office."

"What does *Ozark* mean? Lizzie asked.

Wesley answered. "The Ozarks are the mountains, or more accurately hills, in southern Missouri and northern Arkansas. Tremont is where I attended the country school before it was closed." He shifted his attention to Rita. "Sorry for butting in. Go ahead, Mom."

"Grandma and Grandpa had gone shopping in Pine Grove, a nearby town. I was in the kitchen by myself canning tomatoes." Rita stalled. "Lizzie, are you sure you want to hear this? Wesley has heard it already."

"Yes, please go on, Rita."

"We called Darrell 'Slappy' because when he ran, he flapped his arms up and down, slapping his hips, as if he were a cowboy galloping on a horse."

"Yeah," Wesley said, "then he would yell, 'Hi Ho, Silver,' like the Lone Ranger."

Lizzie's smiling eyes went from Wesley to Rita. "Go on, Rita." The slight frown at Wesley telegraphed an unsubtle cue to quit interrupting.

"Grandma always kept a full bowl of candy on the kitchen table. I think she did it because when she was a child, they were so poor they couldn't even afford penny candy. One afternoon she went to get a piece of candy and said, 'I'll swan, I just filled that bowl the other day and now it's half empty.' I told her I had only eaten two pieces. It stumped her because grandpa never touched candy. But then she said, 'You don't suppose Ol' Slappy sneaked in the house when we were gone yesterday, do you?'"

"Nobody locked their houses in the country." Rita hesitated to gauge her audience's interest.

"Go on, Mom."

"As I was about to say, a neighbor had given us a bushel of dead-ripe Big Boy tomatoes and we had to get them canned. I had parked my car in the garage out back, which didn't have any windows, so when Grandma and Grandpa went to town, I guess it appeared nobody was home.

"A little before noon, I peered out the back window and I see ol' Slappy sneaking through the gate. He was crouched down and scoping all around," Rita chuckled as she spoke.

Lizzie and Wesley both laughed. Rita, with a sparkle in her eyes, continued her tale.

"Then he creeped over to the garage and tried to peek inside through the door jamb, but it was dark inside. Apparently, he didn't see anything. Then he darted behind the big dirt mound over the storm cellar. I saw him peeking around it before he slipped to the back porch door and cracked it open.

"It was early August and about 95 degrees outside and no cooler inside—the old house didn't have air-conditioning. I was standing over a pot of boiling water, with a floor fan blowing steam in my face. With my limp hair hanging in my face and wearing an orange muumuu, I must have looked like a witch stirring a cauldron.

"When Slappy opened the screen door, I heard this little voice say, barely above a whisper, 'Anybody home?' I just kept stirring. And then a little louder, he asked again, 'Anybody home?'

"So, in my most eerie voice I said, 'Nooo, Darrell.'

"It apparently confused him and he blurted, 'Who's there?'

"I said, 'Nobody, Darrell.'

"He tiptoed into the kitchen and saw me. His eyes got as big as saucers. He tried to speak but couldn't. He kept uttering this *ooh ooh* noise that sounded like a hoot owl."

Rita started laughing, and Wesley and Lizzie joined in.

"Finish the story, Mom."

"So finally, ol' Slappy says, 'Is that you, Mrs. Sanders?' I said, 'No, I'm a witch, and I'm boiling up a pot of tomatoes that need the ears of a little boy like yours, Darrell.' He stumbled backwards a couple steps. I worked up my best witch's cackle and said, 'Come here, little boy, I have some candy to give you to get you fat for my kettle.'

"Poor Darrell wailed 'No!' and he whirled around, shoved open the screen door, and galloped across the backyard, slapping his legs and yelling, 'Hi Ho Silver!'"

Lizzie and Wesley burst out laughing. When the mirth subsided, Rita said, "And we didn't lose any more candy after that."

Rita gazed out the window and drew her brows together, as if she were contemplating something in the distance, and then said in a calm voice, "God, it's good to laugh again. It seems all I have done for the last two weeks is cry. You two have boosted my spirits. I think I might be able to manage all this, now."

Lizzie touched Rita's forearm with her hand and gave her a compassionate look. "That's good news, Rita. When we are flying back over the mountains, I will say a high-altitude prayer for you."

"I'd like that. You are a darling girl." She shifted her vision to Wesley. "Treat this girl right." Lizzie mugged an angelic look.

Rita cocked her head to the side. "Wait … you're flying back?"

As Wesley explained the plan, Ray showed up at the door.

Looking at Ray, Rita said, "Come on in."

Wesley stood up. "We are about to leave. We have to meet our ride."

"Whoa, pretty fancy having a *chauffeur*." Ray accented the word in a clear attempt at being clever.

"A friend is driving us," Wesley shot back defensively.

"All the way back to Yellowstone? I could take you as far as Laramie."

"No thanks. We've already made the arrangements."

"That's a shame. I hoped to talk to you before you left."

Wesley thought he saw Rita and Lizzie give each other knowing looks just before Lizzie said, "We've got a few minutes, Wes. And I want to talk to your mom a bit longer—girl talk." Motioning toward the door with her head, she added, "You two can talk outside."

"Go on, son, we'll just be a few minutes," Rita said.

Wesley shuffled toward the door, looking annoyed at the two women.

In the hallway, Ray positioned a couple chairs on either side of a hallway table littered with magazines. Looking apologetic, he said, "Let's sit down for a minute. I won't take much of your time."

Wesley sat on the front edge of the chair as if he might spring up and leave at any second. He faced Ray, but the rest of his body was angled away.

With a solemn face—Smiling Ray was absent—he said, "Wesley, I have made a lot of mistakes in my life—none bigger than with you. And in the last couple years, I have come to realize that."

Wesley held his posture rigid, with his arms crossed in front, in a manner that suggested he wasn't affected by Ray's words.

"The problems that your mother and I had were not your fault. They were mine, but you paid the price. I know now that I did the worst thing a parent can ever do—abandon a child. And that's what I did."

Ray stopped speaking, providing an opportunity for a response, but Wesley remained unyielding, maintaining his stare, which had become stony.

"Yeah, I know it wasn't like an Eskimo setting an unwanted child on a block of ice in the ocean, I mean, you had your grandparents . . . and I sent money . . . at least for a while. Nevertheless, I left you."

"Yes, you did." Wesley said, his contempt apparent.

"I know I did, but I was drinking then. I know that's no excuse, but it's the truth. I haven't had a drop for close to two years now. Before, I could lie and blame everyone else. I never sold my soul to the Devil, but I let him trespass too long."

Wesley continued to glare, uncompromising.

"When I got sober, my past behavior ate at me. An ex-priest I met introduced me to an organization that helps drinkers get their lives back together. And part of that process is to make amends to those we've hurt. That's why I came to Denver to see your mother. And now, it seems God has provided me with an opportunity to see you, and tell you, from the bottom of my heart, that I am truly sorry."

Wesley blinked but said nothing. He realized he had been holding his breath and gradually expelled it. He saw the big man's eyes well up, but only felt the sympathy one might feel for a stranger who was sad. "I hear you have another family . . . and another little boy."

"Yes, I do. His name is Billy. He's four years old and reminds me of you at that age. His mom's name is Rita."

Wesley did a double-take, and his brain clouded. "What?" Was Ray just confusing his mother's name with his new wife? And he didn't like being compared to this half-brother. Having a half-brother was embarrassing. Focusing, he asked, "Your new wife is named Rita?"

"Yeah, don't that just beat all?" said a meeker version of Smiling Ray.

Wesley stood up. "I've got to get going."

Ray extended his hand. "I don't expect to be forgiven, but I've said my piece. And I hope this might be a new beginning."

Wesley contemplated Ray's hand. Why should I shake his hand? But Rita's words, *Give him a chance. You're a Christian, aren't you?* echoed and prevailed. He took Ray's hand with a firm grip, the way Sam had taught him, and made brief eye contact. Adjusting his attitude, he said, "Good luck," turned, and walked away.

If Ray had hoped for more than an apathetic response, he didn't get one. He didn't follow Wesley into Rita's room, but instead allowed his son to say goodbye to his mother in private, with his girlfriend.

As Wesley entered Rita's room, melancholy overcame him. Nothing was resolved. His mother was still seriously ill, maybe dying. And now, he felt shame on top of that. He had sat there, cold and indifferent, as his father poured out his heart seeking forgiveness.

"What's wrong, son?" Rita could read her son's emotions like a printed message.

By now, Lizzie was no slouch in that department either, and for the second time in the hospital she asked, "What's going on?"

Wesley emerged from his own thoughts and said, "Nothing. I'll be back in a few minutes." With purposeful strides, he walked out of the room and reached the elevator in seconds. Twenty minutes later, he was back in Rita's room. Neither woman asked where he had gone.

It was time to go. Wesley and Lizzie hugged Rita, and both promised to write, but sadness was overwhelming Wesley. He knew if he spoke, he would start crying, and he didn't want that. If he cried, so would his mom. And so would Lizzie.

With a mother's intuition, Rita said, "You two need to get going. I will be okay. Don't you worry. Lizzie, say that prayer for me."

Lizzie hugged Rita and said, "I will." Rita kissed her on the cheek. Lizzie responded with her own kiss and said, "Now, you get well, Rita."

"Oh, thank you, darlin. You're the cat's pajamas."

After final hugs, Lizzie and Wesley marched out and began their journey home.

CHAPTER TWENTY

The Yellowstone Park bus stopped in front of the Old Faithful Inn. Arriving tourists, anticipating their summer adventures, chattered like squirrels. Lizzie and Wesley had spoken little after boarding in West Yellowstone. Wesley had dozed off, even though he had slept much of the way from Pocatello. On the other hand, Lizzie remained awake and on edge thinking about seeing her brother.

On the return flight to Pocatello, they had encountered a headwind and after a couple hours realized they would not make the 6:10 bus connection. From his previous travel, Carry recalled a later bus that would put them in West Yellowstone early the next morning.

After landing, Carry rented a Chevy Impala and drove them to the bus station. Lizzie gave him a ferocious hug and kissed him on the cheek. "Thank you, Carry. You're just the best, and I wish you all the luck in the world."

"You are most welcome. And I can always use luck."

Wesley gripped Carry's hand and added his thanks.

From the inside pocket of his leather flight jacket, Carry extracted a business-size envelope and handed it to Lizzie.

She took a quick look and showed it to Wesley. It was addressed to both of them.

Carry nodded at the envelope. "Don't open it until you are on the road." He appeared to be reading their faces. "I don't like goodbyes, so until we meet again." He gave a half-salute, which they had seen before, and did an about-face toward the car.

After they boarded the bus, Lizzie said, "I can't wait any longer." When she ripped open the envelope, a couple of two-toned plastic coins fell onto the seat. They were brown and white and the size of 50-cent pieces.

Wesley picked them up and examined them. "Wow. Two one-dollar poker chips from the Sands Hotel. That's the joint where Sinatra and the Rat Pack hang out."

"I told you he was a gambler!" Lizzie said, with the satisfaction of one who had been proven right in front of skeptics.

"Read the letter."

She unfolded it, exposing two greenbacks. "Holy Moly, Wesley. Forty dollars!"

"What's the letter say?"

"Hold your horses." She held it out so they both could see it.

The quality bond stationery, with an embossed letterhead, showed Carry's address and telephone number. The body of the letter had been written in a tight cursive script, with a fountain pen and vermillion-green ink.

Dear Lizzie and Wesley,

You may not know it, but you two have enriched my life. I met you at a low point in mine. From time to time, I can get swallowed up in dark moods. I start a downward spiral and start thinking there is nothing good in this world. I have been told it is the result of my negative experiences in the War. Whatever the cause, I've always managed to come back to the light. This time, it was meeting you two that helped.

It reminded me of when I first met Leeta. I was on a losing streak and had lost faith in myself, but Leeta stood by my side and we marched forth against the world. It is one thing to have love, but it is more important to have trust. Love can build on trust. I see both in you two.

I'm pretty good at reading people. Lizzie, you are so full of curiosity that you are about to burst, but you are also brave beyond your years, with unblemished kindness. And, Wesley, you are a guarded one. You play your cards close to your vest, but once you trust someone, your strong suit is loyalty—just the kind of guy I would want with me when the chips are down. Keep in mind what I said about war. It is not always smart to lead with your heart ... or your chin.

Enough of my sentimental journey. The two twenties are to help with your travel expenses, and the two chips are for luck and something to remember me by.

Yours truly,
Carry

When Lizzie finished reading, she said, "What a great man. After all he has been through, he is still so kind."

Wesley just nodded, feeling too emotional to speak.

Lizzie wasn't finished reflecting. "I read a story about a man who had been injured in a car accident and had to use a cane afterwards and he became very depressed. Then one day he was walking in a forest and sat down on a log feeling sorry for himself. A huge oak tree that had been split down the middle by lightning caught his attention. He noticed that one side was still green with leaves and full of acorns. And he had an epiphany ... although the tree had been injured, it was still living and productive. That became his parable. He understood that even though he had been hurt, it didn't mean he couldn't thrive and be productive."

Wesley squeezed her hand and said, "That oak tree is a powerful image, and it seems to fit Carry. Maybe, it's something I should remember, too."

"Same here," Lizzie replied. "We can't let something bad in the past cripple us in the future." Her voice became tentative. "Wesley, maybe I shouldn't ask, but when you left Rita's room, did you go see your father?"

The question surprised him, and he hesitated a moment, before simply saying, "Yes."

"What happened?"

"I caught up with him in the cafeteria . . . sitting at a table and staring out the window. As I crossed the room, he looked back at me with red, weepy eyes, and for a moment, I felt his sadness and believed his sincerity. I extended my hand, he took it, and I said, "It's okay. I accept your apology.""

"Oh, Wesley, that is wonderful. What did he do then?"

"He clamped on my hand with his other hand, and said, 'Thank you, son.' I let him hold on for a few seconds and I let him know with my eyes that I meant what I said, but I didn't stick around for a family reunion. I told him I had to get back upstairs and then I left."

"That was a brave and good thing to do, Wesley," said Lizzie. Good for your dad and good for you. I hope you can both let go of that pain eventually."

Wesley and Lizzie stayed in their seat as the tourists got off the bus at the Old Faithful Inn. Then Lizzie sighed and said, "I guess it's time for me to go face the music. The prodigal sister has to seek forgiveness from Dudley Do-Right."

"If your brother is Dudley Do-Right, then I must be Snidely Whiplash, the villain," Wesley said, continuing her reference to the *Rocky and Bullwinkle* TV show. Do you want me to go with you to meet your brother?"

"No, he would have to act like a big shot in front of you, which would only complicate things. Plus, I need to clean up before I see him."

"Well, I'm not worried about the outcome. You're no fainthearted damsel in distress. You've got as much gumption as anyone I know. Maybe Mike should be reminded that in the Bible, the prodigal gets forgiven."

Lizzie put both arms around him and brought her lips to his ear. "Thanks, I needed that." She kissed his ear.

From the front of the bus, the driver called out, "Hey, you two lovebirds, get a move on. It's time to get off."

Back at her dorm, Lizzie stood in the shower for twenty minutes until the water began to turn cold. The soap and hot water had relieved some of her tension. In her heart she knew Mike wouldn't fire her, but he would inflict some big brother retribution.

The shower had also brought clarity and justification. As she dried off, a sense of resolve came over her. Even satisfaction. She smiled. Her own personal, private smile.

It was one heck of an adventure. I went on two airplane flights. I met Carry and Rita. Wesley and I became closer. And I may have met the love of my life.

Lizzie approached the wrangler shack as Mike unsaddled his horse from the morning trail ride. He jerked his head back in surprise when he first saw her, but the surprise on his face immediately morphed into a sneer.

Lizzie met his stare like a gunfighter ready to slap leather. Standing tall, not flinching, waiting for Mike to make his play.

"You're finally back."

"Yep."

"Are you still a virgin?"

In spite of her mental preparation, his sarcasm stunned her. She should have seen this coming. Then she bristled. Mike had just trespassed on sacred ground, and he would pay for the transgression.

"At least I can report that one of us still is." She played her only card, knowing he had lied to their father about his dalliance in France when he was on his two-year Mormon mission.

The color drained from his face. "You don't know anything!"

"Don't I? Like I said before, little sisters have big ears. I heard you whining to our sister when you felt so guilty about lying to Dad. And to think I felt sorry for you . . . you sanctimonious cow pile."

One of the wranglers passed by and tipped his hat. "Hey, Lizzie, glad you're back. Are you going to be on the afternoon ride?"

"Yes, I am . . . unless something has changed since Thursday." She stared at Mike.

Mike glared at the wrangler, avoiding Lizzie's stare. "Nothing has changed." He barked his words. Without looking at Lizzie, Mike hoisted the saddle on his shoulder and stomped off to the tack shed.

"Whew!" the wrangler said. "He's had a burr under his saddle ever since you left."

"Give him a few days. He can't stay mad at his little sister forever."

Hez sprang off his bunk as Wesley entered their room. "Hey, Cuz, good to see you. How's your mom?"

"Not good, but as well as can be expected. Her spirits picked up when we got there."

"Who's *we*?" His hands went to his hips, as his face became a portrait of disbelief. "No, you didn't . . . Oh, crap, you did. You took that Mormon cowgirl with you."

With a sheepish grin, Wesley said, "Yes, I did. And I think I'll hate to see this summer end."

"Sounds to me like you have your tit in a wringer."

"How's that?"

"Those Mormon girls are the marrying kind."

"We're not getting married. And you're one to talk. I don't see that you've excluded Mormon girls from your Top 40 hit list."

"With me it's different. Girls know I'm not the marrying kind when they go out with me. It's part of my reputation. It's part of my *appeal*."

Some things never change, Wesley thought as he chuckled. And he was glad, but then added, "Let's change the subject."

"Good idea. I figured the trip would take longer. I didn't expect you until tomorrow at the earliest."

"We met this interesting guy who flew us from Ogden to Denver and then back to Pocatello in his own plane."

"You're putting me on?"

"Nope, it's true. He had his own Piper Cherokee. We're pretty sure he was a high-rolling gambler."

"That's some tall cotton, son."

"That's for sure. I'll tell you about him later." Wesley threw his pack on his bunk and surveyed for any changes. Satisfied with the order of things, he dumped the contents of his backpack on the bunk. "Anything new at the fountain?"

"Nope. Other than people wagering on whether you'd be back or not."

"What was the conclusion?"

"All the waitresses except Vivian thought you wouldn't be back. Betty said you promised her. Cliff and I said you would, but the girls wouldn't put up any money."

"Turns out the four of you were right."

"Yeah, but my reason was wrong. I said you'd be back because of the cowgirl. I didn't know you took her with you. Son, you need to tell me these things. Hell, you got a Mormon girl to go with you across state lines—you dog." Hez showed a salacious grin.

"It wasn't like that ... " said Wesley, which led him to share the details of the entire trip, including flying over the mountains with Carry, seeing not only his mom but also his real father for the first time in eight years, and ending with Lizzie going to meet her brother.

"I have to confess to being a might envious, but Cliff will be beside himself with jealousy. He is always complaining about not having any adventures or getting any girly action. Every time The Rolling Stones' *Satisfaction* comes on the jukebox, he sings along and gawks at Vivian, which gets him absolutely nowhere."

"Nah, he's just teasing her, but I'll go easy on Cliff. He's a natural-born pessimist, but when things get tough, he's a guy you want on your side."

"Well, on your side or not, he says you owe him a double shift, since he covered for you."

"Like I said, you can count on Cliff to back you up . . . and then remind you about the extent of his goodness."

"He does keep track of things."

"Speaking of Vivian, Hez, what did she actually say?"

"She said you'd be back because you couldn't bear not seeing her again."

"You gotta love Vivian. The girl has confidence."

"And style," Hez added.

"Heck, I better go report to Betty."

At the fountain, Cliff greeted him with a grunt. "It's a good thing you came back, or I would have kicked your ass when I caught up with you. And you owe me a couple shifts."

"Good to see you, too, Cliff." Wesley matched Cliff's grin. "I'll tell you all about the trip later. You won't believe it."

When Betty saw him, she motioned for him to follow her to the storeroom—the official site of all office meetings and confidential conversations. Once inside, without speaking, she corralled him in a mama bear hug. Her full-figure body mashed against his, as she planted a kiss on his cheek.

"Oh, I knew you'd be back," she said. Her grateful eyes showed relief, and widened in surprise, when he handed her a twenty-dollar bill."

"Well, maybe you'll amount to something after all."

"I had to come back to pay my debt. I was afraid you'd get the law after me."

"No, I would have just docked your final paycheck."

Wesley laughed.

Betty's expression became serious. "Is your mother going to be okay? I prayed for her."

He was touched beyond words by her comment. Somehow, the tough ex-marine praying for his mother seemed more powerful than a Baptist prayer. More exotic. And worthy of belief.

Trying to keep his composure, his voice came out in a detached monotone. "We don't know for sure. The doctors told her it was fifty-fifty. The flip of a coin."

"If she is anything like her son, I'd take that bet." The rare compliment from Betty buoyed his spirit.

When he emerged from the storeroom, Vivian waylaid him. Dressed in off-duty shorts and a tennis shirt with Greek sorority letters, she grabbed his shoulders, raised on her tiptoes, and kissed him square on the lips. After the kiss, she kept walking but said, "As I predicted, my boy didn't let me down." She paused, "Now, don't tell your cowgirl about that kiss. I don't want to be the source of any trouble again. And besides, I like her. She's a keeper."

Wesley squinted. "A keeper?" He was confused; he wasn't aware they had ever talked to each other, but he let the comment pass.

After his evening shift was over, Wesley hustled to the OFI and found Lizzie at their table on the balcony. He leaned over and gave her a quick kiss before sitting down in the chair next to her.

"How did it go with Mike?"

"He's angry, but he was angry before I left. He'll get over it. I still have my job, but I'll have to apologize."

"Why?"

"I did take advantage of the fact that I work for my brother. Somebody else might have fired me."

"Somebody else might have let you go under the circumstances."

"Maybe, but I also called him a sanctimonious cow pile."

Wesley burst into laughter. He had never heard Lizzie use language even close to a swear word. "He must have said something horrible."

"He did."

"What?"

Lizzie turned her head to the side. "I don't even want to say."

After a thoughtful pause, Wesley said, "That's okay," even though he wanted to know.

With her eyes still averted to the side, as if surveying the lobby, she said, "He wanted to know if I was still a virgin." Her eyes welled. "He made me feel so cheap, and I started thinking what we did was wrong, when it had seemed so right at the time."

Wesley's face puffed up in anger, and his lips strained to keep the words in his mind from bursting out. After an exasperated groan, he said, "He *is* a sanctimonious cow pile for saying that."

"You don't think I'm a sleazy girl, do you?"

He had never seen a smidgen of self-doubt in Lizzie before—but she could be hurt—and it brought back memories of his own hurtful behavior. "Why would you even ask that question? I'll never forget our trip together. I've never felt so close to anybody in my life."

Lizzie reached over the table and covered his hand with both of hers. "Thank you, I felt the same way."

Wesley felt the urge to kiss her. "Let's go sit in front of the geyser."

They stopped at an unoccupied bench twenty yards away from tourists who loitered on the boardwalk waiting for another faithful display from the famous geyser.

With a slow-dance move, Wesley rotated Lizzie to face him. Their bodies came together, and their lips found home with the same passion of Denver. Wesley slipped his hands around her waist and drew her closer. Her arms draped around his neck as they kissed.

"We better sit down. This isn't the place to get hot and heavy." She pulled his hand to follow her as she sat down.

They sat holding hands when the rumble started. It came in waves as the geyser built up steam. The first spurt of water only got a few feet high, followed in an instant by other spews, each one successively higher and louder, until the eruption blasted full-force with a roar that sent scalding water a hundred feet in the air.

Wesley and Lizzie watched without speaking, as the geyser worked its magic. Something about Old Faithful, which they had seen countless times, still held its magnetism. It was a place of memories. Of reflection. And the anticipation of its eruption could refocus one's thoughts like a meditation. Her brother Mike was not mentioned afterwards.

Instead their conversation turned to the excitement of the past days, reliving the details of their trip. Wesley's mom. The airplane rides. Carry and Leeta. And finally, after all the preliminary stalling, to their intimacy.

"Had you ever slept with a girl before?"

"What do you mean by 'slept'?"

"I mean spent the night in a bed with a girl."

"No. This sounds like show and tell. Have you?"

"Yes."

"You have?" Wesley's voice inflected and sounded disappointed.

"Of course . . . my sister." Her lips spread in a devious smile.

Wesley laughed. "You know what I meant. With a boy."

Lizzie didn't respond for a moment. "I know where this is leading. Don't turn into my brother."

"I'm not."

"I know you're not. And I think we have gone pretty far in our relationship, so I'll tell you if you tell me."

"Is that like *tit for tat*?"

"Don't be funny."

Wesley didn't respond for moment and then said, "No, I haven't gone all the way. Have you?"

"I'm not saying," she said with her usual playful manner that was missing earlier in the evening.

"What?" His mouth opened wide. "No fair!"

With a more pensive inflection, she said. "No, I haven't. Denver was the only time I ever spent a night alone with a boy in a bed."

"Did you want to do more?"

"That's not the point. I knew I wasn't going to. A girl may want to, but we're taught not to until we are married."

"So are boys, at least Baptist boys. As a matter of fact, the day before Cliff and I left town, our minister preached a sermon that even if you had 'lustful thoughts" you had sinned. And earlier that morning in our Sunday school class, he specifically gawked at the two of us and mentioned that God was everywhere, even in Yellowstone Park."

"Then you understand, but enough serious talk. We need to go. As usual, I have an early trail ride tomorrow, and I don't want to be late. I still have some fences to mend."

After walking Lizzie to her dorm, Wesley meandered toward his. His mind drifted, too, and events of the summer flickered by like a movie. It seemed like only yesterday when he had arrived, and now, the movie was already in its last reel.

Chapter Twenty-One

Most of Wesley's free time after Denver revolved around Lizzie, when their schedules allowed. Part of her penance involved working the sunset rides, which meant a late night for the wranglers with the after-ride chores of feeding and brushing the horses. Lizzie wasn't thrilled, but she thought it was a fair punishment. Plus, Mike had nearly overcome his anger about the Denver trip, and she didn't want to rock the boat.

Denver marked the height of their sexual activity. In all their romantic interludes after that, their clothes remained on, leaving Wesley frustrated and Lizzie with conflicting emotions. She feared getting pregnant, and claimed she came from a long line of fertile women.

Wesley suspected that her brother Mike was playing a part, as well as the religious precept of not having sex before marriage. Maybe, Hez had a point when he said, "She's a Mormon girl guarding home plate."

In his more reflective moments, Wesley considered the possibility that she just didn't want to make love for the first time with someone she might never see again. She had hinted at that earlier in their relationship. She underscored that notion when she finally said, "I'm not ready, and I don't want to lead you on." He respected that, but accepting it was harder.

The fountain crew recognized that Wesley and Lizzie had become a "park couple." Because of this, Wesley was thankful he had not gone further with Sue on the camping trip. To her credit, Sue had gone out of her way to introduce herself to Lizzie. And the two girls instantly liked each other. But it was Lizzie's relationship with Vivian that truly surprised him.

More often than not, when Lizzie popped by the fountain, Vivian would dart over to her and start talking. In jest, she would accuse Lizzie of stealing her boyfriend and promise to steal him back if she were mean to him. When Lizzie wasn't around, and her name came up in conversation, Vivian would threaten Wesley with dire consequences if he hurt that "darling" girl. And as a regular afterthought, she'd add how she would kill for those long legs of Lizzie's.

An unforgettable feature of that summer was the jukebox at the fountain. It played continually. If patrons didn't supply the coins, the employees did. Years later, Wesley would claim that if a song had been popular in the summer of 1965, he would remember it.

By August, "(I Can't Get No) Satisfaction" by the Rolling Stones was the number one hit on the Top 40 chart. Cliff had apparently become immune to the song after he started dating a waitress from the OFI. For Wesley, it was the Beach Boys. He knew all the words to "Help Me, Rhonda" and "California Girls" and sang along whenever they played.

Like a sad surfer song, the summer that had seemed endless in May now began to show its age in late August. The crowds in the park had become smaller; Labor Day would be the last hurrah. In two days on Sunday, August 29, Wesley and Cliff would be heading back to Missouri. Lizzie would stay another two weeks, as would Hez and much of the soda fountain staff.

Hez decided to throw a going-away party for the boys from Missouri on their last Saturday night in the park. Lizzie promised to go in spite of the alcohol that would be flowing. She remembered all too well what had happened at Hez's last party, and as Wesley's girlfriend, she wasn't going to take any chances on a repeat performance.

Although billed as Hez's party—Hez rented both sides of a duplex cabin—Vivian assumed the role of hostess and decided it should be a dress-up affair, with cocktails—not just a "tacky beer kegger."

Shortly after her proclamation, Vivian hiked over to Lizzie's dormitory carrying a shopping bag, hoping to catch her at the end of a trail ride. She found Lizzie sitting on the front stoop removing her cowboy boots.

"Hey, Cowgirl."

Without looking up, she recognized the voice. "Hey back, Soda Queen. What brings you to my neck of the woods?"

"I've got something for you." Vivian removed a black cocktail dress from the bag and held it up.

"It's lovely," Lizzie said.

"Lilly Pulitzer—a sleeveless cocktail shift. I saw Jackie Kennedy in one like it. Rayon—it hardly wrinkles. I've never worn it because it's too long for me. I ordered a petite, but it isn't. I thought I could get it shortened out here but never found a seamstress."

"Why did you bring it to me?"

"For Wesley's and Cliff's going away party, silly. We decided it should be a dress-up affair. It's perfect for you."

"I couldn't accept it and—"

"Of course, you can. Consider it a loan. You can give it back to me afterwards. Girls in my sorority borrow each other's clothes all the time. It's no big deal. And I would be honored if you trusted my taste enough to wear it."

"Since you put it that way . . ."

"It's settled then. Let's go inside and try it on."

In her room, Lizzie said, "I should take a shower first. I smell like horses."

"Don't worry, it will be fine."

With no more reluctance, Lizzie stripped down to her underwear and slipped into the dress.

From behind her, Vivian said, "I'll zip you up."

Lizzie faced the mirror to appraise her reflection. She rotated for a side view and then over her shoulder for a rear view.

"It's an A-silhouette with sweetheart straps," Vivian said, "I hate spaghetti straps because you have to wear a strapless bra, and, frankly, my boobs need more support."

Lizzie admired the perfect fit and the elegance of the dress. With the hemline an inch above her knees, the shift framed her figure in a suggestive way, without being too tight.

"I feel awfully fancy."

"Not fancy. Sophisticated."

"Do I need a belt?"

"No. It drapes perfectly." Vivian said, and then sighed. "What I would give for those gorgeous long legs of yours."

Saturday afternoon Wesley finished packing before getting ready for the party. Keeping with Vivian's directive, he wore the only pair of slacks he had brought with him. Sharkskin gray, with no cuffs, and a continental belt. With his black loafers, blue Oxford cloth button-down shirt, and blue blazer, he thought Hugh Heffner would approve. For a finishing touch, he splashed on a little after-shave lotion and left to pick up Lizzie.

When Lizzie appeared at the door of her room, Wesley gaped at her transformation. He had never seen her in a dress or wearing makeup before. With hints of eye shadow and mascara, and her lips accented with a gloss of pink lipstick, her Pygmalion change astonished him. His eyes started on her face and worked their way downward.

The dress revealed perfect legs. Her calves had the long muscles of a distance runner and tapered nicely at her ankles. Beaded Indian moccasins completed the ensemble, which no doubt represented her quiet protest against a complete conversion.

Could this be the same girl who had shunned dolls as a little girl? The girl who had yanked the hair out of a Barbie she received as a Christmas present and stuffed it in a trash barrel because she had wanted a Matt Dillon cap pistol instead?

As he ogled, Lizzie executed a 360-degree twirl. "How do I look?"

"You look beautiful. The dress is super sharp."

"It's a chemise or a shift. It doesn't have a lot of shape to it."

In Wesley's mind, it had just enough to give more than a hint of the shape underneath it. "I think it's sexy."

"Ooh la la, Mr. Standish."

"Did you bring it from home?"

"No, a friend loaned it to me."

He suspected he knew who the friend was, but reasoned it was better not to mention it.

Lizzie held out her hand, and Wesley lifted it to his lips for a kiss. "M'lady, your squire has arrived."

She curtsied and then tiptoed up and tapped his lips with hers. "Hmm, you smell nice."

Wesley leaned his head back to face her. "My mom would say I smell like a night across the tracks."

"That sounds like something your mom would say." She stroked her hand across his cheek. "You cut yourself shaving." She gave it a cursory examination and smiled. "I don't think it will require stitches."

"You should have seen it before the styptic pen."

"I'll kiss it and make it better." She pecked the cut with her lips and then planted them on his mouth for a second kiss.

By now, Wesley thought their kissing was perfection. He slid his arms around her waist and pulled her forward.

Lizzie hugged him and then pushed him to arm's length. "We better go before we get carried away with the PDA."

"What?"

"Public display of affection. At BYU, or as my sister calls it, B-Y-Woo, there are rules against it."

"The way I heard it back home is this: kiss by the door and not the gate—love is blind but the neighbors ain't."

"You are just full of cleverness tonight."

They strolled away arm-in-arm in the mild summer evening like a formal couple promenading to a soiree. The electricity between them made talking unnecessary.

As they sauntered by the Old Faithful Inn, Wesley felt proud as the tourists observed them pass. He saw their expressions and whispers and imagined they were saying, "What a handsome couple."

A slight breeze carried a hint of Lizzie's perfume, which replaced her usual clean smell of Dove soap. He inhaled the scent and said, "You smell wonderful." He leaned his face to her neck and sniffed loudly like a tracking hound.

Lizzie laughed. "Stop, silly."

"What is it?"

"L'aimant by Coty." She pronounced it with an affected French accent.

"It's nice."

They continued walking, enjoying the mild summer air. Suddenly, Lizzie stopped. Wesley was about ask her what was wrong when she extended one of her long legs out in front of him in a choreographed manner, and broke away skipping and singing the theme song from *The Wizard of Oz*. Wesley caught up and synchronized his own steps with hers, and soon they were skipping and singing as a pair.

When they arrived at Hez's cabin, it was already crowded, much like his first party. However, Wesley was relieved to see that some of the partiers had filtered outside, leaving more room inside the cabin to move about.

Vivian, as the self-appointed hostess of the affair, held court just outside the cabin door and greeted everyone as they arrived. Rumor had it that Vivian had been dating Ranger Brett on the sly, but Wesley didn't see him. She opened her arms wide as Lizzie and Wesley approached and gushed, "My two lovely protégées."

She put her cheek next to Lizzie's and made the smacking sound of a smooch, gave her a hug, and then stepped back, admiring her up and down. "Très jolie, mademoiselle Lizzie. You look simply divine. Très sexy. Don't you try to take advantage of my boy."

Lizzie occasioned a coy shrug and smiled.

Directing her attention to Wesley, Vivian said, "And you, you handsome devil, are straight off the cover of *GQ* magazine."

"Why, thank you, Miss Vivian. How nice of you to say so."

"Oh my, you *have* learned something this summer." Another couple approached, two people Wesley didn't recognize. As Vivian excused herself to greet them, Lizzie and Wesley stepped inside the cabin.

In spite of Vivian's wishes, Hez and Cliff had insisted on a pony keg, which sat on a kitchen chair, already tapped, and the suds and conviviality flowed.

Hez mixed cocktails at a makeshift bar by the sink. He held up a Coke, pointed at a bottle of Bacardi rum, and raised his eyebrows at Wesley. Lizzie shifted her eyes without moving her head for a glimpse at Wesley's reaction.

Wesley shook his head and said, "No, thanks, Hez. Just a plain Coke for me and a 7-Up for Lizzie." He wasn't going to make the same mistake twice.

Other partygoers would not be joining the Temperance Movement, at least not until the next morning when the hangovers had kicked in. As the alcohol consumption spiked, so did the decibel level of the chatter in the cabin. Lizzie said, "Why do people get so loud when they drink? I don't understand it. I can barely hear myself think."

"Maybe the booze affects their hearing, and they talk louder, the way old people with bad hearing do."

She raised a cupped hand to her ear, and in the high-pitched voice of an old person, said, "What did you say?"

Wesley laughed wholeheartedly at his clever girl.

"And the cigarette smoke is fogging the place," Lizzie complained, as she waved her hand back and forth in front of her face. "Let's go outside."

"Sounds good to me."

Outside, Cliff waltzed over, holding a mostly empty beer cup. "Wes, ol' buddy, you were a lucky man finding a girl like Lizzie this summer." He extended his hand to Wesley.

After shaking Wesley's hand, Cliff put his arm around Lizzie's shoulders. "You know, Lizzie, I have known Wesley for many years—he's my best friend—and I think you are swell. He couldn't do any better than you."

Wesley suspected the beer Cliff held wasn't his first of the evening.

Lizzie leaned forward and kissed him on the cheek. "Cliff, I think you're pretty swell, too. Wes is fortunate to have a friend like you."

A goofy, tipsy grin spread over Cliff's face. He pivoted to a group of fountain employees and semi-shouted, "Hey, everybody, I just got kissed by Wesley's girlfriend."

Someone yelled, "It's about time you got your first kiss from a girl." Cheers and applause soared, as if Cliff were a conquering hero.

"Speaking of girls," Wesley said, "where's your new honey?"

"She's coming over after she gets off work."

"Sounds good, buddy. We'll catch up later. I just remembered, though, we need to go back inside and talk to Betty."

Inside the other half of the duplex cabin, Betty sat in an upholstered club chair, which had seen better days, holding a drink in her hand. No beer for her, either. Because she no longer smoked, she had taken it upon herself to usher the smokers outside, which accounted for the markedly better atmosphere on her side of the duplex.

As they approached, Betty appeared carefree and relaxed. "Don't you two look gorgeous?" She eyed Lizzie, up and down. "You are a very pretty girl, Lizzie, and as innocent-looking as a prairie flower."

Lizzie beamed. "I should dress up more often. People are saying such nice things, but I think it's just because everyone is used to seeing me in jeans and long-sleeve shirts."

Nodding at Betty, Wesley said, "You're looking pretty snazzy, yourself." Betty wore a belted shirtwaist dress with vertical stripes that had a slimming effect.

"Like Lizzie said, you're just used to seeing me in a uniform and apron." She gazed across the room. "Don't look now, but here comes t-r-o-u-b-l-e." Rather than a worried look, she smiled.

Hez sauntered up without either of his dates. "Are you guys having a meeting without me?" He didn't wait for an answer. "I have to say, this is one of my better parties, and the first time two of my favorite ladies are in attendance."

"I don't recall being invited to any others," Betty said.

"Oh, Betty, you know you wouldn't come to an after-hours employee party."

"That's true. End-of-the-season parties are the exception."

Vivian sashayed next to Hez and nudged him with her shoulder. "Move over and make room for another lady."

Hez bowed with great affectation. His dramatic flair caused the women to chuckle.

"Hez," Betty said, "you do dance to a different drum. By the way, who all did you invite? There must be thirty people here."

Hez cupped his hand to his ear. "You'll have to speak louder. The placc is getting pretty loud." Then his brain apparently filled in the portion he had missed, and he said, "Oh, just a few of my closest friends."

"Miss Lizzie," Vivian said, "will you accompany me to the ladies' room? There's no lock and I need a door guard."

"Sure."

As they walked away, Betty remarked, "There goes an unlikely pair—Mutt and Jeff."

Hez added, "Or, Rocky and Bullwinkle."

"Maybe so," Wesley said, "but it is an odd friendship that I wouldn't have predicted. It's as if Vivian decided to adopt Lizzie."

"She could have a worse friend," Betty said. "Vivian is one of the most sophisticated girls I've ever had here, but behind all that sorority charm and sass is one street-smart woman."

"You've got that right, Betty," Hez said. "But tell me this. Why do girls always go to the bathroom in pairs?

"Hez, I thought you had that figured out," Wesley said.

"I have my theories, but I still don't understand. Personally, I prefer going alone and doing my business in private."

Betty shook her head without a verbal response.

Vivian knocked on the bathroom door, and from inside, a voice said, "Wait a minute. I'll be out in a second."

The door opened and a girl in cut-offs and a Mickey Mouse T-shirt came out. "It's all yours. There's no lock, so—"

"We know." Vivian cringed at the girl's outfit, and lowering her voice, said, "So much for the dress code." She tugged on Lizzie's arm. "Come on in. You can guard the door from the inside."

Lizzie was a bit perplexed, but she accompanied Vivian inside.

"My daddy, who is an Alabama state senator, conducts all his political conversations in the men's room, away from the women."

Lizzie leaned against the door, while Vivian stood in front of the mirror and freshened her lipstick. Vivian rubbed her lips together and, seemingly satisfied with the results, said, "There, that does it."

She turned to Lizzie. "Gussied up, you are one sexy cowgirl."

Lizzie blushed.

"By the way … this may be none of my business . . ." Vivian's lips tightened.

"What?"

"I don't know anything about your sex life, and I would never pry, but I do know something about last dates."

"What do you mean?"

From her purse, she extracted a small envelope and put it in

Lizzie's hand. Put this in your purse and keep it with you."

"What's this?"

"It's a prophylactic. You do know what they are for, don't you?"

"Of course, I do, but I won't be needing this." She attempted to hand the envelope back, but Vivian held up her hand like a traffic cop stopping a car.

"You say that now, and I can tell you mean it, but things have a way of changing unexpectedly. Don't be embarrassed. Put it in your purse. Never go on a date without one. If you were my little sister, that's what I would tell you. Things happen. Believe me, I know."

Lizzie's eye's widened, and she started to speak, but held her tongue.

"I'm not saying use it. I'm just saying be prepared." A sudden gloominess veiled Vivian's face. "A close friend of mine wasn't prepared one time, and it changed her life forever in a very regretful way. She didn't understand that being in love was nature's way of making babies. And it's the girl that pays the price. I just don't want any accidents ruining two friends' lives."

As they moved to the door, Lizzie clutched Vivian's hand and faced her. "Thank you for caring enough to share that with me. I can tell your friend's situation affected you deeply."

"She was a sorority sister—my best friend. She had to drop out of school. Lizzie . . . I would prefer it if you didn't mention what I said about my friend to anyone."

"Of course not. The information is safe with me."

"I knew that before I told you," Vivian replied with a smile.

Outside, they nearly bumped into Ranger Brett. Even though he was off-duty and dressed in civvies, Betty had invited him to ensure things didn't get too rowdy. "Fancy meeting you two here," he said with a big grin.

"Were you following us, Ranger?" Vivian asked in her best sultry, Southern accent.

The soda fountain scuttlebutt became a fact for Lizzie when Vivian playfully asked if he had brought his handcuffs. Lizzie excused herself and made her way back to Wesley, who was still talking to Betty. Hez had moved back to his two dates.

With a wandering gaze past Lizzie, Wesley said, "I see Vivian has Ranger Brett cornered." Trying to appear nonchalant, he asked, "What did you and Vivian talk about? You were in the bathroom a long time."

Betty shot him a dirty look. "Wesley Sanders, haven't you learned anything this summer. You don't look in a woman's purse, and you don't ask what girls talk about in the restroom."

Appropriately chastened, Wesley said, "Never again."

By ten o'clock the music was blasting and conversation was becoming more difficult. For the past thirty minutes Lizzie had been mostly quiet, nodding and smiling, but not speaking. Wesley knew she was partied out.

He put his hand on her shoulder. "Ready for a change of scenery?"

"Yes, let's get some fresh air. I don't want to spend my whole last night with you at a loud drunken party."

"I agree."

CHAPTER TWENTY-TWO

Wesley and Lizzie wandered in the balmy air under a waning crescent moon, seemingly with no apparent destination or purpose, holding hands and chatting. As they passed the YP cabin office, Wesley said. "Wait here, I'm going inside to check something. I'll be right back."

He cruised past the front desk and casually inspected the pegboard where the cabin keys hung behind the check-in counter. He spied a key hanging on space No. 23—the cabin was not occupied. And this late, nobody would be checking in. He felt inside his pants pocket, making sure his skeleton key was there.

When he got back, Lizzie said, "What was that all about?"

"Oh, nothing."

She gave him a suspicious look.

They meandered through the cabins toward the Old Faithful Inn. Lizzie had her arm around his waist. Wesley stopped at cabin 23. After a nervous moment, he said, "I have this cabin for the evening if you want to spend the night together." He tensed and waited for a rejection—he was sure she would say it wasn't a good idea.

"You rented a cabin?"

"Not exactly." He explained how the "Hez system" worked.

"So that's why you went in the cabin office."

"Yes."

Lizzie took both his hands in hers and studied his face, illuminated in the glow of a street light twenty yards away. "Wesley, we may never see each other again. I don't want to believe that, but it may be true. And if we go inside, you understand that it doesn't mean we will go all the way?"

"I understand, but ever since Denver, practically all I've thought about is lying on a bed with you again."

In a flirty voice she said, "I think that can be arranged."

Wesley opened the door and they stepped over the threshold. "We can't turn on the light or we may get caught," he warned. They found their way to the bed in dim light from the streetlamp shining through the window.

Lizzie said, "Don't get any ideas, but I'm going to take off my dress so it doesn't get wrinkled. I have to return it to Vivian."

She placed her purse on the nightstand, kicked off her moccasins, and slipped the dress over her head, folding it neatly on a chair, and then crawled to the far side of the bed.

Wesley stood at the side of the bed as her shadowed form stretched out on the bed. She rolled on her side and folded the pillow to support her head. "Well, are you just going to stand there and stare?"

Wesley hung his blazer on the chair back. Then he removed the rest of his clothes except his undershorts, placing the clothes on top of Lizzie's dress.

"Can you put the dress on top so it doesn't get smashed?" Lizzie asked. He rearranged the folded clothes and then he joined her on the bed, lying down on his side. He propped himself on his elbow and faced her.

"Let's just lie here for a moment," she said. Wesley reclined on his back and put his arm around her shoulders. She rested her head in the crook of his neck. "This is nice."

Lying without speaking, her other senses became more acute. She noticed the muscles of his chest against the softness of her breast. The telltale smoke from the party in his hair. The hint of his aftershave lotion. The smooth firmness of his waist as she rested her hand there.

As her eyes adjusted to the dimness in the room, she angled her head to look at him.

"What are you thinking?" she whispered.

"That I want to kiss you."

She turned on her side and placed a hand on his cheek. Their lips met, open, and with no hesitation, expressing feelings that words would not.

Wesley reached behind her back with one hand and grappled with her bra clasp. She let him undo it, and then pulled it off the rest of the way and let it fall onto the bed.

They continued kissing with their bodies molded together. He moved his hand down to the waistband of her panties.

"Wait." She raised up. Her mind had flashed to Vivian's cautionary words.

I'm not going to get pregnant, she thought.

She reached inside her purse on the nightstand and felt for the small package.

"What are you doing?"

"Here." She handed him the Trojan package. "Put this on. Even if we're not going all the way, we can't leave this place a mess."

Wesley fumbled with the package and dropped it. He picked it up but couldn't get it out of the cellophane. Embarrassed, he began biting at it with his teeth.

Lizzie giggled. "Let me help. I've got fingernails." She opened the package and handed it back to Wesley. He tugged his shorts down with his other hand and put on the condom.

She eased back down on the mattress as they kissed. Their breathing became rapid and shallow. Wesley pulled her closer. Her arms clamped tight around his back.

*   *   *

Just before dawn, Wesley put his arm around her and pulled her to his

211

side. She positioned her head just below his chin, with her cheek on his chest, and they lay silently.

Lizzie remembered what she'd said to Wesley about girls feeling different than guys, and now she wondered how he felt. What he was thinking? Was the experience what he had imagined? Would he still think she was a good girl? A voice from somewhere in her mind told her to be still. Lulled by the rhythm of his breathing, she dozed in and out of dreamlike images.

After a while, he murmured, "Are you asleep?"

"No, just thinking."

"About what?"

"That it's bittersweet. My body is relaxed, but my heart is sad."

"Are you sad because we made love?"

"Oh, no. I wanted to, but in my head, I keep hearing that Floyd Cramer song, *Last Date*."

"It is sad, but we can write, and maybe come up with a way to see each other."

"I know, but you will be at college, with all those girls."

"You'll be at college, too."

"I know, but there will never be another summer like this, and I'll never be in love again for the first time. I'll be lucky if I meet a boy like you again." Her eyes were welling with tears.

She kissed him, and Wesley slid his hand down her thigh. She put her hand over his. "We can't start that again, and we already used the prophylactic."

"I know . . . leave a tender moment alone. By the way, where did you get it? I haven't seen any dispensers in the park."

"A friend gave it to me, just in case." Then, playfully feigning offense, she said, "And why were you looking for prophylactic machines? You were being very presumptuous."

"I was just being cautious."

"While we are on the subject, was your friend a female?"

"Maybe."

"Are you kidding me?" he laughed and then added in his best imitation of Vivian, "'That little hussy,' as she would say. But I doubt that we'll ever find a better friend." They both smiled and laughed at that.

When they closed the cabin behind them, cleaning crews were assembling their wheeled carts loaded with towels and supplies in front of the lodge office. It was nearly seven o'clock. Wesley would be leaving in a few hours, and Lizzie had a trail ride at eight.

With their arms around each other's waist, they made their way toward Lizzie's dorm. Wesley felt a deep sadness. It struck him that the adventure was over. The endless summer was now a setting sun, and he was about to say goodbye to Lizzie. He could see that she was nearly in tears.

Looking straight ahead as she spoke, Lizzie said, "I don't feel tired now, but by ten o'clock, I may have to violate 'The Rule' and have a Coke."

"Your brother might fire you."

"If he sees me walking in with you now, he may anyway."

They trudged the last fifty yards without speaking and stopped at the backside of her dorm. Lizzie pivoted and threw both arms around Wesley's neck. Her eyes flooded. "I love you, Wesley Sanders, and you *are* worthy. I will never forget you. Promise that you won't forget me."

Wesley drew her further into his arms. "I love you, too." He could not stop his tears. He felt her muted sobs against his chest. "I'll never forget you—I promise." Her arms clenched him even tighter.

A moment later, she exhaled a barely audible sigh and whispered, "I have to go." She put both hands on his cheeks and brought her lips to his, but this time, she did not linger long. She pivoted and began walking to the front of her dorm. At the corner of the building, she turned once more to look at him. Their eyes met just before she stepped out of his sight.

Wesley wiped his eyes with the back of his hand and began to trudge toward his dorm. At one point, he looked back over his shoulder, as if she might be there, but of course she wasn't. He bit his lip and kept walking.

I will never forget you, Lizzie Smith.

CHAPTER TWENTY-THREE

Cliff and Wesley boarded the turbo-prop plane in Jackson for the first leg of their journey home.

Neither Cliff nor Wesley had flown on an airliner before, and both remained silent at takeoff. The plane kept circling the airport, spiraling upward like a corkscrew to gain sufficient altitude to clear the Tetons.

After the plane leveled off, Cliff said, "Wes, where did you go after the party last night? I asked around, and everyone said you had left."

"Just out with Lizzie."

"I didn't hear you come in."

"You were snoring."

Their conversation ceased when a stewardess stopped next to their seats with a beverage cart. "Would either of you like something to drink?"

"With no hesitation, Cliff said, "I'd like a Coors."

"May I see your ID?"

Humbled, Cliff sighed and said, "Just give me a Coke."

Wesley ordered a Coke, too.

Then, like two sailors coming home from the sea, they relived their tales of the summer. And as their conversation lulled, Wesley said, "Well, partner, we did it."

They shook hands and leaned back in their seats.

Wesley closed his eyes and the Beach Boys' *California Girls* played in his mind, as it had many times that summer. As he mouthed the words, he thought of Lizzie and smiled. And then he said a silent, high-altitude prayer for his mother.

EPILOGUE

Rita survived Fitzsimmons. God apparently honored his end of the bargain she had made with him. With time, the scars on her abdomen faded, but the trauma of the experimental radiation treatment took its toll on her mental health. Today, it would be called posttraumatic stress disorder. She would only talk about her experience when she was drinking. And, yes, the live radium implants were indeed like having a hot coal shoved up your ass. She lived another thirty years, but ironically, the radiation that saved her life eventually killed her by causing a second primary cancer. God's promise had an expiration date.

Wesley would see his father Ray one more time after Denver—at his grandmother's funeral, during his sophomore year in college. Ray drove to Ridgeview and brought his other son, Billy, who was six. That day, he wasn't "Smiling Ray" but a sad man mourning the loss of the woman he used to call Mom. For once, Wesley was in the same dimension as his father as they shared a common grief.

After the funeral, as he watched his father standing next to Billy outside the church, a chill came over Wesley. For a moment, he saw himself in the place of Billy. Maybe his old man would do a better job as a father the second time around. He hoped so. Another feeling overwhelmed him—shame. If truth be told, deep down, Wesley had never felt right about their last meeting in Denver. Although he professed to having accepted Ray's apology, he had smugly continued to resent him.

Wesley walked over to his father and extended his hand. "Dad," he began, and then his voice cracked as he realized he hadn't called Ray *Dad* in more than a decade. "I'm sorry for your loss . . . and I'm sorry for my attitude back in Denver." Ray looked shocked for a second, but then he pulled him into a smothering hug and broke into sobs. Feeling waves of relief, Wesley let his own tears flow. He thought of something his grandmother used to say. *Sometimes the person you resent is someone you owe an amend, and when you make the amend, the resentment goes away.* At that moment, it rang true for Wesley. His resentment vanished.

For several years after that summer in Yellowstone, Wesley and Lizzie corresponded, but as time passed, the letters became less frequent. He received her last letter during the spring of his junior year of college. She wrote to tell him that she was engaged. He sent a note congratulating her.

Eleven years later, Wesley sat in the St. Louis airport reading a magazine while waiting for a plane. A women's voice, said, "Excuse me." He looked up. A conference name tag on her blouse identified her as Dr. Elizabeth Regan, DVM.

"Lizzie!" He stood up and they hugged.

A little girl about three or four years old tugged at Lizzie's skirt. "Mommy, who are you hugging?"

"Vivian, honey, this is Mr. Sanders, a dear friend of mine from when I worked in Yellowstone Park with Uncle Mike."

After a short visit, they went their separate ways, but the promise he made that last day in Yellowstone remained true. He would never forget Lizzie Smith.

About the Author

Lonnie Whitaker attended a two-room school in the Ozarks and graduated from the University of Missouri School of Law. A retired federal attorney, he now works as a writer and editor. After publication, *Geese to a Poor Market* won the Ozark Writers' League Best Book of the Year Award.

Other stories have been published in Chicken Soup for the Soul, magazines, and anthologies. His children's picture books, Mulligan Meets the Poodlums and Mulligan Runs for Office were published in 2018 and 2020. His Western Stories have been included in Five Star Press anthologies, and he is a contributing writer for the Howell County News.